Yams Do Not Exist

Yams Do Not Exist

Garry Thomas Morse

TURNSTONE PRESS

Yams Do Not Exist
copyright © Garry Thomas Morse 2020

Turnstone Press
Artspace Building
206-100 Arthur Street
Winnipeg, MB
R3B 1H3 Canada
www.TurnstonePress.com

Turnstone Press gratefully acknowledges the assistance of the Canada Council for the Arts, the Manitoba Arts Council, the Government of Canada through the Canada Book Fund, and the Province of Manitoba through the Book Publishing Tax Credit and the Book Publisher Marketing Assistance Program.

Printed and bound in Canada.

Library and Archives Canada Cataloguing in Publication

Title: Yams do not exist / Garry Thomas Morse.
Names: Morse, Garry Thomas, author.
Identifiers: Canadiana (print) 20190150785 | Canadiana (ebook) 20190150793 | ISBN 9780888016775 (softcover) | ISBN 9780888016782 (EPUB) | ISBN 9780888016799 (Kindle) | ISBN 9780888016805 (PDF)
Classification: LCC PS8626.O774 Y36 2020 | DDC C813/.6—dc23

CONTENTS

Yams Do Not Exist

Amortization of the Amatory

Farinata[1] clung to the darkling plain[2] with all his might. He showed great determination not to be the highest wet point for a sliver of lightning. Supine and stricken with fright, he was amazed not to see a whit of life flash before his eyes. More of a blankety-blank. Whatever had happened before his move to the "Land of Living Skies" was incredibly obscure, as was his translation next door to the friendliest province in recent memory. There, a prairie storm was in the offing, and he was nervous about more than just its metaphoric content. Yes, his fear of a fatal bolt from on high was matched only by

---

1. This Latinate name is merely a low-tech Easter egg—or Paschal egg, for that matter—and will be covered in sensuous detail when we have a moment. For now, it is enough to admit that he lays claim to a literary bent. Poetic, if you must know.

2. There have been worse references to "Dover Beach."

a fear that his creative powers would fail him, should he try to recount his life.

To this end, Farinata pictured two pupae that were (securely or precariously) suspended from the top of a fence that had a stony finish. Inside were the women, wriggling with anticipation. Was it a common male fantasy, to bind them in leafy shells like that, hanging from a silken hook? No, nature abhors nothing. The satin bowerbird spares no other bird when collecting feathers and other blue objects with which to adorn the entrance to his bower, cleverly designed to dazzle the azure eye of his prospective mate, she who promptly dispatches him to gather more blue buttons or bottle caps. Farinata suffered countless outbreaks of shame over the fact that there were two of them, dividing the highest caste of beauties. To the best of his knowledge, Muses were single-spined, or went around in nines. Thus, his personal fortitude—his *virtù*—was called into question. Might as well cover them from head to heel, and protect himself from himself.

Yet these two ladies gave him pause for thought, wrapped in delicious colours that mimicked the dominant shades of the substrate with an air of Pre-Raphaelite grace. Naturally, there had been other scrapes with a chorale of capable women he had been obliged to categorize under the rubric of fleshly pursuits. As for these two delicious misses, neither would be caught dead wriggling in a chrysalis. One morning, they had broken free of those chitinous husks and had dried their sopping wings until they were ready to take flight for parts unknown. Poetic usage aside, one Muse was getting on with her decorous life in Queen City. The other, still waving in the foreground, was well on her way to a solid vocation, and had abandoned her former friends to the social milieu in which they still flounder to this day. Look, there is no need to exaggerate. Just a second ago, she had not actually waved, or for that matter, walked arm in arm with her usual chaperone, their steps keeping in perfect time with one of Schubert's dances (D.783 no. 7). Nor had she lorded it over him on a minimalist-chic Scrooser, although that is how he always envisioned her. No, she had mouthed a "hello" meaty enough to feed almost half of Paradiso, with a display of friendliness that was already guaranteed on every provincial license plate.

We need not worry that no one else will turn up. Someone often does. Incidentally, this is known as foreshadowing. While we are here, we might as well appraise his stupefaction. His eyes were screwed up because he had nearly idealized the poor dear out of existence. He clenched his teeth because her bourgeois constraints were quick to cordon off the open manhole he teetered over, namely the Void. Taking into account as many artistic purviews as our budget will allow, we must concede that the Canadian prairie has seldom been expressed as anything more than a whopping *Néant*,[3] and that is how Farinata happened upon her. Stuck with the same old representative models, he lacked the tools to mansplain away the copious amount of desire that had repeatedly tripped him up since reaching the middle of the road of his life. In passing, he lacked enough pluck to suggest that countless exoplanets ultimately had more influence than the perpetual recession that held sway over his most heartfelt inclinations, even the most fleeting infatuation.

Even so, the meaty "hello" of the dark-eyed one had substance, and "infatuation" was too wonderful a word to relinquish whole hog. Besides, it would be nice to leave horndoggery out of it for once. He was bound to take it

---

3. Madeleine or mille-feuille? Within the abyss, every humanistic decision is in danger of turning into literature.

personally once he was informed—he was *well*-informed—
that she had dropped everything to serve at the sister café
of one of his favourite haunts, the former below street level
where tea was served with a strainer that dipped ever so
shallowly within the rim of the affronted cup! Meanwhile,
he was more likely to be found in the front window of the
brother café that faced onto Main, where he could moon
over the architecture and stare up at the faded lettering on
a chimney that read CLEANS & SHINES. Never again
would their paths overlap, save in a staffing emergency, and
the odds were still against him. Otherwise, life lumbered
on. The red squirrels were free to chase each other around
belted elms, just as the black swallowtails were free to flit
about and flirt among the thistle.

Beset by impressive nether-pangs, Farinata took a page
from the white-tailed deer playbook and ignored the TRES-
PASSERS WILL BE PROSECUTED sign. He crept under
a section of torn fence and wandered across the golf course
in a daze. They were sedatives, if not basilisks, her eyes.
Where was the accountability for the stalwart anvil cloud
or bosomy mammatus clouds hanging pertly from the base
of a cumulonimbus?[4] A rumble of thunder and a flash of
lightning introduced a massive downpour. Let a romantic
pneumonia carry him off! He flung himself upon the grass
and lay there and that is how we find him. Supine, just the
way we agreed, and about to take stock of his life. Fortunately, compensation for his nearsightedness came to him in
the form of an otherworldly farsightedness in many an existential matter. He could savour the flavour of recent mis-
adventures yet also taste the fuzzy logic of things to come.

Keep in mind, when a man of letters reflects on his various comings and goings, he is bound to feel short-changed

---

4. Actually, the pathetic fallacy has never been more pathetic.

in the amatory department. Year after year, there is a depreciation of the intangible asset that is so precious to us, we can scarcely amortize it. Mostly a string of close calls, if one is telling home truths. Well, let us abide awhile with his abstruse impressions, involuntary memories,[5] obstinate fetishes, and portentous meanderings, for to find profundity in the laughable—let alone split a gut over the profound—is a fair aim.

---

5. Clearly, we decided on the madeleine, swiftly dipped in a steaming cup of Bergsonian consciousness. To be honest, they were plum out of the mille-feuille.

Cortesia in the Centre

Farinata leaned against the little bridge in Les Sherman Park, tragicomically besotted with the infamous Trish, who by all accounts—her co-worker Donna—had a murky past and more adventures than were allotted to a lady of high standing, in her humble estimation. He called it love because he could only see *her* stately head over the assortment of coffee machines, and if there were a glimpse of anything more, he would redden and avert his eyes at once. He called it love because he caught himself comparing the green of certain waterfowl to the green shock she gave her long black locks. He also believed that she possessed intimate knowledge of the cello. This error in judgment was the divine masterstroke for Farinata, who now heard a gavotte or a gigue whenever he passed the bank façade that stood by itself in the middle of Cornwall Centre, which might as well have been a parapet from which she lowered her hair for inspection.

Such was the luxury of an unemployed poet upon the little bridge—defying with a few tears[6] the integrity of his pants from the Sprawlmart nearest Highway 1—to contemplate her image through flat whites and foam at the mouth of the downtown mall in Grounds for Delight. He cut such a sorry figure that out of sheer pity, a couple dismounted and paid him the courtesy of walking their bicycles across the bridge without subjecting him to any more of the bumps and shocks that flesh is heir to. Expiation came, as it surely did to the first ice age hunter-gatherer who slew a bison and grew a bird-head—or so the cave paintings show us—in the form of a few peerless tears that had no peer because they were unrivalled in their heartfelt dedication to Trish, and also because they had no peer to speak of, which is to say not a friend in the vicinity.

Farinata was so overwrought that he might have cast himself into the shallows of the (debatably artificial) creek, had not a pelican floated into view, appearing for all the world duly satisfied with its own awkward and merry surrealism. This whimsical bird floated right under the little bridge and Farinata did not even notice the yellow cornrows or the bosom heaving through a T-shirt or the thighs swathing his crumpled sad-sack-of-a-self in the passing aura of their continual locomotion.[7] The fact that she was eager for an acquaintance of roughly his length and breadth between the hours of ten and two on business days did not make itself known to him, nor that his plunge into the shallows might have afforded an opportunity for her to fish him out and dry him off over a hot toddy until the time was ripe to

---

6. According to Stanislavski's method of affective memory, we'll soon be joining in just to show how much we care.

7. This may be of minor importance later, but for the time being, let us say that the breathy greeting tickled his ears and nowhere else.

grant him some relief from his irksome passion, had not the happy pelican passed.

There was still a sixty per cent chance the thunder and rain would help matters along, much as *Iuppiter Pluvius* helped along Aeneas at the very instant he was aching to get a leg over. But no, the sublime undulations of those buttocks in Get-A-Grip shapewear were already out of sight. Farinata clutched the bridge railing like a second mate on a sinking ship and gave himself over to a fresh stream of saline discharge and a low, woeful ejaculation that made the pelican look back with something akin to concern. Though the mourning dove appeared to be rubbing it in, ceaseless in sounding its baleful coo, all was not lost! Farinata felt around in his pocket and fingered the pearly white lid of the anonymous supplier, a superfluous token of everything that had remained unspoken between him and his beloved Trish. Indeed, her downcast eyes had instilled in that pale, plastic object an unearthly light at the time of his leave-taking, causing it to shine like a late medieval or early renaissance disc in gold leaf—superfluous because it had no practical utility and would likely as not choke some poor seabird in the near future, no matter where he disposed of it.

Farinata headed for his thinking bench—lacking the Greek or German compound word for such a help—still fingering the Fra Angelico disc, and thought. What did he think of? When the wind had stopped pestering the poplars, he thought of the shell-ish earrings in the delicate pink lobes of Trish that softened the effect of the silver nosering gleaming through her right nostril. Quite the riddle, quite the koan to beat about one's brains, especially for a sentimental autodidact who couldn't get out the compound words he wanted. In the background, beyond the barbecue, a girl waited, baggie in hand, for her pug to do its business, although this was by no means a source of consolation to our friend. Were there ashes in the barbecue, mere remnants of once-tender things burnt to a crisp? No there were not. The pug ran amok, panting, then returned home much refreshed with a wonderful sense of vacuity.

Farinata said aloud that he wanted to go home but he meant go home-ish, meaning back to a micro suite, meaning part of a house that was really too small for mere mortals. He went back to the bridge and peered over the railing but the beaver[8] (muskrat?) that had been chewing leaves was nowhere to be seen. Just then, a stripling paid him a whit of *cortesia*, lifting his skateboard and even tugging out his earbuds with an air of solemnity, leaving Farinata to mumble his greeting after that chivalric shadow in passing. One noble penumbra gave way to another, and a lanky representative of the mounted police appeared in the corner of our friend's eye, a rotating sentinel who was inclined to tolerate the apparition of an Indigenous person[9] in a sports team jersey that in logo and name might be taken for a racial epithet, a jersey upon the crumpled body of a frail paramour that might be taken for an ironic declaration of protest, just the sort of rabble-rousing certain to disturb the riparian peace, artificial or not. Farinata paused, supposing the season to be too early and the weather too mild for starlight tours with a zero point zero zero nine per cent chance of

---

8. Unknown to his conscious processes, this national symbol was perhaps indicative of the amorous indulgences our friend hoped to one day receive from dark-eyed Trish, not to mention the fish that made a sex-obsessed splash behind him, but it was also an undeniable reality of the (debatably artificial) creek, just as the civic statue of a giant beaver was an undeniable reality of the tranquil park.

9. Cops on the beat are not equipped with the latest in blood-quanta kits.

being struck by lightning. And anyway, the officer might have taken sensitivity training. In fact, this inquisitor had taken more than his fair share of sensitivity training, but Farinata had nowhere near a "casebook" profile and "looks good on paper" certainly did not apply here.

Naturally, our hearts fly out to our friend; it was the bread and butter of the officer of the mounted police to remain circumspect, having found the crumpled individual at ten past three in an excitable state, unable to clearly articulate with any exactitude his origin story or even precisely why he had been reduced to such a pitiable condition. Farinata is a funny name for this loon with an out-of-date Status Card, thought the copper,[10] although his actual commentary was a string of muffled dissyllables more along the lines of "there, there" or "uhm hm" or even "uh-oh." Not much grilling, then, to bring about a confession. An argument had ensued, calling the handbook into question, with Trish on the side of freethinking with a trace of freebooting, revealing her rebellious streak in her proposal to reverse the order of the elements for a particular drink, to do it like *this* rather than *that*, afterwards fuming under the chastening glare of her manager. Grist for the mill and grain for the proud elevator of his love[11] in a town so tiny it is the only thing visible, aside from the train rushing ahead to conclude a weepy adieu. Meanwhile, the officer of the mounted police asked him to kindly keep calm and carry himself off. Sensitivity training, indeed!

Once on the other side of the little bridge and on solid cement again, Farinata clung to the DISMOUNT sign and admitted to his crime, for he had, in a sudden fit of

---

10. *Stop, thought the Thought-Police,* is what Farinata thought.

11. This is an enduring symbol of his lonesome ardour. Best get acquainted with it.

desperation—blamed upon very low blood sugar and/or excessive dehydration—permitted a compact bumbershoot to point through his coat, demanding of the wee-hours clerk a small bottle of water and a tired pastry partially smeared with a berry-ish filling. To his credit, they were not saskatoons, imitation or otherwise. This unfortunate incident had appeared on Crime Stoppers on a slow week, but to this day remains unsolved. Sadly, the officer of the mounted police was already well away, the collar never to be his.

The next day found Farinata scarcely improved, save for the prospect of chicken and waffles for elevenses. The second he had seen the bright orange food truck from afar, the sleep had tumbled from his eyes and his heart had leapt towards the public square, shoved forward by the rarified discernment of his impetuous stomach. Fans of *opera seria* will have to forgive this slight digression from the Metastasian order of acts, scenes, and appearances by dramatic personages, because even as Farinata guarded his generous portion of fowl and honeycombed battercake from several bees, his breezy head was full of torporous airs. At the same time, his insides were so full of marvels, love, remorse, and hope that he did not even notice the flames rising about his ears on account of a conversation that was about to take place during a brief lull at Grounds for Delight. Set to harpsichord,[12] the dry recitative was no mere hack work—there was a drop of pathos there!

"Well, I see him in the square or wandering the streets."

"Shy dude that's into you?"

"Now you're being stupid."

"Remember, as staff, you mustn't fraternize—"

"Remember, as staff, you should shut up."

---

12. An instrument that meets the Thomas Beecham measure of two skeletons copulating on a corrugated tin roof in a thunderstorm.

Then the eyes of Trish darkened and the soft *basso continuo* pulsed through her, as faintly as the genteel *recitativo accompagnato* of the grasshopper that had glided into the square, only to land at Farinata's crumb-covered feet, which is to say brogues in sore need of reparation. Birds have augury but what have these stridulating stoics with their songs of love and territorial admonition? Farinata was no wiser then, for a little bird had told him nothing. Having divested the bones of their quantity of dark meat, with sticky fingers clasped together, he vowed to the living skies that his fanciest fancy and he would be united in a world that was probably not this one, however delicious this life could be, especially right before the lunch rush.

Mull in the Mirage

Wisteria wondered aloud about the new regular, or believed she had, and checked herself. That was how it would sound in a book, right? With her behind the glass partition, peering through, brimming over with reflections. She was to be the object of his fascination, which was all right for a lark when no one was looking, something to pack tightly into a ball and tuck in the right place when a spot of shallow breathing occurred, something to fill in the gap like music—no, she was getting carried away. This could never be "real" in The Mirage Club, where docile fantasies occupied the air. She was reminded of this cool movie about a writer who penned a silly story about a man who was warned not to fall in love with these female service robots whose ridiculous heels generated electric sparks. The movie came to mind now and then, when she was behind the glass, looking through at the customers. If she ever ran into the new regular outside, this would be something to bring up. She had various phrases stockpiled, because he looked clever and she wanted to sound clever, or at least not as dopey as some of her coworkers sounded to her.

She knew all about him of course because last time he had left a book in a booth—blatant strategy of the grosser sex?—and Ashley had asked her about that dog-eared keepsake, as it was in her section on her shift and she knew when an intrigue was in the works, but did not force the issue. Taking note of the book and the name, she watched Ashley toss it into the lost and found with special instructions. Wisteria could have reached in and nabbed the book, but that would have felt like pulling a medium-rare twelve ounce out of the oven with her bare hands while everyone was watching through the glass. It was not at Readerz and she felt awkward about ordering it—did she have it right that people liked to make an informed decision before buying the one book they planned to read in a given year? In any case, peeping through the windows of a soul was okay, but climbing in through the window head over feet was a shade extreme. She settled for a few sample patches of it online. He had never met her, but he was writing about her, or someone very like her. How odd, to consider he was scrunching up his face and concentrating on making her into an unfamiliar object for others to examine in private moments while she was looking back at him through the glass and making up her own version of events or non-events, such as pounding the transparent barrier of her observation tank.

They didn't say much whenever he came in—she knew about his allergies that (refreshingly) had no relation to nuts or gluten—but it was clear he saw her as a person of quality, incredibly conscientious. There was no reason to fuss over him. She found him "thinky" and that was something, but it was like that show about the birds—sometimes the female preferred an excellent builder and other times she preferred a clown, as with budgies, if she remembered correctly. He was easy enough on the eyes, and then she supposed she had murmured "pretty" or "thinky" like a heavy breather against the glass because the next order was taking a long time. She was tall, or as she read in a poorly formatted snippet, "too tall to drop forks on a Friday," and she kind of liked that. She was under the impression that he could see her as she was, beyond all this day-to-day twaddle. Some of the men who leered said "hot" when in larger groups. She would smile in response and usually she would receive a decent tip. It was all standardized, along with her tight top and short, dark skirt, with everything decided long ago by the crotchety ancients at corporate headquarters.

The movie came to mind again because it was imitating life, in which you are not supposed to think or feel anything, only suppress your slightest inclination. For one thing, she appreciated that he lowered his eyes when she came closer and did not play games with the water glass, the way some of those tedious goons did. Yes, she was tall and she knew since that first growth spurt early on in high school that she was like an animal—she had no wish to remember which animal—trying to lower itself to take a drink of water, or to pour water out for the new regular. Maybe being "hot" blotted out that memory of herself that sometimes returned with a vengeance, along with those spiteful commentaries. Her sense of self was different in this case, as she thought she could see a tinge of red creeping about his ears and neck and she knew she had caused that with the simplicity of her pour. Maybe he could see something that would surprise her, something more non-objective than her "girls" or her rear. According to his biography, that is how he saw the world.

Wisteria's keen awareness of his perception made her want to press the issue, to squeeze some objective remark out of him, to brush her body against his the way people did so easily in some novels, to make sure everything was understood between them, even without words. Not that it was impossible to make contact. He was wrong about the impossibility, but it was still terribly hard at times, to say what you wanted to say and mean what you wanted to mean, when it counted. Anyway, he would probably write about her and give the impression she aspired to be a cheerleader for the home team, or more likely an actress. She had a Creative Communications degree and had tried a few jobs, but in the end it was less boring to wait on people than it was to sit in an office all day. Somewhere, her funny customer had come up with a citation about Juan Gris the painter becoming a baker to look at people and it was like that, only she was not a painter. On a good day she was a still life, a quick sketch, a study—she did not mind being so. Therefore, it was more than fair to desire the object of a decent perception to come along, to take a look and see her in a light removed, or even as she really was. Reciprocity is the word he would use.

Then she saw him enter, and she stepped out from behind the glass and warned Ashley to watch what she was doing, vacuuming up those crumbs, as she was blocking the way through with her tush—she bit her lip for even thinking of calling attention to it—and returned to fetch the pitcher before he could follow that interfering tush to a seat. Wisteria turned over the empty glass and poured the water in; the new regular looked into her light brown eyes. She had something for him, leaning in closer until he could sense her excitement through her tight top, brushing against the little hairs along his left arm as her mouth found his earlobe and so many warm, clever words flowed out of her right into his ear and right away his fingers found the spot that gave her the most pleasure.

Actually, there was no piloerection to speak of. She was still holding the pitcher of water, standing in a partial crouch, and calling to mind the indigenous sanderlings with their soft little cries and he was looking at her quizzically, his face in the shape of a question mark sidling up against an exclamation mark but more surprised than angry, she hoped. When she returned to take his order, the book hit the table more violently than she expected and fighting off a spot of shallow breathing—a lifelong affliction—she raised her voice and everything came out rough.

"You left this. This is yours, yeah?"

The new regular nodded, not knowing what else to add. She helped him out by wondering aloud if he wanted his usual and he nodded again. Wisteria walked away, taller than usual, and called out his order behind the glass. Remember, no mayo or trademark sauces. Just plain. Plain as the day is long.

Master and the Mounties

"Farinata."

"Farinata? That sounds like something."

"Sir? The kind lady at the front sent me in about the writing program."

"So you want to become a creative writer!"

Professor Klamm opened a drawer and poured some rum into a tumbler. After all, it was a lovely summer's afternoon.

"No, thanks." .

"I wasn't offering. That's just my cliché of the day. Force of habit. One must get oneself into a rigid regime. You write, I trust?"

"A few poems of some small repute to my name, sir. And a few other fragments that might be called novellas, on a good day. If you would be so kind as to—"

"Never mind. Everything will arrive with your application."

"Yes, that was on my mind. How do I apply?"

"How do you apply? Ha! There's no one way to apply. Your things will arrive and in time they will receive a proper gander."

"Gander? By the geese outside, sir?"

"What's that? Oh no, the geese will have gone elsewhere by then."

"And you, you're the head of—"

"Me? I don't know what they told you. I have my papers. Mostly, I like to teach Kafka. Just don't let that get around."

"Kafka, well, that takes the cake! I have a background in—"

"Of course, Kafka's trending like mad nowadays. He would have called it kitsch. How many atrocities are committed in that man's name, I wonder?"

"Atrocities! Not by me, sir!"

"Look, if you are serious about becoming a creative writer ... Farboob ... I will give you a comprehension exercise to take home. I shouldn't be telling you this much, but it is loosely based on a true story. Local colour, you know. If you are serious, you will read it, then make some notes and return to me with a short evaluation. Then we shall see who is the Master of Writing."

"Sir, I never said I was—"

"Too late, Farnoob. It has already begun. Once it has begun, even I cannot stop it. No one can."

~

K had left under a cloud. He had decided on Regina because the city was more or less the sort of sanatorium he had been seeking. He remained hopeful of Thomas Mann-ish scenarios. Snowy walks and cellos sounding. Yes,

that kind of thing. He struggled with nervous
anxiety and mental anguish, and periodically
suffered "manic attacks." Now he was out of
work and only eligible for a temporary residence but not a semi-permanent residence, and
by virtue of these facts, he was K, which is
to say, a character type of the previous century, a person who scarcely existed, without
origin story or traceable lineage. During a
trip to the Yukon, in a faint-hearted attempt
to follow the courageous steps of Jack London,
he had fallen out with BUSTER over the lack
of wireless service in former Gold Rush towns.
An additional month of non-service had been
added to his bill, in accordance with BUSTER
policy. K let a month pass while he waited for
his final bill to arrive, and in the interim,
threatening notes from BUSTER were dispatched.
The threat of a collection agency sent him
running into his bank, where with trembling
hands he instructed the teller to pay for the
month he had never needed or used. It was not
until the love notes arrived that K realized
he was in an abusive relationship. BUSTER was
not sorry in the slightest, and yet BUSTER
wanted him back.

Not that the first tentative call to HEL-
TEL—a union of two telecommunications compa-
nies freshly merged for his convenience—lacked
the remote intimacy of a cavity search. Still,
this was closer to what K thought he needed,
and it would save him from the shame of crawling back to BUSTER. He had decided to order a

smartphone, primarily because he wanted to be able to look up bus times when the sub-zero temperatures arrived, and also because he wanted to have the Saskatchewan Roughriders' cheer team a mere touch away. That was exactly the amount of human contact he wanted, as established at his last counselling session, during which he had recoiled with uncharacteristic vehemence from any thought of *staying connected.* He had gone dark for quite a while, but it was time to return to the global grid. After the call was over, he closed the admittedly clunky borrowed phone and set it down on the table. He had given up everything he had. Personal information and various addresses. Social insurance and credit card numbers, along with intimate details about former employers—and exes. Five business days later, he walked into the main post office and approached the counter.

"Hey K, your box is here."

"But what … how did you—"

"Also, I'm blaming you for the rain. Feels just like home, eh?"

When he opened up the box, K was a trifle stymied, but his neighbour directed him to an entertaining online video in which a scantily-clad anime sprite used a bobby pin and/or other sharp implements to free a tiny metal tray that was to house the precious SIM card he had carefully trimmed down to size. Then nothing. While he could find footage of alleged cheerleaders doing all kinds of things online, he could learn nothing about the Saskatchewan

Roughriders' cheer team on his new phone. Not their area of study or their hobbies or even their favourite dance number. No, the app was not working. Then confusion set in and he felt one of his attacks coming on. Could it be that he was still on the rebound after BUSTER, and it was too soon to hook up with another provider, no matter how attractive they seemed? Had he been hasty and ordered the wrong phone?

Once again, he borrowed the neighbour's clunky phone. After a lifetime of pressing "1" and several songs, a human voice spoke into his ear. At that point, K broke down and told the voice everything—the circumstances of his lingering issues with BUSTER and even about his fear of commitments, at least contractual ones. Two years with a Tetchy 2046 already seemed like a lifetime. It was the new N-Erv phone he wanted—no, needed!—or he wouldn't be able to check the bus schedule or see the Roughriders cheerleaders whenever he wanted and life would be, in fact, over. He had not sat idle, no siree. He had asked for help in two HELTEL stores, one in the North and one in the South, but they had washed their hands of him in accordance with the Pontius Pilot program and its policies clearly stated in small print somewhere or other. Finally, returning to the store in the centre of town where his incredible journey had begun, the two young ladies in hijabs had once again genuinely sympathized with his desire to pull up the eminently flexible cheer-bearers of Rider

Nation at a moment's notice on the iciest of evenings.

"Your address, sir?"

"Yes, I've been through this. I don't have—"

"The Vancouver address, this—"

"Uhm, I don't live there, not anywhere—"

"We will send you a custom mailer."

"But I don't live anywhere … it's not—"

"The custom mailer will get to you, no worries. It will be someone you know …"

K hung up the phone that was not even his and put it down on the table that was also not his. The mailer did arrive, by the time he had nearly forgotten about the whole ordeal. His neighbour had found a soggy envelope on the doorstep, containing the folded box in which to send the Tetchy 2046 back to meet its makers. K apologized profusely for causing one nuisance after another and the neighbour returned home, muttering about folks without jobs or homes or phones or gargantuan trucks. K realized there was another decision to make. As it was Saturday, he could call the courier to pick up his package or he could take a bus, either to the North or the East, and send the box back through an office supplies store like Stickies. Soon, the box would appear in Brampton, and hopefully, this would enable him to start the process all over again. Through the borborygmus, a voice inside him sounded like it was asking him to *choose wisely*.

K was on the Number Seven bound for Regina's East End. The bus was packed with junior athletic fundraisers, and K tried not to stare at the green uniforms they wore, or the phones they were brandishing. Fortunately, he remained ignorant of the fact they were just return-ing from a fundraising visit with a few of the Saskatchewan Roughriders and what is more, their cheer team, who had given them a special demonstration in honour of the cause. Everyone on the bus was abuzz about the evening game, but K was preoccupied with the taped-up box in his hands. Most of the passengers got off at the same stop and K found himself follow-ing the green uniforms; meanwhile, their talk about food reminded him that he had not eaten breakfast.

He was apprehensive upon entering Frieda's Fries, where more than thirty officers of the Royal Canadian Mounted Police examined him with unsmiling eyes. Conversation about the pros and cons of Mountie Barbie dried up. K was extremely shaky, and he was also acutely aware of the enigmatic box he was carrying. He ordered as calmly as he could, but as usual, he got stuck on the onions, his Achilles heel.

"Rahhhr onions?"

"Onions but not cooked onions."

"There are cooked onions and onions."

"Onions then, but raw onions, or … well, onions, yes, onions …"

Yuen the shift leader was not to blame if Customer #47 was having an episode. One of the Mounties (in cavalry blue) got up and asked if he could take a look at the box. K handed it

over and then withdrew, trembling. The Mountie
sniffed the box and clawed at the scotch tape.
Then, in a moment of inspiration, he dropped
it on the floor and raised his right boot. K
shook his head with tears streaming down his
face. A gun had been drawn and suddenly all
of the guns were out. They were firing at the
box on the floor and all the people in green
were cheering and K was running past them and
out the door. He made it across the road and
ducked into Slimbuy's. He watched the front of
the store cautiously and did not notice that
he was backing into a cut-out of Mutt Blimey,
the celebrity chef who was saving the planet
by slaughtering animals humanely. Mounties
were already filing into the store and spread-
ing out. K's fight-or-flight response—hyper-
arousal!—melted away as cheerleaders appeared
here and there, advertising frozen gourmet
selections. Also, if he spent fifty dollars,
he would get a killer deal on Mutt Blimey's
choice tableware. The man from the main post
office came into view and asked him to sign
a petition, because two of the three service
counters were endangered. Strangely, the petition was also asking the government to invest
more heavily in banking. Need we add that
agents of the government were on their way?

~

Professor Klamm looked up at his return visitor and nodded knowingly.

"Flarfydee. A glutton for punishment, hmm?"

"Sir, I'm afraid I didn't really understand that text you gave me."

"All will be clear in time. I hope you aren't too discouraged. It does go with seven volumes that are part of The K Project. It is fortuitous that I happen to have them right here for you."

"You know, I'm not sure this program is right for me."

"Come now, Flirtboob. You want that young lady to look you up on LinkedIn, yes? Well then, there is nothing for it. You are the One. No matter the cost, you *must* become a creative writer."

Dearest J,

At the risk of goading forth gonadic disaster, I must do my best to unburden myself of this wobbly (rib or loin?) tickler that will not slither out of the bittersweet bowels of my being anytime soon. I am subject to the most incredible delusion—whenever I find myself under the spell of your distinct physical advantage or whenever our eyes lock with a faint clang, etc.—that some electron has gone rogue between us, that absence is doing overtime in the name of presence, that there are worse ways to squander a post-prandial moment. Surely you have seen me loping about in lukewarm anguish since the summer, with no solace but an orange truck in the grey square, full of delectable fowl and battercakes, such is my wont.

The rest of it, once comestible has thoroughly greeted fickle diges-tion, is a deep longing for your person. Why? That is a natural kneejerk response and to parse its intention, I would have to wade through countless clichés without really knowing what windows of the soul look like, even if I ordered them to be replaced. I would be glad to toss aside such lofty metaphysics, but then it would appear that I covet your distinct physical advantage too keenly, based solely on a local ad for an item of devil-may-care frivolity that fell open before my eyes. Sweet lady, such strategies of illumined angles and accentuated surface areas are not unknown to me. I would only compound my error in denying the unearthly rattle of the bedroom door in the middle of the night, along with your soft footfalls and the curious apparition of you in such fetching clobber. If only you knew half my excitation at such a confused vision! Such is the lot of man, especially at the crack of dawn, to find himself a sad, sticky, weepy thing in a compromising position over nothing he can quite see or hear.

You know, if I said that your shaded eyelids conveyed all the sensuous wiles of Adele Bloch-Bauer posing for Klimt's Judith, would that make any more sense to you than to say the way you wear that hat reminds me of Proust's darling Albertine, or for that matter, a frieze depicting a hundred thousand Albertines, all in similar hats? I have clung to my sang-froid and silence as much as possible, lest a half-dozen atrocities spill out of my mouth, when a smile or a quick kiss would still better what is done. I could surely map out your excellent dermis or mentally arrange your various accessories and accent pieces into a still life, but none of these things are you, exactly.

By now, your break is probably over; you must resume your shift. We will go on with our routine motions and gesticulations like automatons until one day something snaps. Except when you smile at me in a free moment, and I am so gobsmacked beyond recovery. There I waver and wobble, tremulous all over and about to swoon like one of Mallory's knights in a crisis. Before the wind chill brings a tear to the eye, that is. Though you need not worry. I have enough fortitude not to plunge myself into the nearest slough or storm drain—there I stand on the little bridge in the park and take my licks, with no one to tell my troubles to, save a beaver or muskrat.

Imagine when the Flying Dutchman finally came ashore, and Senta recognized him as the man from the picture she had known all her life; they sang a duet of such rapturous feeling that it seemed his accursed years of wandering the seas would finally be over—but that is sheer shash in this place of imaginary waters and dry harbours. Instead, I imagine lifting the hat from your head and watching the green shock in your dark hair falling free as the usurious layers of gold leaf are pried aside to tenderly give suck to the slavering gob most in need of suck. Then, if the cold, hard stars are sufficiently aligned—in flagrante delicto ad perpetuum—you might observe the swirling preoccupation that delights and damns me to the quick.

Most Humbliciously Yours,
F

It was just Farinata's luck to reach the crying section of the Regina Public Library and find his place taken. Usually, in addition to his own heroic weeping at the downtown branch, there was the ancillary weeping of some poor soul who had just been evicted or a single parent desperate for a late payment, trying through tears to keep up the cheer of their bemused child. He decided on a seat at the next table but could not manage a single blubber. Instead, he studied the stony face of the thirty-something man in his usual place, noting the red-rimmed eyes and moist cheeks. Bravely holding back his own ponderous *gémissements*, Farinata got up and approached the fellow cryface with considerable aplomb.

"A touch of seasonal affect, I trust."

"What? Ah, no. If you knew!"

"Let's get some air."

They stepped out into September. Farinata stared at the orange food truck, absent-mindedly making gentle enquiries regarding his new companion's condition in the simplest of copular terms. How was he and was he peckish for the pick of those pecks clucked through his mind over and over again, but he remembered his manners. Surely his excellency would care to partake of those gourmet wares before spilling his guts in the vacant square? The poor fellow shook his head although Farinata was bent on a spot of dinner theatre—however copacetic it might be—to aid his own persnickety digestion. His last ditch protest was to stress that the hoi polloi feast would be as gluten-less as his newfound friend wished.

A mere paragraph away, Farinata parked himself on the bench opposite the interrogative chair, and did his level best to hide the *veni-vidi-vici* on his glowing kisser, for he loved his food about as much as he loved his love. Aside from his triumph over beating the lunch rush, he was dimly aware of having received what, under the circumstances of fraternal grief, seemed an obscenity: a finely cooked breast of chicken nestled between two waffles doused in the most heavenly homemade gravy. Once he was comfortable, he prodded the man's shoulder with his plastic fork and entreated him to begin.

"They show films at the library, you know. I do like films if a bit of thought goes into it without them being too arty. By arty, I am thinking of one where two guys run around a tree to represent wartime Poland. Anyway, there's a small theatre downstairs—I'm sure you've been. So one night, I decided to see a movie called *Berberian Sound Studio*. If you know Antonioni's *Blow-Up*, then you might appreciate that it's a listener's version of that. A mild-mannered sound engineer works on a tacky horror film in Italy and gets sucked deeper and deeper into his work—there are so many shots of vegetables being chopped in half to create the chilling effects of bodies being hacked to bits. That sort of thing. After a while, he can no longer tell what is real and what is part of the film. I won't give away the end, as I hate it when people do that. But the end came, as it was bound to, and the credits started rolling and the lights came on and then I saw her pass."

"Who?"

"I should preface by saying that four years ago, my wife drowned."

"Sorry."

"She was on a trip. Then she vanished. A policeman notified me … I never saw …"

Farinata nodded and swallowed with care.

"The film upset you in some way."

"It's not that. I saw her! I mean, I saw my wife leaving the theatre."

"You're messing with me."

"No, it was her. She started up the aisle just before the lights came on and I caught her profile. She was more or less the same!"

"In times of stress, we can easily imagine our loved ones are still with us. It's been known to happen. Appetite can also be reduced—"

"That's just the thing. We didn't get along. Not really. I didn't want to hurt her or for anything bad to happen to her. But after the first fires had cooled, we sort of gave up. We were living in a duplex and after the upstairs tenant moved away, my wife took her place and we began to live like strangers. A polite word here and there became the norm. Then she went on that trip. I didn't even know the details. The policeman was the one to tell me it was a trip to Hinchliffe."

Farinata wondered how someone could drown in a place like Hinchliffe, or anywhere on the bald prairie, but kept this to himself as he started on the second waffle.

"It gets weirder, believe me. I thought like you do, that it was just a random symptom of my grief. I stayed away for a week before I dared return to the theatre. Hitchcock's *Vertigo* was showing, a special selection by a visiting curator at the Dunlop Gallery. She gave a long preamble before the film, and I couldn't make much sense of it. Apparently, the movie was based on a French novel where the detective strangles his resurrected lover,[13] ruining his second chance to keep the illusion of his idealized love alive. As I said, I couldn't make much sense of it."

Farinata pushed aside his box of chicken bones. An astute reader will guess that the finely cooked breast contained no bones and will therefore assume that our friend ordered a second helping—this time, a thigh and drumstick—before returning to commiserate with his storyteller. Then he rubbed his sticky hands together and stood up, revealing that which he knew.

"I do know there's a screenplay more in line with the oft-rehashed opera about Orpheus and Eurydice. It's named after part of a Keats poem called 'Ode to a Nightingale' and

---

13. Get a word in edgewise, and it might be apropos to point out that Brian De Palma's primary improvement in his remake of *Crime d'amour* is in changing a movie screening to a ballet performance of Debussy's *Prelude to the Afternoon of a Faun*—also using a split-screen homage—in which the music evokes the lyrical perpetuation of nymphs, as Mallarmé penned them in his poem of the same name, and the dancers, İbrahim Öykü Önal and Polina Semionova, mirror the artificial poses of the characters, not to mention society itself. Horrific as the crime is, it has less of a sexual motif than . in the original film, and embodies the mythic theme of righteous succession.

you are fortunate that I once wrote a none-too-shabby essay
on it because I still remember this much …

Darkling I listen; and, for many a time
I have been half in love with easeful Death …"

The storyteller shook his head and picked up his tale
where he had left off.

"Yes, the preamble was just like that. There was also a
lot of psychobabble about making love to a ghost. Can you
imagine? Then something about a revolving turntable for that
famous kiss scene in the hotel room. And the music …"

"Ah yes, Bernard Herrmann."

"Whatever. When the lights were shut off, the woman
who looked like my wife sat down a little ways in front of
me. I tried to watch the film, but I couldn't help staring at
her instead. I still remember that eerie green light on her
face, and that bizarre music …"

"Bernard Herrmann."

"Whatever. After the leading lady—well, let's face it, she
was a con artist—died a second time, the lights came on
and the woman who looked like my wife turned around and
returned my stare."

"Hang on a minute … did you say it was in Hitchcock?"

"What?"

"Hitchcock, Saskatchewan. Where she drowned. Unless
she fell into Hitchcock Bay."

"Hey man, not cool. I'm opening up to you!"

"Sorry. Do continue."

"So we walked out at the same time and I watched her,
expecting her to light up straight away. It lingered between
us, my expecting her to smoke and that familiar sense of her
wanting to. We kept going without speaking. Then, in the
middle of Victoria Park, she leaned against a tree and looked
at me, as if to enact a scene out of the movie. You know,

where she touches the inside of the tree? It was bizarre to see a face so like another face. Her hair was cut short and her face was different ... I don't know how exactly. She laughed at the way I was looking at her and stuck her tongue out. I told her that she did remind me of someone close to me. I couldn't sleep that night because I was so eager to see her the following day. We met at the MacKenzie Gallery and we were standing in front of a very green Roy Kiyooka when she leaned into me. For a moment, I thought I would black out. She had that same look on her face that I found so irresistible. We kissed softly and then more passionately and it was just like those joyful days when I first met my wife. I was on cloud nine, but I was also impatient to undress her, to examine her body for those particular marks that had become so dear to me. She kept aloof, pointing out that we had just met, even if it did not feel that way."

Farinata dropped his box of bones into the nearest receptacle with a smile.

"Feel better?"

"Huh?"

"Sometimes it's good to get these things off our chest, hmm?"

"I'm not finished yet."

"Oh. Ah."

"After a week, she gave in and returned with me to my apartment. By then, I had examined her face carefully and had even seen her provincial ID. I was ready to believe she was an entirely different woman. In that case, was it lousy of me to use her as a substitute for my genuine love who was gone forever? I suppose, but I didn't care. The look and smell and taste of her told me all I needed to know. Or it might have been my vanity, my wanting to believe that she would go to such lengths just to start over with me, like something out of a fable."

"'A sad tale's best for winter ...'"

"Hmm ... what's that?"

"I was just thinking of *The Winter's Tale*. In spite of his terrible mistakes, Leontes gets a second chance and the wife he thought was dead is returned to him after many years and they are at long last reconciled. It's quite moving, the way the Bard tells it."

"Well, this is real life. Anyway, on our own special night, she had specific instructions for me. She fished out some rope from god-knows-where and tied my wrists together. Then she used a green scarf[14] to blindfold my eyes. I could see the outline of her getting undressed but not in any detail in the dark room—there was only a soft, orange glow from the streetlamp near my window. Believe it or not, everything was like the first days with my wife; the way she kissed my bare skin and got me ready for... well ... what she used to call her 'sensuous ascension.' Soon, I could think of nothing but thrusting up into her as she bounced up and down with her usual frenzy. It had been quite a while for me and I wanted to keep going all night, mainly because I seemed to have more stamina that ever before. Even so, under the green material, my eyes were wet. It was so close to everything I had been dreaming about since her disappearance— it was such a shock, but it was also so familiar and comforting—the way her small hands were clinging to me—that I only wanted to fall asleep beside her ..."

---

14. The mind wanders a bit. Another of De Palma's improvements in his remake was a shot of the black-stockinged feet of the twin sister descending into telltale green heels, blending into artificial turf beside the grave.

Farinata rubbed his fingers with a serviette and patted the man's arm.

"Well, I'm glad for you."

"That's not all. When I woke up, she was gone. I looked out the window and the street was empty except for a police car idling at the end of the block. Then, before I could take a closer look, it sped off."

"Weird. Do you think it was … the same policeman … who …"

"I don't know what to think anymore. When I managed to pull the scarf off, I recognized the same faded birds in the morning light. It was my wife's scarf!"

"So do you figure this for an insurance scheme, or maybe that she has a wicked twin, or what?"

"I've run over everything again and again. I don't understand it at all!"

"Yes, that's an odd duck if there ever was one. Rather like those Russian riddles[15]—ever read Gogol or Dostoyevsky?—yes, more of a riddle and not really a story."

"Not really a story? What's that supposed to mean?"

"Well, a story has a beginning, a middle, and an end. I read that somewhere. Perhaps if she *had* fallen into Hitchcock Bay … but that is neither here nor there. Now, if you'll excuse me, I have my own crying to attend to. It's better, you see, not to cry on an empty stomach."

---

15. According to Richard Peace in his introduction to Nikolai Gogol's *Plays and Petersburg Tales*, a typical device is to set aside plot to make room for *zagadka* ("setting of the riddle"), sometimes without *razgadka* ("the unriddling"). For the record, Farinata employs *zagadka* without *razgadka* in a number of his books, but prefers not to discuss this technique at length while the digestive process is underway.

D r. Cassandra Capellini was waiting in a vacant corner on the sixth floor of the university library. Farinata hurried over to her, at once dispelling his anxiety and shortness of breath.

"*Professoressa,* sorry I'm late!"

"Shhh. Now where were we?"

"The tenth canto, of course."

"Ah yes, your personal obsession must be addressed."

Her thick yellow curls fell over her heavy eyelids as she paged through one of a number of tomes. Earlier that morning, the espresso had been exceptional, although he had been dressed down by more than one of the seraphs surrounding Trish for slipping into Italian, for he was puzzling over the fragment "*A ciò non fu' io sol*"[16] when he blurted

---

16. "In that, I was not alone," a phrase put in Farinata degli Uberti's mouth by Dante in the Circle of the Heretics.

out the wrong thing, accidentally using the terminology of a rival coffee chain from across the 49th that perpetually loomed in the distance, threatening like the famous tornado to wipe out anything in its path. Trish had been unable to protect him from the derision of her co-workers, not even with an impromptu *Canadiano*.

"Let's see here ... Farinata degli Uberti was a great war-chief of the Tuscan Ghibellines, who were anti-papal, and the head of the ancient noble house of the Uberti. He played a large part in driving the Guelphs out of Florence on more than one occasion, and that is Dante Alighieri's main beef with him, historically. His arrogant desire to rule on his own terms created many difficulties, but in his favour, when the general consensus was to destroy Florence, he rose in open counsel and pointed out that he was a native of Florence first and a Ghibelline second. In fact, he would defend his city by himself if necessary. When Dante's Guelphs returned, they were quick to crush the edifices of the Uberti and to issue a special decree against anyone in that family line."

"This is all making perfect sense. Politics, eh? Anything else?"

"Farinata is to be found among the heretics which, in Dante's view, would include skeptics who denied or even cast doubt upon the idea that the soul is immortal. In the *Inferno*, these skeptics occupy giant iron tombs that are heated to extremity. They will be open until the Day of Judgment, when they will be sealed forever. This 'death after death' is quite the 'I told you so,' don't you think?"

"*Professoressa*, I seem to recall from a Milton lecture that in its etymological origins, the word 'heresy' means 'choice.' That was Milton's paradoxical argument; that the true heretic would have to be against heresy."

"Neither your Greek wordplay nor your ad hoc Miltonics will help you through the Middle Ages, my friend. Just a whiff of doubt, and you would be all washed up."

"Ah, my questions have left me. I am far too preoccupied with my fate to come. Please help me focus and guide me through that thorny, vulgar eloquence, so that I may improve. It might help to get some of the Tuscan in my ears."

"Do not be deceived. This is more than *terza rima*, these magnificent images that build with every line or these effects that sound with the teeth. These rhymesters don't stand a chance, but maybe I don't either. I would rather give you the gist of it."

"All right. What is this?"

"Farinata is rising from the flames, erect … um, his top half, I mean. He has a haughty look about him as if he thinks he's better than everybody else in damnation. Virgil warns our poor pilgrim to watch how he talks to him. That's an allegorical thing. Reason must dictate our conduct and that means thinking before speaking."

"And here?"

"Cavalcante dei Cavalcanti, the father of Dante's poet friend, is butting into the conversation. He wonders why his son is not on this poetic adventure and to explain, the pilgrim alludes to the son's alchemical theories and disbelief in heavenly matters. In other words, he throws the other poet under the bus."

"What about this part here?"

"Farinata resumes his speech and justifies his own actions, complaining about savage treatment by the people. Then, ah, this is interesting … in reference to Florence, he says 'I, with bold face, defended her.'"

"And the rest?"

"Farinata explains that he and the other heretics can see the future but not the present. One translator says, 'We see asquint, like those whose twisted sight / can make out only the far off.' On the day of reckoning, the door that is ajar to future knowledge will slam shut and they will know absolutely nothing."

"Oh, nice."

"Cheer up. I will read you this stanza near the end of the canto, because it reminds me of you and your verses."

Through a window, the sun lit up her yellow curls and the page as she read slowly and carefully:

> *quando sarai dinanzi al dolce raggio*
> *di quella il cui bell' occhio tutto vede,*
> *da lei saprai di tua vita il viaggio.*[17]

"That sounds amazing, really. But what—"

"I feel that these lines are here to provide balance for the line about the poet Cavalcanti. When his father utters, 'The sweet light does not strike against his eyes?' it is because he thinks his son is no longer alive, which is a mistake. That contrasts with this part about finding your way without error."

Farinata was too stunned by the softness in her voice to answer.

"I brought you something from Bologna. It's a copy of *La Vita Nuova*, in Italian. So you can keep up your practice."

"*Molte grazie, cara professoressa* ... but you know, for the life of me, I'll never know why you came here to study Canadian poetry."

---

17. "When you bask in the sweet radiance / of the lady whose lovely eye sees all, / then you will know your life's way."

"Nor I, for the life of me, why your adopted family should decide to call you Farinata."

"Ha, I can grasp this bit here! Of the rest, let us keep schtum."

That day, they read no further.

Appassionata on Argyle

When the sixty per cent chance of a thunderstorm was confirmed, Farinata was startled out of his reverie, once again failing to notice the yellow cornrows or the bosom heaving through a T-shirt or the thighs swathing his crumpled sad-sack-of-a-self in the passing aura of their continual locomotion. She might have made the tackle but he was already off the little bridge in Les Sherman Park and hurrying away under the downpour, and besides, it was Lucia, the young woman from the library, who made the catch. At this instant, a stolid Brontëan defense[18] is in order, if not for Thackeray, then for our friend, lest he find himself entirely friendless and soaked through.

Jane Eyre this ain't. We are thus carried away by more

---

18. They say he's like Fielding: they talk of his wit, humor, and comic powers. He resembles Fielding as an eagle does a vulture: Fielding could stoop on carrion, but Thackeray never does.

hyperbole than our own carrion-stooper deserves, perhaps on account of the excitement brought on by the thunderstorm. Metaphysical awareness—unless there are more substantial grounds beyond what passes for omniscience here— enabled the pretty eye of Lucia to discern such a degree of quality in the clammy, sopping thing sprinting along Argyle. Personally, she had never presumed to approach the art or elegance of a defensive block, but in her view it was now or never. *Instinctively,*—as goes the modifier in most erotic yarns—she found the muddled blob in the corner of her eye and knew it must be helped or hindered at once. Her timing was impeccable. The embrace was neither too flimsy nor too firm, and Farinata was bowled over into an open bit of road. He was up to his waist in whatnot and about to let fly interrogatives in the most pejorative sense possible when the radiant face, in some way attached to the comely hand offering help, brought about a flash of recognition.

Lucia! Non è ...[19]

A proper lady might have waited for hailstones the size of your head but after all, it was a new century. Mild tackling and invitations during a downpour were to be expected. He hung his head meekly and followed her inside, unaware that the lady of the yellow cornrows would have made him feel like a warrior without the usual head games. He surrendered up his things for prompt laundering and as collateral, she gave him a floral dressing gown. By the time the green tea had adequately steeped, his sorry tale was ready to pour.

Farinata had been presumptuous; he had flown too near

---

19. "Lucia, you are no more." Compare with a certain Irish author: "Dying to embrace her in his shirt. Last act of Lucia. Shall I nevermore behold thee? Bam! He expires. Gone at last."

the sun. His little book had arrived and he had dared to ask for a reading at the chain store, Readerz. We omit any whit of anticipation he had felt over Trish running across his homemade poster any number of ways, as it adds nothing to the story. Saturday arrived and there was some tiny misunderstanding. He had hoped for a microphone, an inch of elevation, and even a few chairs. Instead, two women in Readerz vests had tucked him behind a display featuring a memoir by a reality show celebrity who ate nothing but a hot new superfood. They had brought him a complimentary espresso from the in-store rival of Grounds for Delight, sealing his fate in terms of brand betrayal (Trish!), and then had used the in-store talking stick to get him going. He had begun to read, slowly and softly at first, and then with more energy and volume, although he was suddenly reminded of the gang of Jehovah's Witnesses in the public square, who had certainly won this round. Mothers had marched their brood along, in some cases, scooping them up as we see in Westerns right before the shooting begins. Other patrons of the store had hidden amid rows of mugs, potpourri holders, scented candles, and picture frames. Then the heckling had begun. Mostly disparate characters, young enough in years, carefully hissing their critiques from behind various accessories. In this economy, it was hard to put together a decent claque, and Farinata had been obliged to take every remark to heart. It was not lost on him that Trish had not swept in at the last minute to purchase a signed copy. His existence was dubious at best.

To be fair to Farinata, he was not bawling like a newborn. That said, a touch of snivelling seldom went amiss. As for Lucia, her timing was once again impeccable, having casually adjusted the humidifier and thrown off her bright sweater before plunking a few choice mnemonics of the

Appassionata in an eminently flattering tank top. Besieged by this emotional barrage, our friend discovered that he was— to attempt an impromptu translation of Catullus—"poking through his cloak." In a sudden panic, he reached out into empty air to caress the pale deliberation of his dark idoless (naturally, several blocks away, grinding beans) but met instead the sanguine kisser of Lucia, whose arms were made to squeeze the sorrow out of him even if it took all afternoon and into the wee hours. No, he had not given chase, but carnality had found and conquered him. It was a bit of a turn up for the books when she bent over a footrest, for even as the floral robe landed on the floor, the thought of anything remotely bestial was beyond him. Arriving at this fateful hour in this house, a stranger out of the rain, he was not to know of the young lady's prelapsarian life that, in itself, was a veritable universe of tastes and routines before such an awkward breach. She offered up a bestiary of terms and he did his best to respond in kind, rationalizing the animality that was seeping into his personal metaphysics. Soon, they did seep, and then a quick sleep, and then more seeping, and then more sleeping, and so on.

And haplessly ever after.[20]

In the common area of the downtown public library, Lucia was explaining away his circumstances. He had gotten close to means, but never quite near enough. He could not get a position as a clerk, although he was reasonably gifted. He had perhaps been too overzealous in having things his own way but that would change. Admittedly, he had been given strange things to do and that was his special province. It was not as if he could read children a story or offer

---

20. Their edge-worn intimacy led to several scenes in which he became the William Makepeace Thackeray to her Charlotte Brontë, but we find it more tasteful to press on with what little story there is.

advice that would lead to a win-win. The argument against him was that he was at times too idealistic, too rigid. Well, what if he was a hard man—at this point, Lucia was blushing slightly—maybe that is what was needed now and again or most of the time? She admitted that he had a reputation; that his difficult and even amorous ways sometimes left a funny taste in everyone's mouth, that he had to move among them, although, in many ways, he was better off left alone. Yes, it was a bit of a riddle, but surely his heart was in the right place. Perhaps, if it was not too forward of her, he could at last occupy that library position that had been open for three years? After all, everyone needed help once in a while. Look at John Newlove.

When Farinata caught sight of Lucia again, she was clasping the hand of a tall, handsome, winsome ESL student named Heurtebise. He knew the young man's name was Heurtebise because Lucia was nearly squealing, "HEURTEBISE!" Farinata waited, eyeing the clock anxiously. When he turned to look again, they were gone.

Porpoises in the Post

When the Copernican upset came, as he guessed it could and would, it revolved around a short and tidy personal ad that had arrived in the letter box that was not really his. A cross word, a cold shoulder, and then the means of revenge were at hand. But by the hand of whom? Not a jealous sow, surely? That was Farinata thinking too highly and mightily of his simple soul once again. To explain to himself or anyone else why Juliette was not the sun would be, in his own warped idiom, to press flowery pillow over smoking muzzle. In short, a lady just shy of nineteen was looking for a gentleman, or a plurality of young gentlemen—Farinata winced at the stipulation that these mere striplings be under the blessed age of twenty-six—who would suit her purposes—the ad read "porpoises"—through their unflopping obeisance and everlasting gratitude when greeting her innumerable toys and mechanisms for causing minor pain.

Each applicant need only agree to call her Mistress Juliette or Mistress J and respond with a picture of his FACE, thus evoking the undeniable mystery of the thing that was not his FACE, yet waiting somewhere in the wings for its bold debut somewhere in the Regina area.

Farinata might have blown off this request for submission as a mere prank, had it not struck him that Mistress Juliette's promise to "humilate" called to mind a note sent to him from his beloved Trish expressing an ardent wish not to "humilate" him on the spot, which had led to a quiet word and many meaningful looks in the deepest recess of the food fair they could find. He might have let sleeping dogs lie, had there not been a hasty coda in Arial Narrow, with something close to the following vernacular:

Sorry not sorry you totes know who this [expletive] is

His beloved Trish—this Juliette who was not the sun but the dark side of the moon and behind closed doors on select afternoons and evenings more than understudy in the role of [expletive]? Farinata felt the blow doubly hard, for he had an inkling of what the omniscient mind would know, of the bosom taped together and the leather corset that was thought a novelty item for aspiring photogs; of the inscrutable tattoo on her left forearm that never failed to catch his eye, although now it was the name or surprised cry of the first wiseacre under twenty-six to stumble into her lair and to be—forgive the expression—pricked by the thorns of tainted love. Then the anklets or cuffs or rope to fasten any number of young gentlemen to any number of headboards for their promised treatment. Could marks made by finger blades or soft fists upon the supple canvas of his juniors live longer than the metaphysical marks her continual absence left inside of him?

It was not the best time for Farinata. Not so long ago, there had been a moving fare-thee-well at the food truck, involving a complimentary helping of chicken and waffles, to mark the occasion of the goodly husband and wife team returning to their "real lives" as postal carrier and hospital nurse. The temperature had dipped just below zero, and he was virtually alone at the night market, shivering and tucking into multiple repasts to try and compensate for what he was about to lose, what now was lost until well into next year's spring. After that parting of sweet crumbs and scattered bones, he had wandered the streets, nibbling into this and that without fulfillment. He needed the moral support of Trish, to have her pour the strong black stuff for him with a look of clear-eyed confidence that would obscure any brewing suspicion that the strength of the espresso was directly proportionate to the mild humiliation promised by Mistress J.

That night, he had a dream that he was on a ship with his hands and legs tied to the mast, only the mast was a family totem with growling and snarling animals on it. He was surrounded by naked young men, although he was certain they were at least eighteen or just shy of nineteen. A few wandered off and clustered around Jean Genet, who did everything he could to maintain their fascination.[21] The rest of them lined up and waited for Mistress J to appear. She was in a mask but it seemed that she could be Trish. She was captain of the ship and it was her duty to administer lashes for insubordination. He struggled in his bonds, but

---

21. Jane Rule has emphasized that Violette Leduc was so fascinated with Jean Genet, she dressed up as a (forthright) penis to get his attention. Suffice it to say, she did.

he remained fixated on the arc of her body as she put all of her might into striking the flesh of each of the young men. At last, she selected one of them and, with a sly grin, led him below deck. Jean Genet remained in the company of his choice acolytes, suggesting that it would be absolutely lovely if someone would slip someone else a length, just for kicks. It was then that the totemic mast seemed to grow taller and taller and shoot up into the sky, although the ship was sinking. Apparently, Mistress J had given the ship's carpenter two-dozen lashes while he was tending to a leak—meanwhile, the circling porpoises were leaping over him and he could not help getting wet ...

Farinata awoke with a start to discover that he was not the figurehead of a ship at the bottom of the ocean. In the first few fuzzy instants after waking, he was aware that he had not known a dream of such extraordinary liquidity since the height of his own wasted heyday. By the time his snoring resumed, he was chasing an orange food truck that kept pulling away at the last second ...

Assignation on Armistice

G emma brought the truck to a stop and tilted her head forward with deictic glee. Farinata looked through the windshield and saw hundreds of Canada geese on the frozen lake. Yes, the common image of our vast nation, a guppy mouth under the ice, going unheard. Otherwise, there was no symbolism in this setting, not even when Gemma seized his lined glove with her mitt.

Such well-protected fingerplay was born of a mild chagrin; she had won the post he had wanted at an adult learning centre on the other side of the lake, and he had realized this when he turned up to withdraw from a painting course. His particulars, which he had seen on the front desk on a happier day, had been replaced by her kindly face, bearing the notice in bold upper caps that the situation had been FILLED. This sorrow came not single-spined; as for personal reasons, his dactylographic daydreams were also to be postponed. She had performed the necessary operation and had promised him reimbursement—oh, what manner of compensation for such an outcome?—leaving him to fold up his tiny grudge and dwell upon its ideal conditions for wet nursing. Then he had heard the bittersweet bellow that piggybacked the letters of his name. He had stopped—one hand had landed gently on his right shoulder, but the other arm had caught him as he spun round, and they had fallen into a fleeting example of the forbidden dance, out of which they did not emerge wholly unenlightened. Impulsively, she had held him, saying he looked so down in the mouth she needed to know if he was okay. With a quaver in his voice, he had spoken so passionately of painting with the tip of his finger that she had redoubled the awkwardness of her embrace, as if carefully burping the assignation out of him.

Since that day, he had stalled as best he could, hoping that Trish would find a way to rescue him from this heat-seeking drone. Ah no, that was not fair! Gemma was indeed kindly with compelling eyes but not a word of a lie, she would absorb him in no time flat. He could not help but think of the brain-eating amoeba he had heard about on the news, the one that had caused him to drop his fork right into his rashers. If a thing like that could prosper when the chlorine levels were low enough, what miscreants could slurp us up at a moment's notice? One more fatal embrace and he would be immobilized. Another source of anxiety was the noble lie dangling between them, that quarrelsome iota that might come out in the middle of a tender scene, causing her to get puffed up and him to get puffed off. The wily old woman knew, because she had taken his application for the painting class and she had placed his particulars upon the desk. It would only take an inebriated FYI—say, at a holiday function over dubious punch—that lover-boy was in reality coveting her position rather than admiring her fair behind, and that's how things worked in these dark times. To sidestep catastrophe, they would have to drive the old woman to the lake and then drop her through one of the holes in the ice, and really, how would that look?

Gemma was at liberty, as the holiday had fallen on the Monday—a day of remembrance, a day of armistice—and the subterfuge that had worked on Saturday and Sunday had failed on this solemn day. She had gunned it right into his temporary cul-de-sac, picked him up, and they had taken the "scenic route" along Elphinstone, passing the giant beaver, turning at College and heading south again down Albert Street, crossing the longest bridge ever to cover the smallest littoral body, and crawled along Lakeshore Drive with sufficient leisure to admire the neoclassical point of the legislature that gingerly poked living sky.[22] Ignoring the insistent paddling of his thinly-lined palm, he gave his full attention to several geese who were standing up and moving slowly across the ice. Farinata might have survived this afternoon spiritually unscathed, were it not for a woman of advanced years who was reaching into a plastic bag and tossing out bread bits onto the ice.

"Whoa ... what's the matter?"

"They have tons of grass to eat. Then they have to make it on such a small amount of fat. But the alchemy of what they eat ... what is that, chuckwagon? Something either too enriched or full of chemicals. That could be the internal cause of the cramp, the blow that changes the life of any number of birds."

"Hey, calm down. She's just some old lady feeding the birds."

---

22. Our navigation system is equipped to store more freeassociation symbolism than you could ever want.

"Ah yes, take charge! You're obviously more qualified!"

"Well yeah, maybe I will take charge."

"Wait, what are you … mmphhht …"

The process had begun. The mitts were underfoot and his belt was curling around them. She appreciated random emotion in the resplendent male of the species. She had scented his and had quickly sped in for the kill. She was a diligent worker and he had no choice but to surrender. In fact, she exhibited a due diligence that was surprising for such a small space in such a bucolic setting. The lady of his bona fide affections could not save him now. Even the woman of advanced years had dispelled all of her crumbs and had doddered off, unaware of the distress signal dotted and dashed upon the steamed-up window of the truck. Wriggling beneath the kindly head and generous mouth, Farinata flushed and swooned, realizing that his time had come—yes, it was the exact sound and sensation of his brain being sucked out.

Fever After Black Friday

Ah, how the soft idyll slips away from us! The original land surveyors and planners were probably to blame for their meanness in doling out narrow parcels of mucky earth—that suits us fine because we are unable to come up with a description to match Keats' languishment before a withered sedge, or Hardy's evocation of a heath, or Gogol's lively treatment of Nevsky Prospect. Best admit the downtown core is flanked by some temple-shaped edifices and is otherwise grey in colour and character. The festivities for the Grey Cup were over and the drinking tents were slowly being dismantled. At the apex of triumphant fanfare, the unofficial edict that no one drink on Dewdney was lifted; for a moment, a group of tipsy rowdies gently jostled a pretty reporter to and fro on camera, but that was about it. The charming quarterback who with the CFL had won a personal triumph over NFL height restrictions and three years of fickle circumspection was given the opportunity during a parade to lead the procession along Albert—Champs-Élysées for a day—and appear at a window of the Saskatchewan Legislative Building with the Grey Cup held aloft over the cheering crowd. The scene lacked only a *Sinfonia Eroica.*

Even that iconic trophy has faded, Grey into grey backdrop. Not long ago, Farinata saw the celebrated Cup sitting in the food fair with one of the players—he could not recognize him from his place in line where he was waiting to buy ten wings. A few people stopped for selfies, but Farinata was wholly absorbed by his purchase of a few dollops of tzatziki from the Greek chain that was rival to the outfit whose own tzatziki and fowl sauces were foul indeed, no doubt because of some transnational trade agreement that stuck them with a teriyaki flavour that smacked of dish detergent. CBC had already reported Black Friday as orderly and quiet in Regina, although that sound bite did not harmonize perfectly with the disgruntled Santa on his break. Farinata found a place and before he had reduced his repast to a heap of bones, he murmured a non-denominational word of thanks for the original place name that had graciously offered up this bit of Indigenous marsh for the mall that had become the centre of his existence, especially without the orange truck to sustain him while he was at the mercy of minus thirty weather.

Still digesting, Farinata kept up his pacing as best as he could around the blue fencing that broke up Victoria Park, and likened himself to Evgeny Onegin being plunged into snowbound despair over the thwarted consummation of his requited but awfully inconvenient brand of passion. Passion; yes, it is worth saying "passion" at least three times to emphasize that his celestial view of Trish, even on these freezing evenings, did not go entirely disabused by carnal assertions that were beyond his control. Much as he would try to eschew any such notions, as one appetite went wanting, even growling, the other—and here the infernal and haptic hydraulic is drawn in boldest felt tip—grew in strength and ambition. In other words, he flew from ideas of uplifting sycophancy to slavering degradation and back again.

To make matters worse, he had caught the seasonal thing that was going around, for no amount of chasteness could shield our hero from the microbes loitering around a bus handrail, and in his fever upon a makeshift bed of Black Friday cushions—his worldly things were still making their way along the #1 amid snow warnings—he called out the name of his lady of the slightly distant demeanour, imploring her to step out of the shadows and alleviate his suffering, so that he could enjoy his own fair share of bliss before he popped off in the night for good, and so on. There was also a grimness in the cold air that even the CFL could not cure, and his own dreamy Russian romance had broken down into a growly bass offset by the strangest interjections:

Nos! Nos!

Yes, the sudden discovery of a "nose" in a loaf of bread—oh why must it be sexual in tone?—the shrill reaction to that oddity, and that erratic underpinning of the orchestra, followed by Stravinskian treatment blossoming into parodic Wagnerian outburst as if Prince Ludwig of Bavaria were going to sponsor a fetching silk peignoir for his lady of a reasonable distance! These musings should be sifted and crafted into an essay that no one will ever read, yeah? But why foist one's notebooks out of doors in minus temperatures without even their waffle smalls on, oh why? He was interrogating his own rhetorical question when he turned towards the dark apparition upon a berm in the distance and observed that her goddessy "augen gneisses" (or glittering eyes) were positively brimming over with the pithiest sehnsüchtig.[23]

At the next-to-penultimate indoor farmer's market, the tomato seller was out of tomatoes, even throwing tomatoes, and Farinata had set his heart upon some root vegetables and a dozen eggs. The garrulous hawker, known in these parts for his gift of the gab, had nothing on this minus thirty-two morning but a piece of gossip about a couple who bought up dozens and dozens of eggs and drank the shells soaked in alcohol. Just imagine that. Not exactly advice to take or leave. On the way home-ish, Farinata stopped in front of a white statue of a woman holding a man in her arms and for the first time, it did not appear to be his inimitable Trish giving him succour in his time of need. Then he knew a poem was on the way and he had to lisp in numbers for a while, even if it was only a fraction of its true potential:

> *break any heart that lacks the subsistence of root vegetables*
> *bury it at sea, or in our choppy grey square during a squall*
> *tell me this is not happening upon squawking bird down*

He went on muttering, attributing widening chorale and floating spots to his fever. If only he knew where Trish hung her famous knit hat; that secret would give him leave to recite a few of his verses, or even a fair chunk of fraudulent Ossian, and then collapse in his best hose at

---

23. Operatic prolongation of yearning. Here, it was necessary to repress another overbearing conceit in which Farinata proves he is the perfect Wagnerite by repeating part of Tristan's baleful invitation to Isolde to join him in his homeland—a land where the sun never shines—where seasonal affect is definitely a concern. Also some weak-kneed metaphors and some Freudian overtones about his mother. Enough said.

her fairer-than-fair feet, same as that operatic basket case, Werther, with something in his semi-pathetic air that would shatter winter faster than a bucket of boiling water overturned upon a frozen car.

Pourquoi me réveiller, ô souffle du printemps?[24]

Once he had coughed up his bittersweet Klopstock, he would then be ready to borrow the first rusty harquebus he happened upon, and to blow out the most nefarious part, to break himself into pieces like those wild horses sorely in need of domestication. Generations would carry about vials of tears in his name to represent their own copious shares of impassioned emotion.

When a Crime Stoppers tip about the infamous water-and-pastry bandit brought out dozens of authorities in red serge—mastering wild steeds that bucked like goats and monkeys, and armed to the teeth to deal with a vaguely artistic disturbance not far from the giant effigy of a beaver—Farinata was too bemused to appreciate their ribald raillery about his lack of a nose in front of his lady love, and they had a point, because for a few seconds in the distance across the snow-laden park and through every one of those whirling spots, he thought he could make out Trish, waving at him, and not at all unlike the Queen.[25]

---

24. Ah yes, "why did you wake me, oh zephyr of spring?" No, it's far too early for that nonsense.

25. Sometimes in profile, with an air of one of Degas' dancers or laundresses, she became wonderfully imperious, in a mauve headband with a Tyrian flavor—for he always envisioned her in Queen City over a bowl of the superfood called "queen-wa," naturally in queenly colours.

A Nightmare on the Street of Elms

S he was laughing in the light of August, if you will forgive this unfortunate phrase, which was really nothing to
do with the tall drink of water in the adjacent suite in the
Cathedral area. A player to be certain, with all his beguiling
talk of Phoenician ancestry. The eldest in a savvy and solid
Muslim family bound to find themselves in the third person, mere adjuncts to our very own T.E. Lawrence gasping
for lemonade. The sister was definitely something to write
home about, the third in command at a landlocked branch
of HELTEL where, in striking contrast with her colleagues,
her alluring locks were there for all and sundry to admire.
Laughing in the light of August over merry cross-polli-
nation—our friend was taking the high road and pushing
down deep any suspicion of mutual pollution—between
Trish and the older brother—pushing down deeper a history of meaningful looks and exchanges at the nearest

collegiate—laughing at her laughter as an enlightened free-thinker, unable to object if the object of his fascination had suddenly turned into something less familiar—pushing down even deeper a surge of scathing epithets.

Farinata was still stewing over the implications of this new development when he noticed a staunch yet supple pair of buttocks on his side of the fence. Tentatively, he addressed them with as much pluck and decorum as he could muster, given the circumstances.

"Can I help?"

"Oof!"

The man had slipped on the back deck and landed in some errant barbecue sauce. He examined the stain closely before touching his soiled finger to his lips.

"I've known worse."

"Are you okay?"

"Why wouldn't I be? This is part of the life. You swear … well, you promise to do what you can. C-A-T, that's what interests me."

"Is this about the cat situation?"

"There's a cat situation?"

"I hear they're eating all the prairie songbirds."

"Sorry. I'm after a different beast. One day I'll catch it. One day …"

"So you have a reason for rooting around my backyard?"

"You haven't seen anything funny, have you?"

Farinata held his tongue. Trish, laughing in the light of August, kicking back next door and accepting a bottle or three of beer before reaching for the handsome elder brother in the third person … He shook his head.

"I don't know what you mean."

"Look, I'll level with you. I'm investigating certain activities in the area. I have reason to believe your neighbours *may* be involved, you know, *allegedly*. I used to be with the boys in red who wear blue, but that was a while back. Now I'm strictly freelance, and I consider myself something of a specialist. Here, take my card, and you have yourself a good afternoon. Just let me know if you do see anything out of the ordinary."

DUTCH MULCH
C.A.T. Investigator

A couple of days later, Farinata ran into the sister of his sworn enemy in the mall and joined her for falafel. He was so swelled up with this rare opportunity that, in combination with a spice or two he had tasted off a tiny spoon, his hopes and schemes began to Hindenburg as the hot air blew out of him. She had barely begun her diatribe about Mostafa and that nervy chick from down below—meaning Grounds for Delight—when Farinata launched into a description of the modern biathlon involved with getting decent tzatziki for one's chicken wings, followed by a lengthy ode to the ameliorative qualities of a particular sandwich containing chicken, fig, brie, and apple shavings that would aid digestion and increase one's quantity of serotonin come winter. Yet as the ineluctable intellect of his stomach reminded him that amorous investment might also enhance digestion, Soma, the lovely sister of Mostafa—regrettably still in the third person—grasshoppered over from the question of the chick down below to the question of chickpeas everywhere. Never had the prospect of soaking garbanzos until they sprouted become such a double entendre, spiced up with an enticing exegesis about a former soldier from Afghanistan who roasted whole lambs in an underground joint in Edmonton.

Though this temptation had not yet been enough to retrieve Farinata from his afternoon reveries at the nearest Mirage Club, where the sweet fig jam graced his palate in a very real and non-symbolic sense and the familiar appari-tion of Ashley's bottom, neatly contained in a paisley grey skirt and yet omnipresent to the point that in remember-ing his bill or soup spoon, this low-key Callipygian Venus would turn and suddenly express a faint hint of a smile, as if to push modesty aside and admit to crushing a best booty competition on a local karaoke outing, while behind her, a tall, nameless woman appeared to throw herself emphati-cally against the glass partition in front of the kitchen.

So it came as a pleasant surprise when Soma directed him to a "chesterfield" and trailed her lovely locks over his right shoulder, those lingering visions of syrupy anasyrmos,[26] coupled with the herbal scent of Soma's hair, took him somewhere that could not be said to be "with Trish"—who was likely downstairs at this very moment, gently glower-ing—because the combined stimuli, slathered in a toonie's worth of the superlative tzatziki passing through his sight-line, elicited the physiological response that the indomitable tush of Ashley could not elicit on its own, by hook or by crook. The crux of the matter is that Trish and her beauty were not thrown under the bus with any deliberation—ladies and gentlemen, there is not a shred of *mens rea* in this regard—and yet the proverbial *actus reus* reached a state of rare prominence that happened to catch the attention of Soma and for once incurred her desire to be in the third person amid her own idea of sesame anasyrmos behind the rattling partition of a boutique changing room down below, only theirs was not a story that could then embrace more

---

26. Ancient lingo for the prospect of a peek under that paisley grey creation.

than hapless blushing and an allergic outbreak. Any pass-
erby with a grain of wisdom could have told them it would
only end in capillary action.

When in line down below, Farinata bowed his head more
than usual. When Trish made an assumption, he quietly
corrected her and she told him point blank that she never
knew what to pour for him anymore and that she had not
seen *her* right away—meaning the gorgeous third wheel in
the third person—with a thorny tone in place of her usual
marivaudage,[27] turning as pale as the Lady of the Camellias as
the floodgates opened and Farinata saw careening through
them a luxurious mane of hair, an omnipotent posterior,
a portion of tzatziki, and many figs in the symbolic sense.
They were smearing fig sauce over their lips and bodies and
necking frantically when a feudal hand came down on his
arm like a new form of taxation and it was Soma, in vindica-
tion of the rights of herself. Politesse went wanting then, as
barista and patron exchanged glances of recognition from
afar that looked like parries at close range. If Farinata really
could get an eyeful of the future, this occasion was ripe for
doing so; the reciprocal effect of this scene on both parties,
even down to the tiny spoons trembling on the saucers he
carried over to our lovely friend in the third person, was not
lost on him.

After consoling himself with the aforementioned sandwich at the nearest Mirage Club and pouring out as many of
his troubles as he dared to the patient owner of the aforementioned booty prize, Farinata returned to the micro suite
in which he was staying. Through his bedroom window, he
was startled but not entirely surprised to see Trish sitting
in the adjacent backyard, sipping from a bottle of beer and

---

27. We tremble to even suggest that Trish might be more style than
substance.

listening to the beguiling sea shanties of the Phoenician. Before long, Mostafa reached for her hands and motioned for her to follow him inside. Without a word, she did! Our friend sagged into half a sofa and turned up the volume of the television to drown out the concert of cats at play, which was what he chose to call those unbearable sounds. Only when the noise had subsided and there was nothing but a gigglicious haze permeating the onset of evening did he remember the card on the kitchen counter with the name and number of Dutch Mulch. If Trish was now mixed up—holding back words like "mingling"—with a person of interest, then it would be best to learn more about his shady activities. After all, *any* injured party would only be doing its civic duty.

It was dark when Dutch Mulch arrived. Farinata assured him that Trish, a good gal gone astray, and Mostafa, the malevolent "perp," had gone out to sate their jaded appetites, and that it would be all right to sit in the backyard if the investigator really needed to smoke his joint. He did. Most plants were beneficial, explained Dutch. Just the other day, he had rinsed his mouth with goldenseal root power to relieve a gum infection, just as his friend *Paff der Zauberdrachen*, as Marlene Dietrich would put it, was often instrumental in relieving on-the-job stress, or in this case, on-the-personal-crusade stress. Dutch was adamant that these methods could stave off a root canal or keep you from the kooky-boos when under pressure. Farinata wondered aloud if Mostafa could have a hydroponics setup for quantities of *Cannabis sativa*, part of which he cultivated to overwhelm any Dantean idoless to cross his path. Dutch laughed and offered his two bits that the trick with weed was to sex your plants and then get rid of the males because their pollination takes something away from the strength of the product. Then before you knew it, the female plants were way too busy with their seeds, saying, "not tonight honey, I'm tired," if that's how it was because no one knew what went on behind closed doors. Dutch laughed some more because his mind was clearing and he felt sharp as a Mack truck slowly backing out of a drive-thru.

"So you think it's drugs?"

"Nah, it's much worse ... nightmare ... street of elms ... the beetles."

"The Beatles? Then he's some kind of digital pirate?"

They went on like this for quite a while. Finally, Dutch was able to convey that when he said "beetle," he meant:

(i) the Native elm bark beetle, *Hylurgopinus rufipes*; or

(ii) the European elm bark beetle, *Scolytus multistriatus*; or

(iii) the Banded elm bark beetle, *Scolytus shevyrewi*.

And when he said "Dutch elm disease," he meant the plant disease caused by the existence in an elm tree of the fungus *Ophiostoma ulmi*, also known as *Ceratocystis ulmi* or *Ophiostoma novo-ulmi*. Clearly, the plant in question was, in one out of three cases, an American elm, also known as *Ulmus americana*, which often was in danger. Dutch Mulch had received a tip that the neighbours were burning elm bark, possibly for firewood. Perhaps it was an honest mistake, but that was where the beetles would lay their eggs, and soon the whole block would be taken out. As a self-appointed C.A.T. Investigator, Dutch had a duty to enact preventative justice if it meant stopping "Crimes Against Trees." Farinata wondered aloud how far he would or could go. Dutch instantly eyed the wiring of a table lamp and admitted that he could not go as far as he used to, following the incident he seldom spoke of. That said, if Farinata believed there was even a shadow of possibility that his neighbours had been storing elm wood or were in some way showing wanton disregard for the more recent release of *The Dutch Elm Disease Regulations*, then he did not even need to say anything, only make some slight gesture in the affirmative, and at the very least, an undignified scene would shortly ensue.

Under the streetlamp, Mostafa and Trish were aglow, enjoying gelato. If anything, the waffle cones capped their effusions like the proverbial stone fruit on top. Suddenly, the front door of the micro suite burst open and Farinata ran out, seized Mostafa, and gave him a lingering kiss[28] for the full benefit of Dutch Mulch. Then Farinata backed away and pointed, his eyes wild.

"I know it was you, Mostafa. You broke my heart. You broke my heart!"

"Whoa. What's going on, you guys?"

"Quarterback sack!"

The tackle was quite an excellent one. The highlight reel showed that Dutch Mulch certainly knew how to observe boundaries. The two men lay on the grass together, each wondering what would or should happen next. Meanwhile, Farinata waved his arms about and gently shooed Trish.

"Bad news, love. Best leave it. You don't wanna know!"

"Weird."

"Drop by tomorrow after work and I'll fill you in."

"Pffft."

Late the following afternoon, Farinata opened the door and was surprised to see the Callipygian Venus, otherwise known as Ashley. She thanked him for lending her a translation of *La Vita Nuova*, although the seventh season of *Vampification*, followed by a few games of *Interurban Smackdown* was more her style, fuelled by good company and a

---

28. Here, the limitations of narrative are indeed heartrending. How to convey the suspension of time or will-they-or-won't-they sensation inherent in Giotto's *Kiss of Judas* in Scrovegni Chapel?

box of wine. His address was (conveniently) written inside so she thought she would bring it by. He invited her in and offered her some fizzy water, scarcely trusting himself to get anywhere near bladdered on such a scorcher in a micro suite with the best booty this side of Dewdney. His suspicions were well warranted. Her sensuous curvature at once began to intrude upon his casual perusal of one of Dante's sonnets, even as he read it aloud.

> *Con l'altre donne mia vista gabbate,*
> *e non pensate, donna, onde si mova*
> *ch'io vi rassembri sì figura nova*
> *quando riguardo la vostra beltate.*[29]

Trish was about to knock on the front door when Soma saw her from next door and hurried out, once again glad to be in the third person and what is more, entirely untackled. They were closer to understanding what had transpired when it was agreed they could try the skivvy's entrance and maybe find a clue or two in Farinata's backyard. The makeshift blind was not drawn and very little mystery remained in that little bedroom. One pair of eyes drank in that lovely man from the mall being repeatedly crushed under the most unquitable entity. Another pair of eyes took in that slightly creepy oddball from the mall deeply mixed up with the business end of hardly the sharpest tool in the shed, although to be fair, that was based on her coursework at the collegiate

---

29. With other ladies you mock my looks,
   and never attempt to grasp why
   I am seized by such a novel figure
   whenever I view your beauty.

and not her questionable antics now and then on karaoke contest nights. Diverse sighs had scarcely mingled with beastly groans when a new scene began that was peculiar enough to draw those four eyes away from the free peep show,[30] killing their colour commentary on the spot.

Trish and Soma turned around to look across the lane and saw a very large man in a white muumuu shaking a burning wand at the ground. If any good can be salvaged from this comedy of errors, it is that Farinata's ears were too snugly ensconced in the sublime folds of his visitant goddess to hear a single word of this man's mooning breed of versification that accompanied each jerk of his wand. The man looked up and saw Mostafa's sister—he did not even know the name of his own heart's idoless—and beamed at her. He did not even notice that another man was encircling him with a hemp lasso of truth.

"It's over, Jed. Drop the elm."

"Dutch? It's not what you think …"

"Drop the elm, Jed. Nice and slow. Into the bucket."

"Dutch, you just don't come between a man and his Wiccan love charm …"

"You're pointing it in the wrong direction. Now into the bucket!"

"Fine. *There*. Happy? By the way, who ratted me out?"

"An anonymous tip. But your family's worried, Jed. A bit of counselling wouldn't go amiss."

"Well, you sure made me look stupid, and just when it was bringing in the young 'uns."

"You should have used birch, Jed. Everyone knows that, you sorry son of a gun."

Jed's wife—Marnie!—wept openly because she had been

---

30. Peeping Thomasinas are derived from certain works of Alice Munro, Margaret Laurence, and Elfriede Jelinek.

the one to call it in, and his two point five children were snivelling because they did not quite know what was happening, or why their beloved father was going to receive a letter of warning from Queen City. Farinata had not yet made manifest his own prideful shame, and Trish decided to follow Soma home to share a doobie they had just found in the backyard and to see where the night would take them because all of this was somehow an unexpected rush, and they were both young with so many amazing adventures ahead of them. Dutch Mulch confiscated the white magic muumuu as a precaution and carried away the smouldering bucket with an air of mild satisfaction—blissfully unaware that he was about to receive more than a warning from Queen City about his profiling methods—still patting himself down in search of a magic dragon that had somehow flown away. Notwithstanding, the neat rows of American elms were each snuggly belted to ward off cankerworms, and in all likelihood, no beetle would pester them tonight.

The nightmare was over. For now …

Ferment/Fermata in February

A white rabbit darted through the fence and disappeared around the other side of the eightplex. Farinata looked out the window at the land reserve and made out two more rabbits doing their utmost to look like snow-covered rocks. They were actually prairie hares, or white-tailed jackrabbits (*Lepus townsendii*), the least social of all hares except when wooing a female in the breeding season. The resultant young are destined to be born in a "form," a shallow depression in the ground. They were ordinarily timid but this changed in February, prior to the month of madness that followed. They appeared rather stubborn in their desire to stay put and feed as much as possible on hidden plants and grasses. Best get on with it. One can only look out the window for so long.

By the way, what was Trish up to? Putting it as gently as possible, she and our stoic friend—frail sad sack in some circles—had not yet reached any common understanding, nor perhaps would they in this world or the next one. The situation, if there had been much of one, had slowly tapered off, leaving within Farinata a grim dehiscence he had to salt nightly with the most craven imaginings to keep the bugger alive and kicking, before, out of sheer forgetfulness and abscondence and whatever the opposite of abstinence is, he felt around for the little wound and found it scabbily healed over. Actually, he might have scratched at it afresh, had he not received new intelligence in affairs that were not his. A new profile picture would have been bad enough, but the sizable upload of an elongated banner containing a reclining kiss was a real horror show. The nearly naked cow bone on the table was a surrealistic touch, to be sure. As for the young gentleman receiving his pleasure, the less said about him the better.

Farinata, having not dared to peep at her profile for over a month, reeled back and rolled about with a few hammy paroxysms of self-loathing. A friend of his would have called this occurrence "old cabbage," relegating the present to the past, although this situation looked like the starting point for a fermentation process he knew only too well. Rotten lovers and their rotting mouths, the decay of long-standing decorum and dying courtesy become cabbage at the mercy of salt urging out the precious moisture after a period of two to three weeks. She would no longer be haughty goddess of the ground beans or furtive mistress of the night—the constituent body was now from dermis down to essential tissue an uncooperative collective of cabbage layers. The size in the nearest retail outlet a size "cabbage." The feet and hands round as cabbages. It was almost too much to bear and that is why he took another breather to look out the window at rabbits, chewing something rather like cabbage.

It would have been convenient for the fated sauerkraut to arrive, large as life, on the side of a bus that failed to pick him up, with his frustrated rage converting into passionate expression on the spot, which is to say in the parking lot of Southland Mall, but that was much later. The glamorous image of Alma Smatterson was not unknown to him. Farinata had first clapped eyes on her in a baggy T-Shirt in a pie eating contest one summer's evening, but he had been too preoccupied to notice how truly snoutfair she was, and besides, it had not been her finest hour—she had not obliterated the competition. He had only pursued her because of a faint mercenary streak that usually kept his bread buttered on the side he most preferred. Then, after accidentally catching her breathless finish of a local marathon at the end of the wooden footbridge we have immortalized in our minds and hearts, well, the truth of his feelings would have been obvious to us, although they looked in absolute ignorance at one another, in a manner akin to the rabbits in February who cannot yet fathom the rapidity of March. We must forgive them, even when calling them out, as it was rather cold and they were relatively indistinguishable faces lost under various layers. His light-hearted pronouncements reached her easily enough, and she did not balk at the prospect of helping him enjoy his own fifteen minutes. Promises were made in the heat of given moments, before they evaporated just as quickly. Each of them—they had a lot on!

Hang on—no, this will not do at all. We can't just topple our potluck Lucien de Rubempré, elbow him out of his airy concerns, and plunge him into new nether-danger. He has been through enough, for a start. To shoo the rabbits when they are most preoccupied and to pluck a tuber out of the ground, hoping to stick it somewhere else, well, that is sleight of hand we do not really condone. Since the baleful affair at Readerz, he had been offered the chance to read his tuneful writ at better venues, including a restaurant lounge in the downtown core, which had been packed to the gills. There may not have been the amount of swooning found in eighteenth-century novels, but it is fair to record an evanescent flutter that passed through the room, especially through a table of ladies sympathetic to a touch of musicality now and then. Never in his life had he heard so much feedback in terms of musical canvases, lyrical cadences, staunch fermatas, and arpeggiated breathings, whatever those might be. Indeed, through the minus fifteen reprieve of that January evening, a light murmur suggested that it might be worth keeping him alive after all. A local MLA and his friends, slightly tipsy on the night in question, made promises, and a few offers for a sporadic capful of tuppence came his way. This was fair to middling stuff, and certainly not the kind of local backstory that would bowl over the new incarnation of Alma Smatterson, once a quiet girl with a penchant for linguistics who had struggled daily with her indifference to small animals and children.

This is a new century and we like to think we can do what we like. Let us say there was a wanton splash of mud—finally, a touch of Zola-worthy realism—and for fear of its conquest and undeniable ruination of his day, Farinata sidestepped the glamorous image of Alma Smatterson, who put her feet up on a cluster of neurons, tidily cushioned behind another cluster of neurons, well out of reach of his latest emotional outburst. It was the last day in February—with no leap year to trouble us—when the bolt out of the blue arrived, meaning a response from Trish to his anonymous campaign of notes in shoes and aprons, not to bring up all manner of scrambled messages in the middle of the night. Yes, she read them, only not in a leap year, waiving her right by his substantial percentage of Celtic blood to propose and be irrevocably accepted.[31]

Ever the pragmatic mule-trader, she wanted to know who he was. This sucker punch threw Farinata for a loop, alluding to an endless supply of hyperliterate suitors playing Cyrano from behind the shrubbery. Since last century's introduction of your garden variety *Homo absurdus* in literature—for some, about as historyless and plentiful as faceless dads and their boys scratching themselves as they purchase bags of potting soil at self-checkouts that may or may not accept some of the polymer bills that ignite for no more than a dirty look—it was impossible to answer that question to anyone's satisfaction. Sometimes he had a funny feeling that everything had happened before, with only slight differences, in another place, or that other selves were conducting themselves in outrageous fashion, as if on the other side of a thin wall he had only to claw apart to glimpse a vision of how life could be, or even *was*, without his conscious knowledge. There was surely a dimension in which he and Alma Smatterson were embracing on the side of a bus and splashing everyone else with mud for a change.

If he were a *Lepus absurdus*, it would be almost nothing to rise from his "form" and dirty his face over prairie forbs in the vicinity of a female counterpart, no questions asked. But this was a young century, and it was entirely possible he would never again leave his own shallow depression that vibrated slightly whenever a jet plane or snow plough made its morning rounds.

---

31. There was a rumour in town that Farinata had been caught by this Leap Day trap once before, and the marital forfeit was a silk peignoir.

Farinata after the Flood

The plane tilted its nose upward and quickly vanished. Farinata cast his eyes away from the disposable headline. Almost a hundred towns declared to be in a state of emergency. The headline guy or gal had to keep it going, the fear and the sense of infinite chaos. A job well done. Of course, he couldn't complain. The consensus was that he was staying in a place built on a slough that would sink into the gooey clay soil before too long. Eighty to ninety millimetres had fallen and he had experienced a mild scare. The water in the storm drain had kept rising, and Farinata had regressed back to his sorry origins, even to the exact instant when the trauma had first formed. Then, out of a cozy, wet nook he had been heaved—screaming—out into a world that probably did not have his best interests at heart.

Farinata sat on the live and dead grass and looked down into the shimmering brown water. Some kids had been wading in the impromptu pool only yesterday, terrified of eels, but was he adult enough to give them two bits worth of advice? After the mild scare, a raven had tired of flight and had walked around instead, picking up bugs and worms. During the rains he was not a threat but a red-winged black-bird didn't split hairs—or feathers—and dive-bombed the bigger bird repeatedly. Often, the same bird could be found warding off iridescent Brewer's blackbirds on for-aging missions. Farinata thought the red-winged blackbird an exemplar of fatherhood, but that thought only brought back the trauma, or more accurately, its harbinger like some unidentified but almost fathomable speck on the horizon that was approaching at top speed. Farinata felt it approach-ing and turned away, turning his mind to anti-matters. He remembered the celebrated painter from these parts who had striven so hard—all her life, in fact—to think of noth-ing. Most folks didn't have to try quite so hard but that judg-ment was only another mood coming on, or so he reckoned, like a funny cloud floating into view. He need not heed its shape nor pore over the prospect of its future outpourings. No, the sun was shining and for the moment, he was happy. Not too happy, as that could knock him off balance just as easily. Climb no mountains and you will find no valleys. The hot hard flat of the path, that was for him, and in his esti-mation, long and substantive and relatively commaless. Vast sections of this dry, unforgiving place were submerged, but that did not matter. The landscape could not all *become ardent aquarium* because he knew that was only a misquoted line in his head. He knew that sun and land were altering him, too.

You couldn't run from your problems and yet, he had done so, or so he figured, and that was quite all right. He was a different person and that was also quite all right. He felt that he had left everything behind, the need for thinking, the need to write, the (stupid) need for money, other needs he dare not name lest he disrupt his fine equilibrium under the sun. Various problems had stowed away with him, but they were friendlier once afloat, and besides, they had nowhere to hide amid all this openness. The trick was to give up everything, to live a life that most folks on two-thirds of the continent would consider a life not worth living, and to no practical purpose, living that "crummy" life for its own sake and somehow deeming it none too shabby. Indeed, he was pacing himself, and taking in things very slowly. Feel around—fumble if you must—for the present, then grab hold gently. That was the best he could do and that was quite all right.

A small grasshopper hopped from one plant stem to another. Then another. Then another. A while back, they had been tiny nymphs, clinging for dear life to a blade of grass. Now they were instars, although the precise stage eluded him. After a long winter, the adults had appeared first, crepitating during spells of intense sunlight. They were band-winged grasshoppers, but their scientific name was like something out of a classical Greek play. The other day, he had seen a small specimen with an intricate pattern on its pronotum and abdomen. The professor's best guess was an immature clear-winged grasshopper, one of the two leading pests. Sharing that title, and sharing the same field of wild barley and thistle right near Urban Barn, was the two-striped grasshopper, who did small penance for wiping out crops by eating up herbicide-resistant kochia (originally a bit of tumbleweed rolling across the landscape, hell-bent on colonizing a relatively yellow landscape). In the same field, the lesser migratory grasshopper and Packard grasshopper were up and about, and doing their part to eat everything in sight. As for the speckled rangeland and northern green-striped grasshoppers, they enjoyed singing in the live and dead grass upon which they dined, preferring this mound in the sun that encouraged their leaps of courtship. Yes, they were also quite all right. They could fly pretty far, but courting slowed them down. The males would crepitate with a flash of red or yellow wings, and then a female would either wave a suitor in or, in Saskatchewan fashion, get into the kick-off position, which as signals go was loud and clear. Anyway, they would all be dead soon. That was the brutal truth and not one of Farinata's mood valleys getting its own back. He was all right with the brutal truth because there was by no means a shortage of them any given summer.

A light breeze blew through clumps of cattails in the middle of the slough, which was not really a slough. Soon, it would dry up again to a mere trickling. Memories would be reduced to garbage that perpetually floated in from construction sites and retail outlets. When the snows had first stopped, Farinata had been caught tidying up around a bush in front of his window and had been warned by passing neighbours that the city did that. Actually, there were two or three people who rode around in a little car to check on each plant. There was also one woman who was never seen doing anything but driving around in circles and talking on her phone. She had turned the role of civic worker into an art form, but she was not the special someone Farinata had taken a shine to when he was in a mood—or in *the* mood. She had given him the glad eye, and had even gossiped about him—wait, that didn't add up to much. He must have heard a few things before his mood had taken him for a "joyride," shooting off on a frolic of its own. In the interim, he had given up coffee, or more accurately, the place had produced a powerful disinclination for the stuff within him. Irish breakfast did the trick, in the rotation with green, jasmine, lemon, hibiscus, blueberry superfruit, chamomile, and licorice spice for those frequent occasions when he required an adaptogen to deal with startling new situations. Passionflower before bed was now reality and not a come-on, honest.

Farinata would have been happy—but not too happy— to explain to the young lady his working theories, were they not an epidemic of overshare or T.M.I. Thanks to her caffeinated contributions and extra-strong cups of Kicking Horse at home, combined with the seasonal shift around the time of, say, a recent stabbing in the downtown mall, his propensity for "manic" behaviour had increased, turning slights, real or imagined, into gushing injuries—in that case, there was little difference if an emotional injury birthed suppression or eradication of a key gene for regulating neuronal production, or let us say, nodal dedication—so that her finger-to-nose pejorative retorts reached his acute hearing—heightened by misappropriated adrenal purpose, and without even buying dinner first—took advantage of his flawed hippocampus—or let us say, cerebral seahorse—and recontextualized this sudden glut of neural data in terms of image, sensation, and mood. For argument's sake, let us suppose that the aftermath from a string of unhealthy relationships—already glomming onto that common trait of Wagnerian heroes, that fear of abandonment engendered by progenitors who had left him on a wobbly hillock (or butte) that one time, or perhaps without umbilical or hand holding for the rest of his days—had cultivated a neatly labelled neuronal garden to which the name of the fair-to-middling barista was appended, like a colourful species pinned right through speckled shield under glass, or a fickle noonflower plunked down in the muck. Given such a loveless *a priori*, the rough-and-tumble *a posteriori* arose from the imbalance of glutamate promoting irritability, to dip our beaks even deeper in the elemental chemistry of Farinata's issues, postulating in step with the school of thought that dopamine agonists have a starring role in precipitating mania. In other words, that red-handed culprit, happiness.

We would have a real story on our hands if Farinata were addicted to counting bathroom tiles, buying irregular shoe sizes, voting against celebrity poker players, or watching golden shower scenarios until his red eyes ached—or eked basalt, whichever comes first. No, he was merely excited by the thought of her and quickly upset by the absence of her, cast down into a despondent quagmire of confused interpretations, what with the mind being its own place, even if it was more purgatorial than ever before. Now he could watch joggers of all shapes and sizes jouncing past his window and no longer feel it was absolutely necessary to mate with each and every one of them, lest he perish before the summer ended. Now he would cease to swagger about playing tarnished knight for splendid ladies between the hours of ten and two on business days,[32] splendid ladies who had already pledged their troth to unresponsive oafs. Now he would seek out his own borage—an abominable turn of phrase—in that field of wild barley where purple thistles nodded over sow thistle and buffalo beans, where he had spent many idle hours in contemplation of surrounding canola or mustard, or incestuous combinations of the two, ignoring that upstart mania waiting in the wings like a brash understudy ready to burst out at the first misstep, provided the killdeer did not kick up the usual fuss. After all, there were plans to move the highway and lengthen his constitutional and that was quite all right.

---

32. Ample evidence will be provided to the contrary, showing that such meetings did not cease; if anything, they increased in frequency and profligacy.

Farinata was famished and that did not help. He opened a small bag of mountain trail mix and knocked back a few handfuls. Fatty acids and selenium, followed by naturally occurring lithium and magnesium sounding far more exciting than nuts, seeds, and a glass of fizzy water. His "stomach" brain would be free to give the all-clear to his "brain" brain, giving him leave to go on a vision quest, although there wasn't quite enough mix for that. Then again, no mountains, no valleys. In some ways, to examine the fifth instar of the infamous *Camnula pellucida* had been his vision quest, a real vision only a few paces away that would lead to a luminous journey inward. Of course, it was not too late to catch a bus to the farmer's market. Then he could buy baby kale and pea shoots from the grumpy hippie type, whose mustard green dreams are besieged by drifting canola and rolling kochia. Farinata had not dared to see if the purveyors of chicken and waffles were back—suddenly, the image of Trish flickered seductively across the packed live screening just above his barking animal brain, downing a waffle that left traces of whipped cream on her lips, revealing the faint apparition of her tongue ...

Hang on, that had not even happened! False idols were a symptom of one of his moods gearing up—yes, the sun was already at a certain angle of intensity. The lone noon-flower had shut up long ago and the grasshoppers around him were crackling to signify their half-mad interest in mating. Farinata heard rapid snaps and caught scarcely perceptible flashes of colour. No, the food truck might not be there. If the food truck was not there, he might sink into a valley and find himself unable to claw his way up and out again, and then the simple trip downtown would become a tragic adventure. No, he did not want to stray too far from the pseudoslough today. Perhaps he would go to the breakfast chain with the grandmotherly icon. No, they would only give him heaps of white flour with a few berries hidden somewhere inside—practically a form of colonization—for an arm and a leg, and that, too, would be tragic. It would also be strange for him to observe countless families enjoying themselves in a great clamour, lifting those suspect objects into "cakehole" as he reminded himself he was the one with the noggin problem.

Two of the city workers passed in their large, orange car that saved them from having to walk more than a few feet along the environmental reserve. They did not return Farinata's smile and in return, he did not think much of them. Still, they were winning the war on mosquito larvae, or so he understood, and that was something. It was good to try and keep happy, but not too happy. Then he thought of the little bird. One night, he had been listening to Cecilia Bartoli's forceful rendition of Vivaldi's *Cessate, omai cessate* when he realized that one of the robin's brood in the bush outside was trying to sing back at the voice it could hear, and with much difficulty. Would the trauma for the little bird be one day learning that Cecilia Bartoli was not its mother and could not—schedule permitting—bring food, perhaps not now or ever? This was not the first example of wildlife outside showing a keen appreciation for music of the baroque era. Why Farinata should feel paternalistic urges towards the tiny boreal chorus frogs and small grasshopper instars was beyond him; another working theory was that his unconditional love for them was connected in some way with his reptilian brain.

It goes without saying that if his thyroid tests came back okay and his endocrine levels were good, then his own metamorphosis might very well be at hand. As for his happiness problem, the field was scheduled to become the newest home for the most familiar shopping and fast food experiences, and that was quite all right with everyone.

Cézanne in the Clerk

Suffused with grey-grim light, singing a mournful *solo perduto abbandonato* here upon a darkling plain, is not how our stumbling hero is to be disposed of.[33] There are quite a few more scenes before the curtain can fall on this head-scratcher of a production. Here we are then, with a choice fragment from the master, who, when not looking down his nose at Cézanne's abstruse monstrosities and lowly penmanship, put ink to paper that with minimal tweaking, suits our purpose:

His soft black eyes, still full of youth, also lent

---

33. We cannot say for sure—one never knows—but it is typical of our drama queen to eschew Massenet's powder and minuets and see himself like Callas in the role of Manon Lescaut, belting out Puccini's swan song to a North American desert, or in this case, a featureless portion of prairie.

delicacy to his otherwise vigorous countenance. The young fellow would probably not have fascinated all women, as he was not what one calls a handsome man; but his features, as a whole, expressed such ardent and sympathetic life, such enthusiasm and energy, that they doubtless engaged the thoughts of the girls of his own part—those sunburnt girls of the South[west quadrant]*—as he passed their doors on sultry July evenings.*[34]

Actually, we have reached another August together, and another scene with the most unpropitious origins. Superficially, the young clerk at Avocet Drugs was nothing to write home about. For some reason, she was the youngest of three clerks to have her hair dyed bright red and among them, her breathy *sotto voce* made the least impression on clientele. Her blue uniform was open just enough to reveal the edges of a winged breastplate, and between knuckle and joint on her ten digits, as Farinata gathered over several handovers of change, ten tattooed letters read G R E A T E X P E K, rather like an unfinished thought. Beyond this drugstore-chain atmosphere that made him feel like the poet Tannhäuser in the sensuous grotto of Venusberg, Farinata was not best pleased with the combined effect of her bright hair, her complexion, and the abundance of makeup that gave her a blotchy, red glow. However, as with *Madame Cézanne in the Conservatory*, a number of successive viewings inexorably altered his perception of her. Some small detail—such as the revelation of a section of cheek or a portion of flesh just above her kneecap—would catch his

---

34. Readers who recognize this slightly adulterated passage from Zola's *The Fortune of the Rougons* will be reassured to know this is not the start of a twenty-volume series, or even a second Manawaka Cycle.

eye and live on in his imagination. This gradual process had begun with the opening of the store months earlier, and had been leading up to the moment when her soft blue eyes reached him and the *sotto voce* achieved a recitative absolutely powdered with meaning.

Crisis turned provender one fateful afternoon when Farinata followed the loud crepitation of a black-winged grasshopper into a wild patch beside the drugstore. The field had been full of males hovering and singing at the same time to prove their individual excellence and suitability for mating. The females tended to offer more of a fashion show, fluttering about with bright yellow wings across the road from the singing match. He had almost made it when, suddenly, the impact of the previous day's rain made itself known in a surprise ambush generally known as "Saskatchewan Foot." Farinata had worked hard to shake loose the collection of thick mud before going into the store. He had been doing fine, with his arms full of bags of trail mix and bottles of Happy Water™, when tragedy struck. A giant glob of mud came loose on the immaculate white floor. He stole away, but then at the checkout, a pang of conscience overwhelmed him.

"Uhm, miss ... I've had an accident."

"My name is Piper and I am here to help you."

"No, I mean, I've left some mud by the trail mix and, with all due respect, *inferior* literature."

"Cleanup in Aisle Three. There's some ... mud."

"Sorry."

"No worries."

After her shift ended, she found him in a particularly vulnerable position in the parking lot, still trying to scrape mud off his boots, although he also had his eye on a katydid on the stalk of a plant in the field. Decidedly, she loomed closer.

"Won't come off?"

"Shhh ... come here ..."

"_?"

"That's a gladiator meadow katydid."

"My name is Piper. My mother really liked that movie. You know the one."

"It keeps trying to hide on the other side of the stalk. Their ancestor is a very ancient bush cricket. They sing over the field crickets with a long sustained note, not a chirp."

"That's my blue car. Need a ride somewhere?"

"Wouldn't I get your car dirty?"

"Yes."

Farinata hazarded suggesting the lake—the fake lake according to some locals—the scene of Gemma's immoral victory over him. Piper drove in silence, and he did not know what to say, as books were often a flop as a conversation starter, and besides, he was too opinionated for that topic to lead anywhere good. He glanced over at her and she felt herself being admired. She stopped for some pedestrians crossing to take a closer look at the Louis XVI Beaux-Arts Legislative Building; they bought her enough time to unbutton her uniform.

"Wanna see Bettie?"

"Bettie?"

Farinata stared at the woman on Piper's right arm as she sped ahead. Naturally, he was familiar with Bettie Page, "Miss Pinup Girl of the World," but this was perhaps the first warning sign, as should have been the first whiff of Trish's own craving for fantastical exhibitionism. Not that he was one to disapprove, but this small, lovely shoulder threatened to pull him into her world, or worse yet, Piper's frail pipe dream threatened to attach to his side like a suckerfish and siphon what it could. Fortunately, he was not quite so terrified of women as Cézanne and he refrained from blowing on his whistle at a mere wink from Bettie. He indicated where he wished to stop. The Canada geese had already returned to the lake months ago. Once she had parked, Piper launched into her life story in a nutshell, including her time in Morse, Saskatchewan, where there is little to do but park in the middle of the main road and look at the grain elevator because that is what must be done to grasp the essence of Morse. At once, Farinata began to shift nervously in the passenger seat, dreading the unfolding of a rich inner life, like the gleams in dark prairie soil when it is suddenly turned up. To her credit, she did not pounce. At some point, she fell silent and leaned against his shoulder and stayed that way for a long time. Behind her, a happy pelican passed.

That night, Farinata dreamed he was an *Orchelimum gladiator* climbing up a winding stalk that led to an attic. Trish appeared abundantly taped together in her leather corset, but she was tied hands and feet to a hard chair. He reached for the pink ball gag in the ghostly white attic, but she shook her head emphatically. Then a riding crop struck him and all his katydid armour fell to the attic floor. In spite of the shock, his aedeagus was primed to pass along the spermatophore when he felt hands upon his abdomen. The fingers and thumbs spelled G R E A T E X P E K. Farinata surrendered in front of a captive Trish, and the last thing he remembered was Bettie's sly wink.

Ephemera in Etobicoke

Sigmund Institute had the privilege of occupying the unceded territory of the Wendat, the Anishinaabeg, the Haudenosaunee, and the Mississaugas of the New Credit First Nation, which was acknowledged at the slightest gathering of high-fiving settlers. Farinata was a guest at this bucolic setting outside of Toronto, and primed to take part in discussions about Indigenous writings. Indeed, we are drooling already, although it was a closed-circle affair, and it would be unseemly for interlopers to eavesdrop on the confidences taken within those grey institutional walls. There was a Cree word whispered—not to be repeated here—that roughly meant "to step gently around," and we must step gingerly here because you never know who might be listening.[35] Such was the price being paid by innumerable goodly

---

35. CSIS through a blushing, blinking rose, for example.

Natives for the grotesque transgressions of one blackguard known as The Pretender, The Offendigo, or He-Who-Takes-Everything-Away. Sadly, we must shy away from paying homage to the collective brilliance and talent of the Okanagan, Cree, Métis, and Stó:lō participants. Firstly, we lack the permissions to gape at yet another "living exhibit" with our anthropological bias at play; secondly, we are bound to trip ourselves up somewhere.

For this reason, we come crawling back to a far comfier Western orality—that proud tradition in which scarcely anything ever happens—and why not tone it down for a minor bard who, for three quarters of a given week, behaved like a Celt, if not a Gallic subaltern placed in charge of a food cart? Though we would be remiss not to take note of an isolated incident that possibly transcends culture. A venerable participant had admitted to Farinata that not one but two of his daughters were from the same West Coast Nation—we sidestep the historical mistakes involved in naming conventions here—and neither beauty was allergic to poetry. In short, he was not too hideous to have at table, and if he wanted to look into a riparian wedding for next summer, he'd best get cracking gathering his swag to potlatch. His intestinal issues with eulachon grease he kept in a locked, kerfed box, which is to say, to himself. The potential for future blunders did not best please the Creator, who had more interesting aetiological designs on standby, including a grand wave of melancholia our friend was to blubber out, resulting in a chain of nearby islands.

In other words, the same old story. Farinata was nibbling on a bit of bannock when he noticed her. Straightaway, nuptial torches scorched his eye hollows, torches that were presumably known to the Angles, Saxons, and Jutes. He whirled away at once, well aware that the most alluring part of a gentleman is the back of his head, but even with his eyes fixed to a matte wall, her red dress remained a source of overstimulation. The welcome song and the steady beating of a drum did nothing to nip this sensation in the bud. At this point, we are inclined to usher the Creator towards our stage left and stick with the Dantean imagery that has gotten us this far. In his mind's eye, Farinata saw her as virtually popping out of a stretch of crimson cloth while a shadowy figure handed her a burning heart to snack back. Well, it would be equally absurd to evoke the male pronghorn who presents gland secretions to the doe with an expectant air, but we are getting warmer. In fact, he was so far gone, he nearly overturned his plate of crudité.

Fatidic is our worry-word, and we must take care not to overuse it. Even keeping to the common ordinances of story, how else could Farinata happen upon her again, unless one of them was craftily perving on the other? No, it was typical of him to lose his way, and typical of her to linger in a wing of the Creative Arts Centre under renovation. She was staring at a piano, and for a moment, he fully expected her to jump into the hot dog moment of the "Pathétique Sonata." Nothing of the kind. Though the situation was straight out of *La Rondine,*[36] our perfect Wagnerite was practically foaming lowly tones to keep up the rump of the duet.[37]

---

36. An opera in which the archetypal young lovers from the world of *La Bohème* have become jaded, damaged cynics, or at the very least, far more *comfortable.*

37. For purists, a snippet from the libretto that reconciles mythopoeic universals with our poet's perpetual canoe-hopping:

Wohl hub auch ich voll Sehnsucht meine Blicke
aus tiefer Nacht empor zu einem Weib;
ein schlagend Herz ließ, ach! mir Satans Tücke,
daß eingedenk ich meiner Qualen bleib!

Here we go again. Exquisite as this may sound, any attempt at

"Not bad. I wish I could accompany you, but I've lost the knack."

"You could hum along."

"There used to be such music here. The piano's been out of tune for ages."

"That is easily remedied."

"This place is crawling with storytellers, but I hear you are a poet."

"A man could wait a lifetime to meet someone who knows the difference."

"The poet ends his days at the edge of a tent city. Baudelaire's clown."

"Clearly, you are a danger to my person!"

"Klopstock. You're waiting for me to say 'Klopstock,' or is that wrong?"

"Right in the innards! But whatever does the lady do when she's at home?"

"Write. Paint. What have you."

"Then I'm curious about your impressions. Your perceptions. That sort of thing."

"Here's one. At the reception, I saw blue flickened light reactions greening the latent summer skin of your shoulders. It must have been the China Green tips."

---

translation would only lead us astray. Skittish as ever, we must hug the deconstructivist wall and wait for Roland Barthes to save us from the uphill battle of any more experimental writing. The poet cannot help but pull us kicking and screaming into his nightly repertoire of images with a bonus matinee on Sunday. This myth of roving from one port of call to another—hunting for a reply that can never quite satisfy—can never be fulfilled, thus ensuring its continuity. "Trobar" the troubadour must, just as the Flying Dutchman must wander forever to complete the "accursed" cycle of song. Best to back away slowly.

"Gunpowder Green, when in my native element. Yet your vision sets my nethers aquiver."

"Not to geld the moment, but there are more than a few obstacles ..."

"Good."

A regular Pelléas and Mélisande, although we have already squandered such observations on Trish, believing her to be the one. Comparatively, this was the real deal, and they behaved like the two principals in the Zurich production, staring outward at a mummified audience.[38] That was when she was not letting her mane of gilt-ash sweep back for his benefit, with its fragrance washing over him like so many elusive harmonies arranged in an orchestral pit only they could perceive. It is hardly a spoiler to hypothesize that any amount of extravagant behaviour went against doctor's orders for either of them. Otherwise, our omniscience has reached the end of the line.

Balk we will, but this operatic interlude is better than reams of fluff in a discerning eye, and serves as kindly crib to the folio of iambic pentameter that continually passed between them, along with tender heaps of dirty laundry that were run through a wringer before cannonballing out of the window. Naturally, he saw in her the bright exaggerations of Rossetti, just as she saw in him a non-representational work-in-progress, and admired him as she would have a

---

38. First, music is time passing through space. Second, the instant the signifier makes contact with the signified, it ceases to exist. Therefore, these operatic interludes are merely a mode of waiting for the labial proffering of a few words. Whispers that lead to filthy lies, probably. Let's leave the syntactical subterfuge on the shelf for once. Let's stick to our side of the fourth wall for a change. The slightest hint of oral consummation and the stage will go up in smoke until the next performance.

cloisonné enamel on a gilt copper hat stand[39] with a hint of Cubism. Every chance he got, Farinata strayed from the solemn proceedings inside to take another constitutional in her company. She put him at his ease, and the environs became nearly as non-representational as himself: the sky was blue; the clouds were cumulus; the lake stank; the sooty brown line of adjacent industry did not hold them back from the horizon any more than a pair of cormorants. What is more, she gave him leave to read choice passages from his books, and was by turns, alarmed, aghast, or astonied. Deep within the tear-stained cleavage of her own journal, she found ample room for her own neologisms, and as if to increase our exasperation, she confessed that she, too, indulged in experimentations that straddled the bobbed wire between poetry and prose.

For Farinata, these strolls were (figuratively) a breath of fresh air. Wait, we must not look for enmity or divisiveness where there is none. Even with a de jure and not a de facto elder on the premises, the workshops were still chockablock with lucidity and sagacity, not to mention Cree and Michif. If we allow him one whimper, it is only that in the presence of so many traditional knowledge-holders and doctorate-seekers, he was unable to explain how his life as a roving saga poet had led to yet another island romance that had soured, putting him on the blade-side of a carving family who were sitting on his ancestral tongue like a precious egg. Anything more than signing up for a distance course would deliver up his head upon a ceremonial platter. The literati sometimes took him for a savant or even a prophet, but on account of his disorder, there were still days when a double knot in a shoelace seemed a daunting prospect. However,

---

39. Here, we forgo preciously wrought bats overloaded with peaches and other auspicious symbols.

this woman—her name turned out to be Juniper—could appreciate his tendency towards incoherence in a world beyond understanding. When he read her a snippet from a rare review—describing one work as having jargon-laden prose that yanked the reader in, overwhelming with its physicality and earthiness when not offering a synaesthetic experience as intimate and tangible as the smell of food or the texture of mud, infused with irrepressible ticklers—she drew comparisons to the way in which she approached a canvas.

A saw-whet owl took refuge in a tree and a cottontail hopped into a nearby bush, perhaps to evade the blather-skite that was skittering out of our friend. A dot of eczema in the middle of his left palm was the least of his troubles; indeed, such a winky-wink in polite company over a predilection for wanking on the sinister side was a minor infraction that paled in comparison with various afflictions (albeit fairly sanitary ones) that singled him out as a limping mud-der, a peacock hobbled by his own outlandish decorations, a heedless hopper under tread of tire. Yes, she whirled in the same circles. She could grasp what it was to plant oneself upon a settee while it dreamed of a Louis XVI loveseat, or even an illustrious *cheval d'amour* that went by Fitzpart-ner, when not ambling from upstart salon to gallery space, always keeping a frozen smile on ice for the next vernissage. Or worse, trembling atop the most splendid lectern before the most knock-kneed of academics. Farinata laughed and conveyed himself behind a Beckettian conceit, singing the sorry ballad of seventeen copies sold to free circulating libraries beyond the seas, the sorry ballad of *getting known.*[40]

One afternoon by the pond, he recited a poem in her

---

40. Really? Surely we can do better than such a self-deprecating pose. Yes, we can fail better.

honour. There was the litmus: she did not sigh to punctuate every line break; she did not wonder aloud where his
ideas came from; she did not ask him what one whit of the
blighter meant. No, she prodded where he most loved to
be probed. When she made clement enquiry of each caesura, he felt a powerful urge to retire to his lodging and root
around for his gentleman's handkerchief. The poem itself
had already laid the groundwork for such an eventuality.
Then she coaxed him towards discussion of the VERGE,
and he did his utmost to emphasize its quasi-mystical nature.
Imagine a barrel full of words sailing over a waterfall. She
did. There were several precedents, of course. Concentrated
projections of energy and compositions of breath alone.
How unfortunate for either of them that valuation arose
out of so much expository flub-dub. How exclamatory that
last sentence seems, but it was hissed more than shouted.
Though her gentle critique of his (approximately) twelve
labours was soon cloven into a dichotomy of form. The
more common CLOSED form nipped at his backside, with
its bull's eye deliberation dropped into a bottom-heavy final
cadence, not unlike offal[41] into a greasy sack. And/that/
has/made/all/the/difference. OPEN form, his obvious
preference, moved up in the bed to make room for a more
democratic arrangement of words and letters, sometimes
treating the page as a canvas upon which an interruptive,
ejaculatory, or even eructative blot would not go amiss. In
short, he appreciated her attention paid to those phano-
sonic splotches that frequented the air between them. Once
the seal of lyrical wax was ruptured, anything was possible,

---

41. Farinata's views on poetic form have nothing to do with his
ambivalence about Canada lifting its ban on the importation of
haggis.

whether for economical whittlers or for those who suffered from continual logorrhea.

That evening panned out as badly as the others. Since he had moved into the smelly dorm room, Farinata had been plagued by nightmares, mostly about being "taken down" as some kind of "Pretendian," and having his keepsakes taken away, forcing him to relive the historical confiscation of familial property that was now beyond repatriation. The Okanagan, Cree, Métis, and Stó:lō participants were also sleeping fitfully, and most of them believed the place to be haunted. Here, we must hold a dim view of our restless poet, who for all his early afternoon tributes to "ladies who intellectualize their love,"[42] became a bundle of dissolute cravings after dark. If she would not remotely egg on the tactual, he was left with little choice but to cop a feel in his dream, where she was waiting for him in the cramped shower stall. He stared into her dark eyes and pressed closer for a kiss. He was vaguely aware that the grey concrete walls were dripping; water was covering the floor. He went on caressing her breasts, but had a fright as part of her body appeared to fall away. She turned around and he saw her skeleton. Faced with this unexpected deal-breaker, he turned tail and started dog-paddling towards the front door. Her hollowing eyes followed him. When he woke with a scream, he was clutching the tobacco tie one of the facilitators had made for him to ward off any malevolent energy, thoughts, or spirits. Farinata told himself that flipping through examples of Klimt's florid style was bound to give anyone the jim-jams, even the most stoic arts undergrad.

The next day, Farinata was looking for Juniper when he was thrown off the scent by a pair of wasps who prized his outdoor lunch. Having abandoned his honeyed sandwich

---

42. Sadly, Dantean sonnets cannot get you out of every scrape.

quarters, he came to the edge of some shady greenery, where a man was waving at him. Reclining on the grass in his whites the way he was, the scene approached a *Déjeuner sur l'herbe* for cricketers. Tentatively, our man stepped into the picture with his latent summer shoulders brushing the frame. Please note there was irrecoverable loss in translation from the first "howzat." In the cricketer's own jargon, the modest dibbly-dobbly had just pitched a verbal Yorker at the toes of our bunny who was expecting a rhetorical belter or bumper or, if he was lucky, a periphrastic loosener. That lordly fellow on the lawn was anticipating a textbook response, possibly a Dilscoop or a switch hit, but certainly not a chronic quack for the entire knock. No, for our friend mooning about cow corner, everything was jaffa. After a few more figurative zooters for the village, the bowler ceased to carrom and raised his straw hat in renewed greeting. It struck him on the spot that the colonies had their own piecemeal patois, and he made short shrift of the matter.

"So you're the chap making a waft at my woman?"

"Excuse me?"

"That's quite the googly."

"I'm sorry, I don't—"

"Walking the loop with Jupe-Jupe ... ring any bells?"

"Ah, you must mean Juniper."

"Not to spin you a flipper, ol' boy. The thing is, Jupe-Jupe is here for her moral betterment."

"Here, at the institute? I thought she worked for one of the faculties."

"Faculties, now there's a wounded word. Yes, we give her odds and ends to do, but that's part of her treatment. There have been ... incidents."

"I had no idea."

"Yes, it's the saddest story ever told ... but don't take it too badly. I mean, pitch your woo all you like. Just don't introduce her to a briar patch of funny ideas, if you catch me."

"No sticky wicket, either?"

"There you are. We understand each other. We'll make an anchor of you yet, my lad."

Whether it was tepid obsession or wry whimfulness, Farinata was once again drawn to the Creative Arts Centre, which was still under renovation. To his surprise, he found two men there, standing in front of the piano. For all practical uses, they were identical, and clearly deep in thought. A modest clearing of throat dropped a pebble into their meditative pool.

"I am Jim McQuigg."

"And I am Jamie McQuigg."

"The McQuigg Brothers, at your service."

"It was once said there was little we could not tune. Very little."

"Sadly, business is not about once upon a time."

"Speaking of business, let's get down to it."

Though Farinata had not uttered a peep, the McQuigg Brothers made elaborate shushing gestures. He froze; their idea of talking shop turned out to be a disjointed seminar. They went all the way back to 204 ab urbe condita, sifting cent by cent through the problem of the Pythagorean comma to such a degree that their solitary auditor believed he could hear the hammers that had pounded out the first octaves in human history. They went on to the Meantone, a stopgap attempt to crack the circle of fifths with an inordinate emphasis on thirds. There would be no discussion worth its salt without a mention of *The Well-Tempered Clavier* and the compromise therein between the flatness of

Meantone and the sharpness of the Pythagorean. Farinata could not help but tune them out for a bit, and began teetering to and fro under the influence of the Prelude and Fugue in F-sharp minor from Book II. There is no need to name-drop the composer or the instrumentalist, even with his controversial staccato of the semi-quavers in our poet's head; this information is akin to breathing in this country, and borders upon a ghostly hum of pianistic jingoism, although the harpsichord version is better. To return to the McQuiggs, they wondered if the backslide towards the bland, muddy dissonance—and hence, chaos!—of Equal Temperament was not a betrayal of the tension created by key colour, even if it made Chopin sound brighter than he was. Dissonant ninths in the "Moonlight" were one thing, but the recommended temperament for those ponderous silences in Beethoven that punctuated other silences was quite another. This conversation took place—if it took place at all!—ages before Farinata was to become the most blatant swain draped over the Bösendorfer of Laura Horowitz.[43] Therefore, we can forgive him for naively aligning himself with the German Masters and bringing the lid down on those even-tempered Romantic virtuosi. Though, for all his lack of mechanics, he did find it curious that the McQuigg Brothers appeared to have sufficient expertise to tune a piano without laying a finger upon it.

"Our young-old man can look lively now."

"Soon his Junie Moon will be eating out of the palm of his hand."

"You mean Juniper?"

Their retorts did not reach him, nor their quips and jibes. Even after the McQuiggs had fallen silent, with each lost to his own private reflections, the woman's name became

---

43. We will probably have to sit through some of that later.

a false cadence. The scene did not end and the recapitu-
lation got underway in Farinata's head, mingling with the
tinny echoes of some third-hand philosophy. For start-
ers, the dumb, unconscious tendency of mass to betray a
furtive inclination this way or that, not counting the yellow blobs that troubled Feynman's vision for some days
after the first atomic bomb was detonated when forswear-
ing his attempted reconciliation of aural tuning and tuning by absolute frequency because what did the impact of
wire-stiffness on ear-created harmonies have on the matter
in question? The aesthetic effect must be the criterion; off
the gravel into a parlous wood that way led, struggling to
coat-hanger representational analogies out of the depths of
music, especially when the show model was a section of
spotty dialogue, no more than an allusion to the frame of
mind that might one day set a piano on the path to self-ac-
tualization. Against his better judgment, Farinata gave himself up to this impression in all its forms, an impression
from which he could derive the—forgive us—fatidic note
he needed to dress up as a resounding motivic chord that
would hint at the inner nature of an elusive phenomenon
interpreted as the *principium individuationis,* casting aside the
fetid sawhorse of illicit deliberation—no matter how well
that whinnied along with the illustrious *cheval d'amour* known
as Fitzpartner—that rode shotgun (seated ideally in a Western to ward off Apaches?) with his fever and chills every
fortnight—the sickness of Eros?—until his one surviving
whim was to beckon the most recent source of turbulence
towards that sonic cue and to serve as surtitle to the con-
tralto raising a tiny flashlight over her score in the nose-
bleeds and with her ethereal voice—*you, to whom love's dream
laughs*—compounding the unmistakable sense of inevitabil-
ity. The hypocrite! He was more than comfortable in ditch

or fen, acquainting himself with deep or subtle tones alike
while wading through unorganized nature or cavorting in
the company of shameless chirpers and songsters, grasping
at the slightest vibration to rise from that murky, inchoate eco-
system, and yet it was the unusual exchange between the piano
tuners that informed against himself. Yes, the lack of tactility
sounded a high note that had its counterpart across the bass
clef divide of Farinata's most disputable associations. Or several steps along the modulating bridge, his callow query about
Juniper contained within its foliage all the interrogative mys-
tique of Ives' *Unanswered Question.* The second he snapped out
of this reverie, he knew that he would touch her no sooner
than the oddball brothers would tune the piano.

On Friday morning, Farinata was polishing off a non-representational red apple when he saw Juniper heading outside. He followed her and joined her in the large circle of
workshop participants. The facilitator who had graciously
provided the apotropaic tobacco ties was lighting sage and
stoking it in an abalone bowl. He was not best pleased about
performing any kind of ceremony outside of his traditional
territory, but he was rising to the occasion and filling in for
the faux-elder. When it was his turn, Farinata accepted the
smoke and did his ablutions, palming smell and substance
into his face and along his limbs. Though his eyes were
half-closed, the next thing he was aware of was Juniper's
right hand extending out towards him and smudging him
with a green *sfumato* effect. The facilitator said a few words
and then, going counter-clockwise, each person offered a
greeting and expression of gratitude. After he had done
likewise, Farinata suddenly realized that Juniper was no longer standing to his left. When everyone had dispersed, he
rushed towards the facilitator and found himself drawn into
an ursine embrace.

"Wait, where is she?"

"The Elder-Advisor? She's probably around here somewhere."

"No, I mean the woman who was standing beside me."

"Well, there'll be plenty of time for the ladies, but I want to say something."

"_?"

"Farina, I want you to go on Facebook and I want you to send me a Friend request."

"_?"

"Then I'll accept your Friend request and we'll be connected as Friends."

Anxious as he was, Farinata could scarcely wolf down his complimentary lunch, which is really saying something. Then his name was called for the campus tour. Others had signed up, but they were loath to abandon the trust exercise that had somehow morphed into an orgiastic group hug also working its way counter-clockwise. He was paired up with JJ, a woman who had injured her left leg and was relying on a knee scooter to propel herself forward, sometimes at unexpected speeds. He had to work double time to metabolize the lunch that would help him keep up with her. She led him into the underground and cheerily recounted how the grounds had formerly housed a mental asylum. Well, not exactly. It had been Indigenous territory—and still was!—and then farmland that would scarcely till, and then a retreat for anyone declared insane. She wheeled her leg along one of the service tunnels, explaining that a Quaker ethos had resulted in the assignment of various labours to each patient. While he was staring at the clastic rock that had been repeatedly plastered over, Farinata was tempted to confide in this psychiatric specialist and tell her about his own issues; he would have done so, except for a sneaking suspicion he would then not be allowed to go home. Instead, he wondered aloud about the number of cases that had been all too easily labelled over a century ago.

The faculty buildings were made out of red bricks and had originally served as cottages for guests at Sigmund Lakeside Hospital. JJ brought him up in an elevator to one of these edifices that contained a modest archive. She followed his trembling finger with enthusiasm and knee-scootered towards a display case.

"Props for pointing out this photo. That's one of the administrators with his wife. Beside the two music masters. Poor dear. She was one of the first Torontonians to be admitted. You know, there's an interesting synchronicity there because just like me, her name's Juniper. She had to spend her entire adult life here, where she hopefully found peace at last. But was she even ill? The admission records are all long gone ..."

"Juniper?"

"You know, her husband was mad about cricket. He recommended it to all the residents as a cure-all. Eventually, they petitioned for soccer, but for the longest time, it was cricket."

"But he was right up to date about the Dilscoop!"

A flight attendant put Farinata in the upright position and her perfume and French braid revived him somewhat. He stared vacantly at the instructional video glowing on the small screen. For once, he did not ask himself why a handful of attractive passengers were taking that celestial flight upon which each compartment had room for multiple rolling cases and a bag of 9-grain bagels. He did not speculate whether two grinning guys were work chums or much more, or why one of them was stowing a box of lobster under the seat in front of him. He did not question the gleeful mood of the mother placing an oxygen mask over her daughter's mouth. Other than a good view of the flight attendant's fluid choreography in relation to the emergency exits, one consolation was that the woman who had made his week was not, to his knowledge, a traditional spirit of which he could not speak, still lacking the appropriate permissions. If he was not being "gaslighted," then she had indeed been the ghost of a beautiful settler, and a chapter in his memoir would not be verboten. He tilted back and began to relax. The majority of passengers in front of him had selected a movie featuring a green woman and a talking raccoon who was piloting some kind of spaceship.

Life, he thought, was already getting back to normal.

Billet-doux from Bunty

far far far

yr not heer snug as bug. yr words overwelm me then wut? oky doky smoky thats wut its lyk. stoopid rite

btwn 10 an 2 my post sed no all day yr wurds fill me tall dark an lothsome. tooday the pesant top u love pulls down eesy cheerleeder skirt to

ya i love yr pomes my head spyralls my body when u mone. madd maybee yr playin sum chick in swift currant or stoon herting us all

dreds shaved qwik jog qwik cos thats how u lyk me in showur what thots! no wut hapened runing down my leggs how u lyk it ya yes u doo. feel my shurn head befor i loose it. yr notty qween in qween sitee needs u

yr bossmann in stoon kalls this a fuken hole? awfull. poor qween sitee

born an razed not so bad dont fret ofer anny whyte powur thing unkle wont freek u dont look lyk won ok. tho his spehshul job dont hold yr breth

cum owt an play in fuken hole cos i need u so bad beggin how you lyk it ya

wanna tell blade butt stayj wurst he tayks riley then wut? mostlee laym not lyk u deer sweet far! for instants he wood ownlee gitt fuken part not wurds how spehshul yr sole is

pulees cum tmrw its no lye wut I sed durin hawt fuken part

hope yr feelin it deep

yr yumy scrumy bunt

Whispers around Wascana

Farinata crumpled up the form letter and made a half-hearted rim shot. His epistolary contribution to a national anthology of bipolaric billets-doux had been politely declined. Tack on swift rejection from the mental health issue of a journal; the editor could not see what so much scientific nomenclature had to do with field reports about his condition, let alone temperature regulation among grasshoppers. A magazine in the middle of an identity crisis—too subtle?—too soon?—offered him a kill fee to dig a hole in the same field and bury his submission therein. Then, in the same week, a scheduling conflict had come to the attention of the organizers of the Indigi-Enable conference, and amid profuse outpourings of regret, he had been turned away as a presenter and a panellist.

He could chalk it all up to coincidence, or face facts. Certain incidents were not going to fade into the prehistoric landscape of his metadata any time soon. The first whiff of trouble reached the horizon when a bucolic meditation on paved paths and surrounding shrubbery was passed his way. Once again, his mysterious source had come up with an article, this time by a prominent member of a provincial political party. The limp paean to cultivated nature did not have enough scientific nomenclature in it for Farinata's liking, but he was wary not to jeopardize funding for *Mudflap*, the literary newsletter he had decided to devote himself to—the dying animal his sick desire was fastened to, or so a wit at one of the papers would say. After the first wave of distribution,[44] a significant leak—pardon this phrase—reached the media, asserting that the favourite pastime of this popular candidate was to don a mask that showed the outward face of a former Conservative Party leader and expose the rest of himself to early morning joggers in Wascana Park. Naturally, *Mudflap* took the heat for printing a poem that (inadvertently) celebrated his lifestyle choices, not to mention accepting inappropriate submissions from its very own "Deep Throat" at the back of a multiplex in Golden Mile.[45]

---

44. Who could anticipate this publishing decision would throw him under the #9, which is to say the Albert Park, named after an area that, in its newsletter postal radius, approaches the distance between our friend and a certain lady between ten and two, even with the adjustments that account for the cheeky little dip into Hillsdale, an anomaly that draws the perfect analogy to such an outbreak of repressed passion amid the quotidian throng who loved and hated to hear about it?

45. Farinata first made contact with his source at a packed screening of *Blue is the Warmest Colour*. Little did he know that Wisteria was sitting eight seats away, or that she saw him in the company of a woman in a floppy hat and sunglasses who resembled Faye Dunaway in *The Thomas Crown Affair*, or so it would occur to her in later years; it was quite a memorable night for her.

All of this we can readily believe; the rest was hard to work out, even for Farinata. The way he remembered it, his inamorata between the hours of ten and two had texted him, expressing dread about the electoral flash in the pan, to use a phrase that would follow him into the grave. He had texted Bunty at once, assuring her there was nothing to fear because the whole thing had been blown out of proportion. Autocorrect had for reasons unknown adjusted the clipped phrases to infer there would be something to fear if the recipient did not blow him like a contortionist—or like a property owner, depending on which news source you preferred. Such a high margin of error would not have bothered Bunty in the slightest; this message was tame, going by the naughty yardstick of the consensual sexts they sent back and forth throughout the day. The problem was that he had accidentally[46] sent the autocorrected text to his editorial assistant, Bunny. Unprepared for even a bat's squeak of sex emanating from the only man in the office, she did a quick capture and shared the text with the Organization for Love and Empathy (OLE). The respective members responded at once with suggestions ranging from swift condemnation to painstaking castration. The hunt was already on when she figured out what had happened. On her lunch break, she took Farinata's phone out with her and found all the sexts that had been sent to Bunty, along with all the eager replies. She captured them with every intention of clearing the name of her pervy but innocent[47] colleague. Every

---

46. According to Mark Twain, "there are no accidents. All things that happen, happen for a purpose. They are foreseen from the beginning of time, they are ordained from the beginning of time." Autocorrect's getting a "kick in the A" from the foot of Providence is beyond the scope of this text.

47. The naïveté behind such an awkward construction is noted.

image and emoji from this down-and-dirty repository was to become invaluable on an otherwise slow—the subtext is "sexless"—news day.

Alma Smatterson was the first to get the lead she needed to blow Wascanagate wide open. It may have been the result of neocolonization that led her to assume an Indigenous copy editor would get her own name wrong, and to recast every "Bunty" in the editorial copy as "Bunny." It was more of a mystery how Farinata came to be known as "Fartnoob the Poet" in each of the Postmedia repeats. One paper even enlisted Hannah Hackinen to do one of her exceedingly long articles about all of the players. On the surface, she was wholly objective and gave everyone their say; blink a few times and traces of her trompe l'oeil technique came into focus; scroll down a while longer, and the experience was soon akin to studying Goya's treatment of Charles IV and his family. Was Hannah Hackinen lending these interviewees aspects of her own humanity, or casting them in a satiric light? The giant photographs of Bunny and Bunty, placed side-by-side above captions extracted from the original sexts, immortalized them as "Hunny-Bunny" and "Bunt-Eats." The blunt conversation with Bunty's common-law partner did not take place in his house; the picture of Blade—no nickname needed—grimly holding up young Riley in his Bro-Cave, or paralytic trailer, in front of a Nickelback poster was the epitome of damnation. The equity officers for OLE were persuaded to slip into skin-tight unitards and adopt Wonder Woman poses in front of a brick wall they were just about to punch into smithereens. Though "Fartnoob the Poet" was given the opportunity to clarify his position—ahem—in no less than 1000 words, his stirring discourse was skewered somewhat by the unearthed selfie of him standing in front of a full-length mirror in his long underwear—agitated by the ratio of polyester to cotton, no less—with a Wile E. Coyote mask tied over what the viewer must take for his untamed excitement. Hannah Hackinen dubbed the controversy "The Bunny and Coyote Affair," although the headline—MUDFLAP'S SEX-SUBS IN SASK—had been brainstormed by a sleepy underling.[48]

The Pen-Friend Forum carried on for months, and was less a legal process than an amiable gathering of what sufficed as local peers of the "transgressive" entity. They believed that a concentrated process of inquiry would give the "transgressive" a chance to come to terms with his errant behaviour and reach a reasonable conclusion about the matter at hand. After all, it was one thing to expose yourself in the park—possibly a cry for help from their committee—and quite another to try and orchestrate a sex ring out of a newsletter office amid the sticky clamour of . sloppy three-ways, as one online source put it. The function of this impromptu body was not so much to ascertain the level of guilt as put their findings towards a rating system for similar examples of malfeasance. On account of his disorder, Farinata was soon fatigued by the proceedings and could not hold back a number of highly emotional outbursts, video of which was instantly uploaded for the viewers at home, who generally tended towards a thumbs-down. His peers took note of his continual vacillation between two dominant humours, namely the choleric and the sanguine. Even his capillary action during their stimulus-response tests was indicative of lascivious monstrosities just waiting to happen. Two representatives of OLE took it upon themselves to evaluate his written works. Whatever

---

48. 407 comments expressing outrage vindicate the choice of headline, not including all the blocked comments expressing the "hotness" of the situation.

they could understand corrupted them at once—violating several NO-GO zones upon each of their persons, respectively—confirming their suspicions that all of his poems, stories, novels, and especially his stabs at impossible theatre, were unduly preoccupied with incorrect forms of love. Once the OLE reps had been secured and reprogrammed, they would be ready to exorcise these illicit inklings, plucking them one by one from the "transgressive's" frontal lobe as if they were the midsection of a unibrow. In the interim, a statement of culpability would be assembled for him to sign at his earliest convenience.

Farinata entered into a period of intense self-flagellation. In retrospect, he might have behaved better; to tell himself his overweening adoration of women had turned him into something of a womanizer—well, that was pretty feeble. Nor could he refute OLE's critique of his general disposition. There had been more than one occasion on which his rage and/or despair had resulted in an impulse towards self-harm. He had always considered himself—at worst—merely a danger to the aforementioned, but that was without taking into account a number of unforeseen circumstances.[49] Though he had kept his "nudie cards" close to his chest, he could not deny that working closely with Bunny—a beautiful Indigenous woman who knew what she was about—amid so many flowing fonts had prompted more than one inappropriate thought, perhaps enough to turn him into a slavering Rougarou. The undelivered sequence of poems about unrequited infatuation, like many of his gimcrack satires, was proof of the ill-intentioned pudding between his

---

49. Probably not the best time to reflect on John Huston's insistence in *Chinatown* that most people never have to face the fact that at the right time and the right place, they are capable of anything.

ears. Not only had he secretly coveted his attractive colleague, but he had indulged in countless acts of mutual
objectification with Bunty—a lovely woman of indefinite
extract—between the hours of ten and two without any
regard for her young family, or the charming nanny from
Trinidad who minded Riley at this time of day, possibly next in his shameless sights for a rapid-fire sonnet
sequence, if that's the phrase. Signing a public statement
of contrition was all well and good, but it would not even
scratch the surface of his deviant psyche. Equally damn-
ing was his keen awareness that Trish would have been
perfect to administer the necessary lashes as an unforget-
table reprimand.

Though it was late summer, every residual aftershock of
Farinata's peer-grilling gave him chills. For once, it was not
the conductivity of the salinity of the soil that was detri-
mentally electrifying his mental processes; it was, for lack of
a perfectly apt expression, the hell of others.[50] At first, he
sloughed off Oskana Society's failure to include his name on
their banderole as a harmless oversight. A rootless poet of
modest repute loitering on Treaty 4 Territory was not worth
much more than his traditional connections.[51] Yet there was
a new development, a supersubtle[52] sense of being unwel-
come. Trish would no longer raise her eyes to meet his in

---

50. Farinata had devoured Sartre's *Huis Clos* and he had proudly
sported the T-shirt.

51. One of the advantages of snuggling up with Marcel Proust's *À
la recherche du temps perdu* and familiarizing oneself with all the phyla
of snubbing, shunning, and snobbery is that each taxonomic feature
can be identified in environs beyond the hegemonic scope of
neocolonial social constructs.

52. Forgive this Henry James favourite, but we have need of it just
now.

the coffee queue; Piper disappeared behind a noxious cloud of Deter whenever he passed her cosmetic counter in the drugstore; Lucia had nothing greener for him than a defensive block; Wisteria had quit waiting on the appetites of others to dedicate herself to a local theatre troupe; Ashley had followed suit, chipping in with administrative duties while keeping the dream alive of becoming the body double of her stately bestie. At the food trucks, the choice pieces of chicken and portions of roast were no longer his. At the farmer's market, his usual stockpile of vibrant greens was full of holes, and the tomato seller no longer talked up his wares, but handed over a bag of overripes in stony silence. Farinata expected to find refuge at the Environment Canada information seminar on grasshoppers and other insects of economic importance, but his attendance only resulted in another bizarre headline: SEX PEST CRASHES PEST CON.

Everything came to a head at Prairie Packhorse, as if at the whim of some nouveau-baroque opera god. Bunny was the first to see him. She stared, open-mouthed, and a ripple of unresolved tension passed through the scarlet rashguards. Her parents started into their denunciation from afar, filling the store with their imaginary grievances. Riley rolled into view,[53] and Bunty (not Bunny) reddened right down to the roots of her shorn cornrows. Blade strode over to Farinata and slapped his face with a pair of junior hockey gloves that happened to be within reach, inviting our "transgressive" to settle things like a proper dude in the parking lot. In one of those coincidences we usually only find in a work of fiction, the two representatives from OLE—if you've forgotten, this is the Organization for Love and Empathy—who had evaluated his written works began to give their findings

---

53. The boy was clearly old enough to walk by himself, but not old enough to understand what was happening.

at the highest possible volume. Never had there been such a need for a hero capable of righteous vengeance, some unthinking man of action. Fortunately, there were two such individuals on the payroll at Prairie Packhorse, and one of them was skulking[54] behind a vast array of waterfowl decoys. Though he had never heard the word before, he would have readily agreed it was within his "pervyoo" to throw one punch and then another. A rallying cry followed, possibly "*Olé!*"

Alma Smatterson was the first to arrive at the mouth of the corn maze, and it was up to her to extract the five Ws from a clump of unreliable witnesses. The one H was particularly elusive. A Scrooser-jacking, with the moral re-educators in hot—if unbelievably slow—pursuit. The pervy perp was running on fumes just outside of Regina, and sought refuge in the maze. STALKER IN THE STALKS was just waiting for the headline guy. Though getting the denouement out of anyone there was like trying to pry stray niblets from crowded teeth. "Fartnoob the Poet" did not emerge—naked and starving?—and Roy Cobb, the man who knew the maze like the back of his hand, could find neither hide nor hair of him. In the end, only *Mudflap*—now controlled by OLE's internal task force—was prepared to go to print with the curious tale, providing a headline with a hit-worthy new moniker: UFO CAPTURES UNI-GROPER.

---

54. Nazi or Nazi-basher, he was not allowed anywhere near the semi-automatic rifles or pump-action shotguns.

Visit in Victoria Square

"**W**ell, here we are, then."

"Natch."

"Do you still feel the same ... remember?"

"I think so, but I don't really remember. Besides, it doesn't change a thing."

"If you came back now, I do not know what we would have."

"Came back?"

"How much you forget! You left your home and job without a bye or leave, for ... this."

"Really!? It's not so bad. You have to learn to tell soft-sell from hard-sell Hutterite, meaning the man with the sunglasses at the market. You'll find yourself five bags of corn the richer and poorer. Also, I've switched from the chicken and waffles to a lovely meat van. The closest to Blackfoot pemmican I can get in these parts."

"You've mentioned a 'condition.' Do you want to fill me in?"

"Neither fatal nor transmitted, but chronic. I have a diagnosis that sheds light on very little. It's about as mild as a summer breeze laced with carbon monoxide. Can't complain, only the GP could not trace the paterfamilial line as far back as the schismatic struggle of Puritans, wringing their hands of their sorry trade in exchange for the oldest trick in the book, from Cromwell on down ..."

"You don't think you are Cromwell, do you?"

"Of course not."

"Then are you suggesting the Lord Protector was divided against himself?"

"Only he should not have forsook Constable's picturesque slough or bog to chase such a vacant dream. Better to hawk tickets to leopard frog races, in my experience! The same goes for that bewildered teacher lured back into the Métis struggle just when he was on the mend. By the time his mania died down, his troubled head was on the end of a rope. I am only saying, please do not ask me to run for the Saskatchewan Party or they'll have my guts for garters—"

"Garter brings back memories. You know, I miss your funny mind."

"Nastasya Filippovna! Imagine, here on the humid-continental!"

"If you like, although I never took English."

"You have more than a hunch for business and its sinewed trappings. Live not in thy shame on account of your luxury condo or BMW, because I forgive you these devil-brood of fascism and capitalism, however stylish the product of their coupling."

"Why bring them up, then?"

"The same goes for my affliction and my privation, the

low-hanging fruit of Art, a sorry discipline that leaves me open to all manner of attacks, from pitiless S'tooners to beautiful stoners to petulant baristas! The other day, a man from the rival town denied that his dog would ever in his life, even when pressed, eat a turd."

"Yes, you are here and I miss your funny mind."

"Could the floor displays and trade shows and chichi soirées and faux-royal *perfumiers* from abroad really lack this awfully wobbly noggin? Could frequent appearances on idiot boxes in a 'world-class city' still leave one wanting?"

"You remember a few things, then. Let's say that my BS meter is quite finely attuned nowadays. But do you even remember who I am?"

"You healed man and boy à la Iseult. You often talked shamanics and often heard me without modern technology, even post-DARPA and without circuit boards jury-rigged with more than a few lines of C. Neurology and psychology took a backseat to psychometry. You frequently advocated echinacea and tea-tree oil when I was aching for selenium and magnesium. You were once struck by lightning and that is part of your origin story, or is it that you once got lost in a wood and were touched by Poludnitsa? Hence, your influence over henges. Black flatters you best and emboldens you to comment honestly on my swagger. You once suffered, like all fair maids of quality, a stomach-wrenching heartache in a place of turbid waters. Then you found yourself in a desert, and held an undeniable gala-do in chaparral or upon mesa. You once sang a patch of Verdi or Purcell that was so stirring, we did not even notice your dress was inside-out. You once sent me a card involving a sharp, sexual conceit about a female praying mantis—"

"You are getting warmer, but I must admit, you are more than a little bit mixed-up."

"Sorry, somewhere between the Proustian composite and the Eternal Feminine running through fields of canola or mustard, I have gone astray. Like salt-water taffy in a pocket forever, suddenly converted into a questionable gas."

"Not your finest image."

"Didn't you tell me I used to put notes in the pocket of your coat in the cloakroom?"

"Not on your life!"

"Did I ever moon about you when I was in my cups, making a monkey out of Aeschylus while you had Swinburne plastered across your noble brow? Out of nowhere, you said the picture over your head was like some demented carnival."

"No, you once muttered something about that—we were on the bed in your 'cockloft.' You had just knocked another job on the head and without thinking, I ... *comforted* you."

"What presumptuousness!"

"Then I fell into your arms ..."

"A time of tactility, yes? Only we were surely cuckolding some common-law adjunct—"

"Do you know that I have only strayed once ... for you?"

"But you didn't appreciate the films of Radu Muntean? You didn't go back to Latvia or Bulgaria or Romania or Serbia to declare your illicit intentions to a near and dear relation and return with a proverbial thumbs-up, giving the entire affair a feudal air?"

"I would be glad if you at least got the place right, if not the scenario."

"So we weren't caught *in flagrante delicto*, resulting in a hunger strike and an inter-tribal blood feud?"

"I would have remembered *that*."

"Natch. You know, I've fallen in love with this stupid place but I must let it go, if only to preserve its good name."

Intermezzo in the Air

Fortunately for us, the entr'acte did not yet threaten to erupt into full blown Walpurgisnacht,[55] although the horizons of our airborne scribe were matchless under the influence of a potent relaxant, or perhaps two or three when no one was prying into his affairs, say, when the flight plan did not load due to a certain spell resulting in a nefarious glitch. Parasitically—its root glossing roughly as "beside the food"—he was bent on heading—fleeing?—to a host city three times the size where a poet could sing for a decent supper; surely winning an arugula house salad was not beyond his abilities. Upon hearing the news, his beloved Trish, much as we

---

55. With every respect to Goethe, the literary convention of a Walpurgis Night dream sequence will be scheduled later than usual. Please enjoy this complimentary portion of *spoudogeloion*—according to Aristophanes, "seriously laughable stuff"—on us.

would expect, had dived into a slough;[56] the gods had changed her into a rusalka to spare her, and Piper, who was not prone to desperate acts, being from Morse, merely beat her bosom and scratched out Bettie Page's inked eyes before smashing all the mirrors at the cosmetics counter that bore the first three letters of his name written in Stay Put Rampage.

Wow, that is some relaxant, no fooling. Compared to the rest, these two got off lightly. There is a prize-winning posterior in the background somewhere, landing about as obscurely as Icarus. Though we begin to weary of this dramatic fail—the boarding and the waiting and the disembarking and the reboarding and the de-icing and the sorry folks kindly get off again. Would Wicca not let the man go already? Not yet, according to the enchanted cabin rubric that read: HOW A HARRIDAN IN WOMAN'S LIKENESS TRIES THE VIRTU OF FARINATA UNTIL HE WRIGGLES FREE WITH A VOUCHER GOOD AT ANY AIRPORT FRANCHISE.

Alack, said she without delimiters, shall ye not humour my latest and greatest whim? Dominique, said Farinata, since the second or third time you have demonstrated use of the oxygen mask,[57] and double so *en français*, there is no lady in this world whose whims I would rather entertain. Ah poet, said she, beyond even the glossy confines of this in-flight magazine, I have clapped peepers upon the beauty of thy words that seldom cease to touch upon the hardiness of the male specimen, that needs ye must grant me vertical tribute before the beverage cart renews its celestial proces-

---

56. Compare David Cronenberg's treatment of *Naked Lunch*: "Don't give up though. It's—It's a good sign ... the courtship period can involve years of passionate ambivalence."

57. The return of this image after only so many pages would suggest a powerful symbolic significance.

sion. Truly, said he, I shall not do it in no manner wise. Then she made him such sorrow as though there were so much invested in the offbeat dilation of his eyes. Well then, said she, unto this have ye brought me, and the happiness of this domain. She made him to understand crackers would be handed out, but not one pair of cookies while the slightest taste of ashes still haunted her soft, smoochable kisser.

Yet it was her colleague Emmanuelle who patted—petted?—him out of a dazzling flashback. Good sir, said she, there be something in the lost and found for ye. A book, I believe with all my heart! Tush,[58] said Farinata, be it never mine. Then a pair of drugstore reading glasses, said she. I am not your man, said Farinata, balking at the word "drugstore"[59] and putting to bed any discussion of his nearsightedness while pert silhouettes moved in and out of focus. Do not let me be beguiled a second longer, he begged the nearest unbelted elm.

Verily, I need to pee terribly, said a familiar voice, and it was the lady of his heart and traitorous loins. Trish, cried Farinata, how are you transported here to this window seat? Hemlock is what you need, and I could not bear the thought of you going like a rogue in the night without a proper fare-thee-well, said the short goddess, savouring the longest sentence she had ever uttered in her young life. A sucker for any attempt at periphrastic excess, he rose with unsteady obstinacy—she called it an opportune show of spunk, whispering deal-sweeteners into his ear—and escorted

---

58. Archaic homograph subject to psychoanalytic interpretation. Ashley in Scat 16C!

59. By all means, take flight, Farinata, but you're bound to wash up at another cosmetics counter at another Avocet Drugs less than 600 km away, when all the fight has gone out of you. A seriously laughable situation, with all the pathos of a Greek tragedy.

her down the aisle to the tail feathers of the medium-sized bird. Dominique and Emmanuelle hissed and booed before ascending the secret stairway that led to their crypt-like sleeping quarters, where they surrendered to one another with impressive efficiency. Trish promptly propped open the unisex door and raised the hem of her emerald fée frock, enticing him into the heady world of YA series modelling.[60] It was surely by the grace of something greater than himself that a suspect kebab began to revolt and cry havoc within his intestinal tract. Modesty drove him to wobble away to reach the other lavatory near the beak of the medium-sized bird—no doubt enraging it!—only to discover that the beverage cart had renewed its celestial procession; his path was barred. Farinata's only option was to take refuge in a free seat where the whole sorry business came up all over a man in a seersucker suit and his glowing tablet. The raccoon pilot[61] was furious and stormed out of the head of the bird to personally admonish our troublemaker.

Anon, Farinata heard a great noise and a great cry, as though all the fiends of hell had been about him; and therewith he saw not Dominique nor Emmanuelle, nor his beloved Trish, nor the overt provocation of a right arm bearing Bettie Page with the eyes scratched out. To his surprise, he lay upon a wide path that bordered the bifurcation of two rivers, clutching a blue cheese and fig empanada like his life depended on it.

---

60. Even to appear in this relaxant-induced hallucination, Trish is required by law to be more than a few moons into her eighteen years.

61. In one of the deleted scenes, he retires to the secret bedroom with his crew. Canadian surrealism!

Mädchen among the Mennonites

Around the time Farinata had reached a short-lived equilibrium, the redux fell into his lap. "Huzza!" screamed a young lady in Stonewall before falling silent again. Huzza, indeed. Getting to a nunnery or even a cloister was simply not in the cards for *cet enfant maudit*, so he settled on a bucolic summer in an apartment at the Mennonite University, where long strolls, according to Rousseau, would revive his rather addled sensorium, and discreetly cuspidor his Pavlovian reaction to shinier aspects of the material universe. If he happened to cross paths with a student, rather than kick up any dirt on Flinck the Mennonite—that student of Rembrandt whose commercial success with genre art was like a slash at the canvas of his former teacher—Farinata would wag a finger and give her or him a mild lecture on the biblical significance of grasshoppers, citing their beneficial metaphoric and gustatory usage.

Not that he could avoid his reputation as a complete pest, when he was the first to be defeated by a clingy pair of cycling shorts. The first! To his credit, where he had once clambered after beauty's dozy blink, now he turned tail and did a runner, given half a chance. Really, it adds nothing to our tale that our laureate of little things had once penned a very similar sentiment upon a serviette that ended up wiping an enviable mouth whose owner abhorred gossamer-winged poesy to the point of making snoring noises whenever it threatened her slumberous life, which was, to speak her truth, one continual WOOT after another.

> *You there, you will no longer go a-*
> *courting, clambering after fateful peignoir*
> *open to every suggestion save this one:*
> *allow me by this eventide but one aureola!*
> *Hey, you there! You will no longer raise*
> *your eyelids from my quizzical bulk*
> *stunned by that hobbling hook*
>   *of the unrequited ...*

Farinata was cocking his head and keeping excellent time with the tooth-leggèd music of a male *Chloealtis* when the first flutter caught his attention. Not to say he felt so much as saw butterflies. To go from the modest cabbage white to this incredible painter's box of hindwings was an unexpected boon. He did not even see the raised behind in breathable synthetics—she was standing on the pedals— that belonged to a young woman about to become his own endorphin-fanner. "On your left, on your left!" she cried. She managed a passing joust that dislodged the spore-ridden cadaver of a rare species of grasshopper and narrowly avoided the white admiral flapping awkwardly in the middle of the gravelly route of their lives. Flap, flap, it went, like a wounded bird, but even this was a perfectly sensible demonstration of affection. By now, it was common knowledge that Farinata was looking for a place to hang his hat in the Peg, and what is more, he had taken refuge in a light wood. If you were still a bit wet behind the ears, he might be just the fellow to towel you off.

Worse luck for the Mädchen—Maddy to her bestest besties—still relatively fresh from the Fatherland with more than a few oats to sow.[62] Sad, we say, that such a cunning linguist in the offing should not be in the slightest acquainted with the life-affirming texture belonging to the variegated tongue of Farinata, which held its own when put under a microscope. Sad, we insist, to think of each soul wriggling in a wet paper bag because there had never been a better time for such an exceptional Fräulein to gloss him right down to the roots of his supercilious being. Natural light streamed in through the large windows of her workplace and became a bit epiphanical—please, not fanatical!—until a mere snatching of scripture was transfigured into the following gibberish for anyone within earshot: *So this is how I was enchanted by an ass.*[63]

Yet with cart before horse(!), we rush ahead of ourselves. For countless meanwhiles, the Mädchen had her hands full with his budding tea fetish, when not glamming up coffee and sandwiches for members of staff, along with the reasonably handsome student body. As for our friend, he could taste the green fruit of her dreams in every cup of

---

62. Our poet would surely chafe at these rhetorical flourishes, as with "wet behind the ears" or "hang his hat" or "oats to sow." Best not to let on.

63. This allusion to Nick Bottom's misquote of 1 Corinthians 2 is a rather complicated way of saying that Farinata did not like his odds.

Manitoba Rooibos she served him—a heady draught that for no clear reason contained the Saskatoon berry—and wrung out of him an overripe nostalgia for the province he had so abruptly left behind for this decidedly deciduous promise of aspen parkland. *Sweet, moist, slightly tart,* piped up the piping tea. However, on the subject of a loyalty card, his view was downright adamantine. This was their first real conversation and their first real spat, if either noun is even remotely credible. Had the Mädchen waited on him even five or seven or nine times before she made her claim on him and drove the point home? At the end of his days, after so many punches, he would be able to enjoy a complimentary cup of tea, no questions asked. He could not put into human words (or even subject, predicate, object) the principle of the thing, namely that such a token of inessential itemization was bound to systematize and annihilate its original purpose to the point that even this pecuniary reduction would, in effect, suffer an abstract depreciation. What was next, a punch card for fidelity? That way, boggles and stumpers lay! In short, if there happened to be a next world, this loyalty card would do nothing to unite them there. All the same, on a quiet afternoon, he would go through the whole gamete of emblems in the history of Western civilization that positively oozed allegiance.

By now, we have gathered that once they were deprived of their precious phonemes, morphemes, and particles, metaphysical economics did not become them. Farinata itched to relate the tale of Étaín, who, in some versions of the myth, had been turned into a butterfly larva and had passed through the innards of so many unprepared Irish before being reunited with her intended. As for the white admiral flapping about the gravelly path, it was the scourge of Québécois kitchens in the nineteenth century. Yes, that little butter thief! Farinata was shrewd enough to rein in these bubbling tangentials in favour of a weighty caesura, lest she cotton on from the get-go that he was—let's be candid—a bit *touched*. Not to say the Wagnerian cellos started up the moment their dark eyes met. No, it was more of an *Ungarische Melodie* in the hurried hands of Imogen Cooper yet somehow with the painstaking delicacy of Dora Deliyska, until it was entirely possible to visualize "Tubby" himself, peeking into the Esterhazy larder for goodies and overhearing the first few bars being hummed by a Hungarian kitchen maid. Heaven help us! Somewhere between a racing gallop and the plunk of a wonky heartbeat, a sort of Schubertian giggle-fit took hold and did its damage. A trifle, a mere bagatelle, to be sure, but when a mayfly pressed itself against one of the large window panes, sorely aching for the fluorescents inside the building—if only to advertise his last day upon this blessed earth—Farinata got the distinct impression that he, too, was luminously doomed.

It is the gentleman's prerogative to betray a touch of caddishness, and admit that Trish would have bested her any day of the week—and twice on Sunday—for pride of place in an atrophied Sears catalogue, and yet the prospect of a Norman brow marching into his Roman-Celtic ruins—if not ultimately establishing dominion over his heathen ways—truly beggared belief. In laymen's terms, he was into her something awful and he was up for it like we dare not admit. On paper—where he cast the finest profile and stood half a chance—the perpetual mobility of her distinct features had a pleasing effect that could be called beauty, provided the eye of the beholder had gleaned the remnants of many mosaics and frescoes, especially those eaten away by the salt of the sea.

Now we can appreciate his uproar over the loyalty card

that would only have punched holes in his most sincere outpourings that were sweet as the sap of the Manitoba maple
to the red admiral, or beguiling as Tubby's Piano Sonata
in A major, for all its opening plangency, outpourings that
were well documented in numerous studies of aberrant
psychology, not to disparage an unutterable impulse that
flitted and fluttered between these two, inconvenient as
all get out because he tended to evoke her erudite pater-
familias—though he did not look a day over thirty when
dewhiskered, we promise!—with his fancifully wrought nest
of preverbal idiosyncrasies, still teetering on the cusp of
ordering fashionable hiking attire, could he lay claim to an
ounce of sang-froid compulsory for the role, aping woeful
dotard with a caravan of chattel, which is to say a man of
property without the canny wherewithal to dicker over the
dowry, being more like a peacock hobbled by his own outlandish decorations—though we have used this comparison
before, and to no great effect—leaving us with the post-
modern contiguity of this modest pair—for such a modifier
in lieu of "hapless" we must bear witness to her lowered
eyes and hem clinging to soft shin and his pressing need to
adore her in the old high-handed way as if he were pushing
one hundred and ninety-three rather than thirty—a suspect
attraction easily likened to silver gleams on the underside
of the great spangled fritillary, or various other fritillaries
our budding Nabokov would gladly fritter away his spare
moments on, each of them a divertimento from the usual
pangs of heart and loin, which is not to say that even if he
had the permissions, he would go in for the Navajo emblem
of vanity in favour of the more grounded Caterpillar of
Plains culture, or would, on a whim, install her in lacy stays
and tatting for the sake of a quick cuddle—no, not even in
painful peignoir or shoes that pinch—when the fauxhemian

blouse of a street mime and piped racer leggings—over jeggings distressed by chemical preparation that would only pollute the waters between them—would signify another verboten unspoken that permeated the air with sufficient toxicity to animate their fine limbs, which clearly kept track of such fearful symmetries, not to draw a comparison with the monarch who tries to mount other males of his species and is bitten forever shy for his efforts, forever destined to colonize milkweed from Mexico to Labrador, were we not horribly bored of forecasts and anticipating some kind of courtship as a natural progression from all this pedestrian *babillage* about heat and rain and storm, by the time the scoop could scarcely inch through the lime gelato for the amount of lustful dissonance their brown limbs were generating, even when he was fishing out the freshly tribalized coins of the realm, still stuck in the mull over a prospective union that insinuated not one shred of the Eternal Feminine, partly because—virtue signalling aside—he fought vocal fry at every turn, and generally subscribed to the much desired trifecta of freethinking, freewheeling, and freebooting—although a portion less of the freebooting this time round would put colour in his cheeks!—but it was hearing tell of her zeal for tongues that netted him in the wood, so to speak, surpassing the usual vicissitudes at top speed and fast-tracking the issue, which was pouring inner onto outer—not to overtly imply the fluid pleasure of the admirals, who are notorious mud-puddlers—reflecting a pair of dark eyes to steady his wobble and an enchanting smile to lead him out of sketchy or even nasty scrapes when push came to shove.

Then in a bizarre and unexpected twist, an artful teacher of more James than Austen decided without circumlocution or ambiguity that it would be a splendid idea for Farinata to escort the Mädchen through the thickest regions of the forest on the hottest of afternoons, barring weekends and civic holidays. They were each too polite to refuse outright, having not the clear grounds to do so with the violence of a beating heart.

Crowley and the Cheapbook

The antiquarian peered out her front window, a case for operatic Valhalla if there ever was one.[64] Psychoanalysis—going by her fiery red hair—would say a projection of Piper had gripped our friend about the ghoulies, but let's leave such flimsy conjecture for the time being. A familiar face craned out of a crowd of Norns. Yes, it came back to her ... he had purchased a facsimile of news from the Battle of Batoche, a horrific bit of historical reportage that now seemed amusing in an ironical way, depending on whom one asked. Aside from the crowing voice of Empire, the illustrations depicted Native people as chronic loungers, even in the heat of battle while shots whizzed overhead.

---

64. Memories shuffle in and out of order. Fritillaries flit about and take our eye off the ball, or for that matter, the goldenrod gall ball with gaps in the bracts full of katydid brood. Not a walk in the park then, or, for that matter, a walk in the forest. Not quite yet.

Was such an Ensoresque picaresque intentional? As for the ne'er-do-well, he had clearly gone downhill since that transaction. Proof of poet as Baudelaire's withered clown, if there ever was.[65]

Asquint, the potential menace was examining a chapbook that had been found in the collection of a national supernova who had passed away before his time, sadly but helpfully! There had not been much left when the antiquarian had arrived on the scene and it was not as if she had pried the item in question out of a tightly locked fist. The item in question, not being a vital Menno-tract of yore, had been mistaken for a speckled coaster and she had gotten it for a song; she hoped to turn it over for at least two or three songs because all was fair in love and decent binding. There was no bench to speak of outside her window—thank her lucky stars!—and yet this "Indigenteel" poet appeared to be lounging where he stood beneath a gaudy sun umbrella. No, that was obviously straight out of illustrated Batoche, if not the race memory out of which historical phantoms were always cropping up. No, this poet to someone was erect, if one could call it that, and not like that homeless man who had really been erect one spring morning. Still, you couldn't go around throwing cold water on such enthusiasm like once upon a time.

She stared down at *The Invention of Morel*, but kept a roving eye on the poet, mainly because she had a growing concern about the Aleister Crowley. Now that was what she called a

---

65. There is absolutely no proof that this bookseller would reach the same conclusion as our protagonist, even in a novel full of such concurrences. Would it be any more believable that she was reminded of "An Epigram of Fealty" by Javier Marías while opening a box of books by Jorge Luis Borges and Adolfo Bioy Casares? Perhaps it was not too late for her to marry the King of Redonda.

chapbook proper. Two hundred and fifty loons worth, and this upward-scuttler was sidling up to it. Not that he would get far, even with the new airport extension. Lake Michigan, maybe, and then the manhunt would be on. Ack! The bell! The poet was calling to her from inside the store!

"Good afternoon."

"Afternoon. How much is that chappie in the window?"

"Ah yes, let me just look up the entry."

She was not judging. Maybe he had stashed two hundred and fifty smackeroos in a mattress or moth-eaten sock. What she liked about the entry book, in addition to the presence of her fountain pen within its contents and the delicious description that accompanied it, was its proximity to the silent alarm. Not to signal the district patrol, per se, but some well-meaning toughs from the back of a falafel shop. They happened to be Bosnian but the ringleader—her sometimes paramour—was Moroccan. Not that she was judging! No, she was besotted with her own entry for the moment.

Hand-bound in full terracotta-coloured leather, with gilt lettering to front board. Marbled endpapers. Glue used on frontispiece at production has caused some rippling. Paper bound in against the grain, causing some minor rippling throughout. Lettering entirely in green, with limitation numbering by hand in red. Lightest rubbing to extremities, no other flaws other than a few noted production errors; near fine. Leather bound. Scarce. Utterly filthy!

Here we go. The poet was mounting his creaky soapbox and spouting off like the incomprehensible fount that Plato describes somewhere. The chapbook worth only three songs—more like cheapbook—was the source of his excitement. He was standing to his full height, which was almost her height, and laying claim to the cheapbook, adding salt to wound with his denigration of the Crowley verses as not worth the paper they were printed upon. In spite of her chagrin, she knew this to be true, deep down. The rippled paper was munificent, and deserved every word of her paean to it, author or not. But the cheapbook had belonged to the late So-and-So, who had won prizes, and besides, a scraggly man was attacking her trade. Too soon to ring for Assoun? No, there was surely a Socratic way out. *Talk him down, girlie*, or so her limited-edition interior monologue went.

A tepid standoff ensued. The antiquarian held her position with her trigger finger upon the Crowley entry. The poet's eyes were moist and he was stammering his name, which only came out as "Fffffff" at first, and eventually, they agreed on Farley Nuttat to conserve time and energy. Then he drew a bit of folded paper out of the back pocket of his abominable khaki cutoffs, and she accepted it like any squirrel accepting an acorn from fingers. Sorry, that is the best image that springs to mind under such harrowing circumstances, and we shall live with it. Or maybe you simply had to be there. She unfolded it gingerly and her face lit up. It was a letter of some kind. A letter long enough to buy her time, once she had thumbed the silent alarm.

Flame in the Folds

Dear Fare-thee-nought,

This is a surprise but eventide is for wine and trees (and thee, a freaking soliloquy). Finally, at long last, you've got me on the grass under that sentimental catalpa and where in blazes are ye? A buddy of yours filled me in on the deets. They will run you out of my hometown if I have anything to do with it. Don't think I fancy you, no, not that old chestnut! My friend thought you were a laugh only it takes more than falling off a stool to sway me. I hearken back to experimental heydays but even then. Just not my type.

Wait, a wee confession. The words in that little paper book were A-OK by me. I carried it around with me along the Liffey and in piazzas full of pigeons with no shortage of chaps to pinch the merchandise. Then, after a bottle, I got thinking it would be sweet to sit across from Swinburne and get a gander at the goods, or what he means by such-and-such. Well, I figured you would be disappointed to sit down over a cuppa and find out the bloody sun doesn't rise out of my

Never you mind. I am pretty great! Fellas go mad for me, or didn't you know that? A ghastly mandemic if you follow. Pure magic, from auditions to posing for ultra-product. Empty promises galore. Scam capital and don't I know it! Then your fine words and what do you want with me? Queue up with the rest of 'em! Nutters all! Wanting one thing. What about you, master of alabaster, did you just want one thing? You never said, not once.

There we have it. A leg over. But you would get consumed all over again, right? Prolly not the best for Brolleywood. You know, I do miss the bright winters. All right, another wee tell-all. Maybe you were the one to see the real me. How on earth? I want to understand but those tricks with the words give me the willies. Even so, thank you for keeping me in your heart. That's the best a gal can do, then get right back to lining up her ducks.

Wait, what? Service is not what it was. Another glass for the lady. Yes, me! Look, I'm going to mail this before I wake up tomorrow with a nasty head. The unvarnished is definitely not into you. In case you didn't guess, it's your biuuuuuuutifull Muse

Muck in the Meadow

FYI: this is a new century.[66] Narrative and dialogue have given way to their non-representative betters. Yes, rejoice in the conceptual squiggle instead of all that dusty old humbug of days gone past! Another way of saying that similitudes, like delicate études, were passing between our taciturn pair. The thunderstorm had passed and yet the muck remained. Though intensely conscious of the silent Fräulein who followed his tread along the narrow meadow path, his aural memory was turning over the sod of a section of Schubertian *Silbertönen*, which is to confess a moribund sliver had gotten stuck somewhere about his heart. An

---

66. Once again, with particular daring, we pan away and cut the scene. Was our poet chased, beaten, left for dead, or did he lose his memory and end up in this section of terrestrial paradise? That is between him and the falafel shop. Back to this contrivance of Farinata escorting the Mädchen through the forest.

orange fritillary—such terse inaccuracy!—landed upon a
bunch of—rigid?—goldenrod within view. Farinata pointed
at it and she nodded, assuming that stillness was the order
of the evening.

It was. In all likelihood, they were looking at a great spangled
fritillary, but he was not ready to commit himself at this early
stage of their relations. What if the fluttering beauty turned
out to be the Atlantis or Aphrodite fritillary, and at some
later date, his error came to light? Or what if she only heard
"Aphrodite"—a continual preoccupation—and fled from the
meadow, ne'er to be seen again? Size was the decider, along
with its penchant for *Liatris ligulistylis* that led to a territorial tus-
sle with a ravenous monarch who was a bit of a bully in these
parts. Farinata would be the first to point out the sheer lack of
symbolism. Even that monarch—say, when failing to mount
another male (a mistake?) and getting nothing but a clipped
wing for all his hovering[67]—had little to do with Farinata's min-
imalist ache. As for the butterfly's own appetite, it would be
loath to leave this vast array of meadow blazing star, but the
Mädchen did not know that. Farinata used this fragile scene
as a pretext to speak in hushed tones, inching close enough to
study constellations of sun-browned freckles upon and around
her nose. Even in a G-rated movie, a monumental kiss would
have ensued but in life, Farinata would have had to overcome
being forgetful and possibly forgotten about. Let us give him
credit where credit is due. Her prolonged survey of his pores
did not repulse her. Anywhere else, hands might have clasped;
their owners had not thought the problem through, and had
already committed to first-in-first-out single file. Then a white
species with a green tinge caught his eye, and the moment

---

67. Your guess is as good as ours why we have to hear about this
again.

tumbled like moth into meadow,[68] where that comely *Komm, beglücke mich* was sputtering delicately in its own reflux.

Farinata had cooked up an incredible escape plan to an area in the Peg that he alone referred to as "Little Regina"; the plan was to nestle in among its big box outlets and industrial zones and nature preserve. There, indulging in habits we by now know so well, he would haunt the Greek outfit and nibble skewers of lamb and stare at the same pictures hanging on the wall in Regina and Winnipeg and elsewhere, those tidy Mediterranean scenes devoid of stray dogs and unnecessary surcharges. Even a tree cricket came with the densely packed condo development, chiming in with katydid evensong and matching its seasonal counterpart in Queen City. Only on the long hike home did he see a pelican in shadow, passing overhead. A reminder of former troubles and a portent of future muddles? No, that was his funny-looking heart flapping overhead. Presumably, the poem began to form at this prompting, a poem that would sooner congeal in amber than suffer brute exteriorization in this breathing world, scarce half made up, in spite of the opportunity for revealing the spiritual evisceration caused by frequent meditation on a plucky tea wench still too green in years to offer him the raspy imploration that would soon spur him on towards recitation, whether in alehouse or aspen meadow. We need only review the slightly inebriated letter from his former Muse to estimate what a fire she would light under him, although it is hardly four contradictory versions of the fourteen books of *The Prelude!*[69] Well past the flammable peignoir stage, the poem waited in the left

---

68. Alternatively, "tumbled like toothed somberwing into their shared silence."

69. Evidence that the growth of a poet's mind still needs a hard-nosed editor.

pocket of his abominable khaki cutoffs, damp and lonely as
a cloud that had not been touched in quite a while.

Deep in Gular Pouch

          too long in the tooth
for pursuit, at least
        on paper [still none
        too shabby a place to dwell]
leaving the only decent thing to
            circle
    like pelican over Assiniboine
Park, to defy augury
      draining water for fodder
    in huge gular pouch
        gulping down
        any oneiric ideas
that gleam
upon massive
panes [illumination of
    that constellation
of freckles]
      to which the mayfly
      clings on his last day
        on the planet
half in love
    with easeful
        fluorescents
  the second a cloud
  obscures sunlight
      that vatic muttering
    pipes up
      Ὀφθάλμοισ

δὲ μέλαισ[70]

another epithet for
the dark-eyed one
who makes heavy
our drowsy looks
   as sandalled feet brush through frond
   after frond, a penitent for affection in the
presence of large monarchs and fritillaries
   curling
        proboscis into meadow
                   blazing star
      sucking
           each of them dry
yet these bright apparitions
     lack the power to haunt
held by the fingertips of a certain
silhouette
       aloof   among   slender   poplars
denuded
    of green
poised almost nervously
                at edge of wetland
like *Ständchen* in *Schwanengesang*
aching to find a common tongue

      In den stillen Hain hernieder
      Liebchen, komm zu mir!

before mosquitos spoil everything
we must yank ourselves out of funk
picture Schubert peckish, sneaking
into Esterhazy kitchen, overhearing

---

70. More dribble about her dark eyes, etc.

young woman humming the
nonchalant whimsy of the
                    Ungarische
plunked rapidly
                    in the fashion of a
                              galloping passion
one cannot quite take in stride
since so much is semi-comic
the uneven yet welcome din
upstairs
          of a Bach partita for solo
                              violin
before these wee hours
when a chipping sparrow
crows about multiple nests
when deer are in clover
outside this window
only never the one
that is wanted, no

only these tenuous
                    ideas
are hardly additive
    tied together like
                    sheets
                              out of window
workable only in
              the finest surrealist
       paintings

Flüsternd schlanke Wipfel rauschen
In des Mondes Licht
In des Mondes Licht

if only winter would be a different story

if, on a snowy, sunny day, the dark wings
of a mourning cloak appear, its veins
full of glucose antifreeze, let that be
a sign that all is not hopeless or lost

before brazen light penetrates drape
scolds reading lamp, reminds of her
stirring, beginning her day
            while he is fading fast

on the other side of the road, a
female katydid on the pavement
                  with her sword-shaped ovipositor
listens high and low to frequencies
of green suitors scaling reed or plantain
still not ready to make up her mind

while eyelids droop
in Irish myth where
a prospective lover
fails to meet the lady
who was turned into
a butterfly, sunk by
enchanted slumber
before each
            encounter

missing her every time

she watches a storm rolling in
through those massive panes
perhaps unaware of all this
marvelous folderol
　　that revolves around her
　　　　　　acute rarity
　like that pair of pelicans
　　　　　circling
overhead
　their gullets full of
　　water, slime, everything
　　　　　　but what they most
　　　　　　　　crave

None of this lonesome poem did he utter, not a whit.
They could press on without blunder. Farinata chose that
moment, with the verses still hovering upon his lips, to
break the silence. He described how the male monarch
attacks the female monarch in the air before he pins her
down on the ground, and locks into her delicate insides with
a pincher attached to his equipment, before he drags her up
into the trees for uninterrupted consummation. Toxic love,
for any creature who should dare to bite them when caught
in flagrante delicto, or really on any other occasion. The Mädchen said a few words, and one of them was a savage blow,
a sucker punch called "boyfriend." Then something about
a bicycle and her own sincere efforts to master the same
conveyance in all weathers. Farinata balked, and threw all his
energy into vehement admonitions about the perils of winter cycling, which left him spent of more tender sentiments.

The elderly couple on the tandem recumbent bicycle[71] was clearly her ideal.

Yes, a savage blow, and they had not even reached the clumps of bergamot that were so irresistible to fritillaries! Sweating then, and attempting to regain his composure, Farinata launched into a milder tirade about the invention of Lady Grey, something of an *entente cordiale* designed to appease the Norwegians who found the amount of bergamot in Earl Grey excessive, and desired at the very least a touch of citrus for balance. Debatable, but this erratic factoid threw her for a loop, and for a few seconds, she forgot about the pleasure a lady can derive from her bicycle.[72] None of this grazed the surface of his personal dilemma, for he stuttered between her indivisible uniformity in the sense of the Platonic atomic and the erratic whims of the demented hydraulic that responded to her nightly visit as if with the fanfare of a royal fount, keeping in mind that Farinata was no royalist.[73] Yet in this case, it was not for him to genuflect without distinct reciprocal direction from the female of the species, which would hazard another historical ambush by wood ticks, even on the path less beaten by mammalian beasts. Honestly, how could he convey in the Queen's English that the poignancy lacing his bareheaded passion was not that of a mere lacewing, or for that matter, was not down to an abrupt turn of mood?

Horribly addled as our local nomad was, it stood to reason that the Norns would no longer isolate him in a distant suburb. Nurturing a certain percentage of Yiddishkeit in his

---

71. A two-headed organism who made regular appearances at the café—just never really blossomed into anything.

72. This theme of love and bicycles will receive proper treatment around the bend.

73. We would only need to review his hallucinations of the RCMP or authority figures in general.

blood, our staunch carnivore would find himself only steps away from not one but two Jewish delis[74] with a number of decades behind them. In other words, his escape plan was soundly quashed. He would get no farther than River Heights, which was still within cycling distance of the Mädchen. Nor could silent profundities be plucked out of the air between them to combat the lovely ambiguity of her left eyebrow, whenever raised to maximum height. From an early age, on the most taxing comprehension quizzes, she had known enough to efface an equals sign between sex and ice cream. If we are to get into specifics and talk Argentinian gelato,[75] the tower of two flavours she would erect on his behalf was constructed according to sound formulae she never failed to describe at length. Whether his preference was insubstantial or not was perhaps an ecclesiastical issue. In any case, the ornery in line behind him would find more than a scoop of favoritism in that gargantuan heap of raspberry packed onto blackberry, whereas the more literary would see in this cold monstrosity more than a foreshadow of their inevitable melting together.

Being on the whole fastidious, and for the most part a person of quality, the Mädchen found something in Farinata's manner that made her eager to please him. Old World idiocy, perhaps. Though this atavistic urge had no place in any other walk of life. Gentlemanly slaver could be confined to the small jar for "eating in," thank you very much. In another life—well, why not?—but not in this one where a holistic courier did not pedal into your life every day and

---

74. Once again, our existential humanism will have a schmear of romantic consequences, just you wait.

75. Marcel Proust would have been horrified to return to the scene, only to discover that, during the interim of his absence, the local provider of gelato had changed.

was not to be strung along. Should she unpack her concerns before this eccentric stranger, who would only have a field day, impressing upon her the stirring gravity of that Schubert serenade pushed through the throat of a baritone while fully expecting her to renounce her solemn cares for her intended's frozen tires? Furthermore, to risk losing that sublime prospect of the tandem recumbent would be too much to bear! No, there would be plenty of love and lime gelato to be had in the great beyond.[76]

They stopped. A plump bumblebee was drinking its fill of blazing star. A wasp arrived in time to remind us that when it came to an idyllic summer, *tempus fugit*. The lips resting upon her cheek or the nose nuzzling her nose did not surprise her, but the hand did. Straight to the heart of her predicament. It was probably her imagination, but the fingers seemed to melt right through the pleather. She was indeed melting in the heat she hated and losing her head over the sense of urgency in that carnal touch. What is more, the *Komm, beglücke mich*[77] had returned with a vengeance.

Admittedly, it was not long after that short, sharp gasp before they were congealed in awkwardness once again. Then they were two lonely figures on a woodcut at the height of the Expressionist Movement, with a pelican passing overhead.

---

76. Possibly a misreading of the Gospels, but who are we to get on our high horse?

77. Possibly the most dubious use of a Schubert serenade. Ever.

Yella and the Yams

Farinata was, as usual, deep in contemplation about the precarious future of *ars longa* in the popcorn aisle when it occurred to him that the Osborne Village Safeway was busier than usual. Was it a murder or a parliament or a gaggle of prairie gals who were checking him out to such a degree that he dropped his bag of mountain trail mix and made himself scarce? Something like that. He accepted a few pieces of cheese on sticks before returning to the abandoned trail mix. On the spot, he was handed a predicament in the form of a rose just as the dazzler came into view, with her excellent legs descending into Louis XV heels. The second she caught his eye, she stashed a burger in a box and macaroni accompaniment behind a display pyramid of toilet tissue rolls. With nary a greeting, she accepted the rose and leaned her intriguing head against his right shoulder.

"I'm Yella. Walk me to the fruit and veg?"

"_?"

"Is this rose for me? Aw, thanks."

Yella happened to be an aspiring actress—actor!—who gave each of her pronouncements an elaborate nasal inflection. This charming quirk is not beyond our powers of description, or even our comprehension, but why bother?— surely you know the type. In any case, her nuanced explanation tickled Farinata to the toes. Apparently, the Safeway in Osborne Village had agreed not to eject or maim participants in a massive Singles Night that invoked a glam game of romantic rollerball that had taken place at some point in the sparkly 1980s. Once his general mirth had subsided, he began to feel a vague moral crisis slinking closer and closer—or was that Yella?—that posed a threat to his vague arrangement with the Mädchen. Could he, in perfectly clear conscience, sidle up to such a phenomenal pair of legs while fondling a pair of mammoth yams? He elected to broach the subject with Yella so that they knew from the starting gun[78] how things would roll, but she cut him short.

"Nonsense. They don't even exist."

"Excuse me?"

"Yams, silly! Yams do not exist."

"Then what am I stroking?"

"Good sir, that is a sweet potato. Okay, so maybe yams *do* exist. But not on this continent, except in very rare cases. Yams are just part of this major marketing ploy. Don't you see ... that's how they get you. Don't let them get you!"

"Really? I had no idea."

"The folks at Yam Fest know the truth but someone got to them. I tried to bring them down from the inside until they canned me to get me out of the way. Now they claim

---

78. Okay, we have introduced a starting gun, but that doesn't necessarily mean anyone will use it!

that 'Sweet Potato Fest' is too long to put on their posters
but I know better."

The grudgingly handsome pair soon forsook all thought
of commerce for the evening. Yella led him along River
Avenue, pressing close to ward off what was only very mild
minus weather. After she had described the potential threat
to the Gas Station Theatre in the form of a combined arts
centre and living complex that would demolish her youthful
memories, she brought him to a little snowy park, where
by the light of the moon, she unpacked her heart. She
told him everything, or at least as much as she had been
able to piece together. She revealed that the yam, which
is a monocot at a veritable distance, has but one embry-
onic seed leaf to its name. On the other hand, the sweet
potato—our near and dear friend—is a dicot with two such
seed leaves, and politely disassociated itself around 200 million years ago. Surely we can forgive African slaves, say, on
George Washington's farm, for finding comfort in this soft
member of the morning glory family and bestowing upon
it the moniker of something they had adored in their homeland, namely the yam. Controversy over the sweet potato's
false name waged on until the 1930s when the truth of
the matter was definitively quashed—or squashed—by the
promotion of beneficial qualities of these popular orange
products, a widespread scheme cooked up—ooh!—by the
Louisiana Agricultural Experiment Station, although the
tines of fate left their mark in 1937 when the Louisiana
industry officially appropriated the term "yam" as part of
a national marketing campaign. Sweet potato vines were
swiftly trellised onto fences so that stress would compel
them to flower for this insatiability on the rise. The genetic
recombination that followed was inevitable—such is the
bittersweet legacy of the breeding program that will not

cease until we have tasted the perfect sweet potato in yam's clothing. Until that glorious day, the world must make do with Acadian, Beauregard, Bienville, Bonita, Centennial, Darby, Earlyport, Eureka, Goldrush, Heartogold, Hernandez, Jasper, Julian, Lakan, Murasaki-29, Pelican Processor, ˙Queen Mary, Ranger, Travis, and Whitestar. She would not even get into 05-111, 07-146, or the elongated stigma of clone 96-117. Yet by any other name, the yam was still a lie. The truth was confined to small print, next to invisible beside the grossly enlarged lettering for that mendacious word YAMS. Not only was the consumer cheated—even in the ontological sense—out of the yam in reality, but it was entirely possible for allergic unfortunates to perish, with the root cause—sorry!—being mislabelled sweet potatoes. She was only comfortable with sharing this much on a first date. A second date might involve guerilla action at the Safeway where they had first met. Farinata stared at the semi-frozen Assiniboine thoughtfully.

"Evangeline."

Yella nodded with a small, sweet smile and clasped his hand tightly. She had forgotten the Evangeline sweet potato and the gentlemen had conveniently dredged up this obscure fact about *Convolvulaceae* from somewhere in the vast supraconsciousness.

They soon found their way across the bridge that led into Norwood. Farinata measured this comradely experience with care against his usual solipsism. By now, he was quite at home with his own extremes. He could not recall a time when he had not been a yo-yo between decadent indulgence and ascetic aestheticism, even on those innumerable nights when the naked page would not have him or his delicate scribblings. If the Furies thought they could catch him napping, they would have to arrange themselves around

his erratic spells of segmented sleep, for he was all hunter-gatherer with nothing left to hunt or gather. Still, it was
a pleasant shock to run across a rose in a heaving bosom,
a wonderful addition to his nocturnal peregrination. They
passed St. Boniface Hospital, reflecting on personal losses
and questions of mortality. Then, along Tache Avenue, they
came to the illuminated façade of the old church, where
for a nominal fee, people could have their wedding photos
taken beside a barrel of safety sand that was not far from the
former remains of Kapeyakwaskonam (Kah-pah-yak-as-
to-cum). The Cree Chief, otherwise known as One Arrow,
had been convicted of treason for his participation in the
North-West Rebellion of 1885. Farinata liked the ambiguity
of this upstart—considered a minor figure in Manitoba—
who had returned to Saskatchewan a hero after his spirit
had made a special request to do so. His tombstone bore his
last words: *Do not mistreat my people.* Yella squeezed Farinata's hand tighter, steering the conversation back to wedding
photos.[79] They strolled on. Then she stopped in her tracks
and pointed. The Furies? No, she was trying to stare down
the candified man who appeared perpetually ready to doff
his candified top hat.

"The Nutty Club man. How I hate having his eyes on
me."

Yella tugged Farinata along and led him across Esplanade
Riel. He absorbed its tension forces and expounded his best
theories on why the tourtière in the restaurant at the middle of the bridge was scarcely better than torture. Chronic
walking kept them in sync, virtually hip to hip and of one
mood. The kismet fail did not rear its ugly head until they
had nearly doubled back to their origin point on the other

---

79. Regarding this omniscient divination, we are getting a green
light.

side of the Assiniboine. Near the giant statue of Louis Riel, Farinata gestured at a totem pole that was the only sign of his own tribe in these parts, although for some reason, he felt more of a kinship with the statue of the Ukrainian poet Taras Shevchenko. On impulse, he quoted the only lines he knew by heart:

> *It makes no difference to me,*
> *If I shall live or not in Ukraine*
> *Or whether any one shall think*
> *Of me in foreign snow and rain.*

Yella's eyes burned brightly. Surely this man was the one to understand what must be done. Without delay, she went through the finer points of her plan, or more correctly, the universe's plan. If the gods were with them, breaking into the Manitoba Legislature would not present a problem. She had enough equipment in her bag for a short séance, one that would stir up at least a few minor deities. Then she and the chosen one would conduct themselves into the Pool of the Black Star, that perfect circle of a room where their copulatory cries would resonate with the musical fifth, otherwise known as the Hermetic constant. Then, if Lady Manitoba was willing to bestow real yams upon her, fertility would abound.[80] Farinata was too fired up to grapple with her razzlegab for very long, and made his own Hermetic calculations, working out the amount of time it would take him to cross the Osborne Bridge and nip back to the Safeway Single's Night for—complimentary?—ultra-sensitive safes. With infinite care, he asked if she happened to be on the pill, or if she at least had the latest update of the Swedish

---

80. Even Chinua Achebe had found Yam, king of crops, to be a very exacting king.

fertility-tracking app. Yella soured, and the glow temporarily abandoned her cheeks to adorn the shiny buttocks of the Golden Boy, who cared nothing for the disappointments of grounded lovers. Ironically, the real yams that would help Yella give birth to twins were also the chief ingredient in the birth control that would prevent the conception of those future guerilla warriors. Yes, a modicum of wild yam would keep those crusaders from striking at the very heart of the yam/sweet potato conspiracy. Arm in arm, those loyal brothers or sisters would charge the Louisiana Agricultural Experiment Station with massive forks, screaming what else but, "YAMS DO NOT EXIST!"

Yella had not finished raving before Farinata recognized her. Soon after his strange arrival in Winnipeg, he had wandered into Tie-Dye Curios, a small space packed with new-agey paraphernalia. He had first stumbled upon Yella at the very back of the store, seated on the floor beside a scented candle, paging blithely through *The Eagle's Gift*. He was just the sort to fall under the spell of her glazed peepers and all her murmurs about her missing *nagual*, although the primal howl that arose from her throat was something of a turnoff. An alto, too. Yes, it had definitely been Yella yelling her head off. With great difficulty, Farinata had navigated past a number of obstructions to return to the front of the store, where a Maine coon had begged him with red eyes to take him away from that doleful prison of so much unrestrained incense-uousness. He vowed to come back for the cat and then he rushed away, pitiably stung for life. This scene closed in a similar fashion. Farinata pledged an oath to one day return to undertake the dual siring she so ardently desired and then he hightailed it across the Osborne Bridge without looking back.

A full week passed before Farinata would dare show his

face in the Safeway that had nudged so many lonely people into new and unexpected situations. He was admiring the beet greens in his basket when he heard a hissing sound. A young lady in a beret was trying to get his attention. Once he had inched closer, she handed him a Freudian dream of a sweet potato and slapped a sticker over the product label. Naturally, it read like so:

Then she flew into a rapturous ecstasy over this *fait d'ac-compli* and reached down low beneath her bright red slicker. As soon as she began to shudder all over, Farinata legged it towards the exit. The beet greens were perfectly acceptable to the self-checkout machine, but when he tried to scan the gargantuan *not-yam*, a shrill alarm sounded.

A cashier fell into step with what had to be a produce clerk, and they pointed out Farinata to a man in dark glasses and an orange suit. The moving target was not to know that the man had just laid aside a tabloid featuring a woman who had just given birth to a sweet potato—with the help of George Washington's ghost!—because the moving target was preoccupied with the problem of getting through the automatic doors as fast as possible without the beet greens or *not-yam*. Perhaps it was only a matter of relinquishing his prize for being the trillionth customer to do such-and-such or perhaps there was a little more to it than met the eye at first glance. One thing was for certain. This was not the first yam cleanup announced that evening, nor would it be the last.

Beaverbrook and the Bilious Attack

Farinata leaned on the side of the footbridge and watched the lone train car pass. Aloof of the locomotive were a swallowtail perched upon a dandelion, a goatsbeard in full bloom, and a pelican in the Assiniboine River. He suspected that these natural elements had their spiritual counterparts in Dalí's *Equestrian Fantasy*. Not that he could boast a noble profile, seated sidesaddle upon a Palomino charger with a falcon perched atop his gloved arm.[81] Yet the painted creatures in the shadows—a frog, a rabbit, a squirrel, a salamander, and two deer—corresponded to the inhabitants of his own laid-back portrait. Surely to confirm this fancy, a red squirrel shot up a tree to hoard its choice nut, just as a small cottontail stopped to reflect on its palatial edifice of unadulterated burdock. His internal chronometer

81. Yet it is in Salvador Dalí's portrait of Lady Dunn that we find the general disposition of our poet friend.

gave him a quarter of an hour in which to dwell on some metaphysical trifle or other. Why not crouch over Omand's Creek and wheeze out the death knell for literature too?

Bless him, Farinata had found an environment that was reasonably pliant to his philosophical stance, the epitome of "standing fast"—to be in continual motion without becoming a function of goals or aims. Yes, work he could, and work he had wrangled for himself! Yet in the middle of the road of his life, he was no longer reliable when it came to chucking a sabot into the gears to better the conditions of his brethren. His nocturnal stint at the post office during the holiday rush had not resulted in a single incident of pulling a Bartleby or "going postal." Though he had avoided becoming one of the walking undead like some of his colleagues, he found that for a man of letters in the age of new media, there were few places to turn. In a pinch, he could be counted on to pluck a gem out of the slush. There was no evidence to the contrary. However, due to the exponential increase in writing programs, there was way more money (still not much) in rejection, something of a growth industry.

We cannot pinpoint the root cause—either too deeply buried in our protagonist's unhappy childhood or under heaps of misdirected adulation—for why Farinata should find that he experienced few greater sensations comparable to those of papery dreams crinkling underfoot. One trade secret he would take to his incineration was that a good editor never takes a step without a gun dog at his or her side. If the publishing house does not provide one, then one will appear within a fortnight. For gun dogs, you see, there are also few places to turn. Once a letter-sized envelope has been opened and your furry friend has established it does not contain a treat, he or she will go to work in a flurry of nose and eyes. A muddy paw print may signify a submission of interest. On the other hand, slobber is not so good. The latter might be a cue for Farinata to begin a slow Baroque dance over the query letter, preferably a tortuous minuet or slow sarabande. Ringing phones were for the birds, but over the years, he had learned that one must always answer a barking dog.

Rabid fans of that natty deconstruction of the "author"[82] seldom took into account that new ones came into being with alarming frequency, laying siege to the avoirdupois of our literary gatekeeper with all manner of stratagems. Any sort of favour was filed under bribery, if not sexploitation. Gift baskets and engagement rings were promptly returned by post. He could not put it succinctly enough, that with the exception of only the most innovative works, the elevated language of poesy could not be equated with applying lotion to a back (or elsewhere). An invitation to submit to a themed issue was seldom more than a game of footsie under the table. Soon conversation would turn to the status of a manuscript, the smoothing of the rugged path, and the greasing of the splintery hamster wheel—an admittedly meagre analogy for the publishing cycle—whose spin could induce roller coaster sickness, and for which reason Farinata was equipped with a broad-rimmed bucket next to his desk. However, the volume of his upheavals would not seem to

---

82. Farinata successfully skewered Roland Barthes in his handwritten essay, "The Death of the Reader," challenging the existence of even the slightest receptor that could receive stimulus from any text, except in cases where a route to self-destruction was mapped out. His supervisor—having just got to the part about neurotransmitters and dressed as Charlie Chaplin at the time—had left this monumental paper in his bag of tricks, which was stolen from his hybrid along with a number of personal items best left unmentioned.

qualify a one-and-a-half-day-a-week gig. A sensitive disposition, then.

Barthes or Bartleby—that was the question. Farinata gave up on his beneficial squat and posed beside a quaking aspen. The shift in position cleared his neural pathways, but he was leery of the murky marbles that rolled forth. A woman stood on the narrow track, leaning against a long stretch of psychedelic graffiti and enjoying her slender joint, scarcely mindful of any locomotive in her future, or the dozens of locks whose links through the footbridge were symbolic of romantic unions, be they eternal or hairpinned open. Her flowing blond mane and the cheap locks were sufficient to evoke the inimitable Aisling. Thus far, he had managed to repress the haziest recollection of her, even that she had once contrived to meet him in the middle of a bridge. Other than sharing a tendency towards waking dreaminess, they were united by a Puritan streak that betrayed them like a sliver in the foot. Even in those operatic times, her pre-programming would never have permitted her to drop the man she was promised to for a few dubious notes from a passing troubadour. Farinata had waited in the wee hours on the bridge, as agreed, for the comely young catch to appear until he became disconsolate, with the wind whipping his hair about, etc. In other words, a Bartleby situation without a whit of closure.

Barthes might have approved of his theory that her narcolepsy had gotten the upper hand at that fateful hour. La sonnambula had wandered into another bed by mistake! Those were operatic times, indeed. Though proponents of any form of psychoanalytic "hot mess" will remind us there are no accidents. That she should flee such a dark city to nestle snugly into what she insisted was the "armpit of Canada," only to one day be followed by a (sleepwalking?)

Farinata—well, let us give subconscious deliberation an ounce of credit. Wait, we are getting ahead of the carrot. Long before his arrival, Aisling had renewed their acquaintanceship from afar. In a Bovaryish twist, once she had assured her standing in relation to a certain neurosurgeon with a marvelous brain-side manner—he could talk a clarino trumpet prodigy into a lobotomy, if need be—she discovered that her high principles could bend just enough to receive an indeterminate number of billets-doux at a time when Farinata was positively itching to pen them. Nor was she the first legal assistant at Fillmore Piddell & Soake to make use of such prurient fare to liven up her lunch hour, although in this case, she contented herself with moder-ate exaggerations of an aristocratic "pego,"[83] faintly trac-ing a rather immaculately constructed *mons veneris*. As for vulval verve in the shape of a Victorian garden, she could "trowel" that part herself! Though once our makeshift rake got going, pen firmly in hand, his exposition of the Pan-glossian method[84] was without parallel.

It so happened that our discount Abelard and Heloise had once taken a course together in which they were peri-odically exposed to the Miltonic theory that the conscience is a book scribbled in by the Powers-That-Be. A fresh entry of noughts and crosses prompted the fair Aisling to come clean and make a hazardous *confessio amantis*. That she made it to the good doctor—thus depriving him of a nap essential

---

83. This was some time before Winnipeg Transit's introduction of the Peggo card.

84. Evocation of Voltaire's libidinous quack is intended to show that Farinata disapproved of what is known as the "podium effect" in public institutions and preferred to operate—at little cost to the taxpayer—out of downtown cloisters. A portable knowledge booth or kissing booth, depending on the time of day.

to his vocation and sidestepping her wifely duty—gives us pause for thought. Happily, beyond the gloomy isles of her ancestors, there was a common solution to be found in sunnier climes. A dreamy look overwhelmed her as she asked him how one should pronounce "cicisbeo," never suspecting that the can of worms was still asquirm. The good doctor had a confession of his own to make, chiefly that he was not so much good as he was a man. Slowly but surely, his mansplain began to fill the room. After all, he was the product of a society that worshipped the superficial image in a century when a gentleman's peers were bound to foster debauchery more than himself, especially after the third period jug of the game day special. Add to that the dynamic of an events planner, a sanitation supplier, and a sandwich artist, whereby some unknown weak force accumulated (per beverage) until there was an irresistible trajectory leading towards the man of medicine. Add to that the extended hockey season.

Aisling could scarcely absorb any of the answers to her barbed questions. The extent of her splooshery she could count on her fingers, at least in terms of pseudo-spiritual errancy. She had blundered no worse than Effi Briest, only to find herself waiting up for a low-budget Lothario. Sadly, driving straight to the overpriced basement suite of her long-distance lover was not on. She would simply drive until she could drive no longer. That she did, bashing the snout of the hybrid into a vintage sign. It was generally accepted that she had merely nodded off.

A young doctor reconstructed her lovely face with devilish care, even to the point of becoming enchanted with his own handiwork. In spite of his technical admiration she had come to respect, the mere prospect of Farinata's presence in the Peg, even years later, was sufficient to make her redress the dining table and the piano legs. That is meant figuratively, although her skirts *had* gained an inch or two in length. She was wiser for her camping experience with the reconstructionist, and knew that when one practical match strikes another, the last thing needed was a soulmate to leap out of the brambles—or burdock in this case—and metaphorically rain torrents on the whole operation. The only bridge she required was the nasal bridge her fiancé had built for her. As for our clumsy-starred poet, he was not one to talk of delicacies that once dampened from elastic corner to corner because of a torrid word. So far as he was concerned, even if it was an abysmal idiom, that sopping pseudo-cotton was all in the past.

The imperfect denouement of this threadbare tryst had a splendid venue. He was at the Winnipeg Art Gallery one January, specifically to take in the Beaverbrook exhibit, when the legal assistant re-entered the frame. The intimacy of a warm yet stormy Tissot had captured his full attention. The painter's mistress was staring outward with an inviting look. Meanwhile, a man stood outside the cozy room, and looked away from the viewer at a funny angle. Caught in the middle of a spat on a sex holiday? Still, you wished to linger there, thumbing through the heap of newspapers and helping yourself to that silver tea tray. Farinata first noticed her standing in front of *The Fountain of Indolence*, one of Turner's stranger experiments. As she scrutinized those nebulous nudes and flying *putti*, he studied the sturdy lines of her wholesale Nygård Slims™, the very kind advertised on a billboard beside the airport that welcomed you into the city. He shadowed her[85] past the array of Salvador Dalí

---

85. We are obliged to add that Farinata was not really the sort to stalk old flames through galleries. We might also take note of Farinata's clenched teeth as he passed that Paul Kane painting of

moustaches and by the time she had already been shocked by the transparent hole in the torso of *The Madonna of Port Lligat*, she was trembling slightly and looked unsteady on her feet. Next, she reached the wall where Santiago El Grande loomed over her; this illusion is only an effect built into the painting, so that you feel you are staring up

———————

Native nudes lounging around beside a Renaissance-style tree, or his reaction to the Emily Carr of a village in Alert Bay that the gallery guaranteed was a faithful portrayal of the culture of the Kwakwaka'wakw (Kwakiutl) nation at the beginning of the twentieth century. Those sad and sullen brown dolls huddled up were a bit Fauve to say the least. As he looked around for *Shaman Never Die: Return to Your Ancestral Roots*, a triptych that was part of the permanent WAG collection, he recalled that its creator, Jane Ash Poitras, had gotten in some hot water for painting some poor Native kids playing with their dogs on the reserve.

A work by Poitras could combine visual quotations of cave paintings, Renaissance frescoes, or abstract expressionist panels, replete with important collagist touches, such as topical newspaper clippings about residential schools. Farinata felt that the dark panel of deeply engraved Cree in *Life is a Tenderly Feeling* was one of her finest accomplishments. He could readily appreciate her painting's commentary on the Black Death, Boccaccio's storytelling, and the spread of colonization as an epidemic passed from Europe to Turtle Island with the arrival of Columbus, but he still found that dark panel of Cree letters as stirring as many a Rothko.

As for the pallid settler up for a spot of hand-wringing, Farinata would have waved off any worries about cultural agency and authenticity where he was concerned, and would have directed the teary onlooker to his metaphysical disposition in *The Mud Clinic*. Therein, one can see fragments of undermined culture and historical narrative. Percy Wyndham Lewis indicated that his figures were made of mud, and characterized by apathy. In this psycho/ socio/economic climate, was there a better way to describe our protagonist?

at a painted cupola in a Renaissance-period edifice. She was stuck on a contorted atomic cloud that hovered over the white stallion's genitals when her legs began to wobble. She put her hands out and eased down onto a bench provided for exactly this sort of stupefied contemplation.

"Aisling. Easy does it."

"Fuh ... Fuh ... Fuh ..."

It was not until he had helped her back to her car that she could relate her experience, from the twiddling of curlicue moustaches to the pounding of the horse's hooves to the indecent flap of the loincloth over the impressive "junk" of the ascendant Saint James, who was holding himself, metaphorically. He tried to comfort her with some trivia about Florence Syndrome, otherwise known as Stendhal Syndrome. Indeed, the nervous system of Henri Brulard, author of *The Red and the Black* and *The Charterhouse of Parma*, had been the most famous victim of overindulgence in art. It was quite common for art lovers to become overwhelmed to the point of delirium after taking in too many master-pieces at once, and in the hospitals in Florence, they put aside beds for frequent victims of the Uffizi. So far, Beaver-brook Syndrome was not a raging epidemic in their proud nation, but that is not to say the greatest painting since the age of Raphael could not bring on a mild bilious attack. Not one to miss a trick, our apathetic figure of mud found the moment ripe for disclosing that since he had seen her again, he had heard nothing but Bruch's adagio from his violin concerto, and even while they spoke softly, he could hear those sweet, bright trills. Aisling granted him her wistful smile before retreating to a corner of the multistory park-ade where she delicately heaved up her guts.

Back in Omand Park, Farinata looked up the quak-ing aspen and read augury into the inquisitive eye of an upside-down nuthatch. Though the child was not his and could never be his, Farinata somehow knew that he or she would never grow up to become a reconstructive surgeon. More likely a full-time poet who would run riot against the inflexible wishes of a domineering father, and that would result in a near-fatal complex, although the dreamy mother would see to it that a phantom imprint of her former paramour remained.

Yes, the best revenge was to live well, unless, he told himself, you were already three-quarters of an hour late for work! As he hurried along Wolseley, he counted his blessings, thinking cheerily of the rejection letters he had yet to write, and reassuring himself that the paws of a gun dog were still not ideal for generating a form reply.

Marriage in Faulkner, MB

From a little after two until almost sundown of that waning, yellow October afternoon, the Mädchen sat in what Missus Ainsley Thiessen called her "office away from her office," which sounded like luxury to one who had called it her "chorehole" for nearly one calendar year, give or take. Her circumstances had not changed, and her partner in crime was holding the fort while she indulged a bona fide regular who naturally assumed the role of mentor, or casual life coach. Cheerful light that shone through the broad glass panes could not touch the matte summer dress of Missus Thiessen, who did not strike one as mourning her recent separation that cleanly yet cruelly sliced through the "us" in Missus, but struck one as mourning painfully ripe prairie summers that were long gone with no enchanted almanac to conjure them back. The Mädchen squeezed generosity—even feeling—into her smile although she had always found

Missus Thiessen a mite pretentious. Besides, papers had been marked and extensions had been doled out and exams had been processed ages ago so why on earth this formal request in the shape of a note left at her place of work, with a hint of alarm tucked into its crinkly folds? Sure, she would heed this otherworldly summons for a brief spell, but she would meditate on the best way to extricate herself at the first opportunity.

You have more than one alma mater now, began the professor, and I expect to see less and less of you. Scrabbling back to this perfect little place is out of the question because we don't have what you want. Keep in mind—that is mighty important—what you want. Never lose sight of that. Only, I have noticed that a stranger has come among us, one of those characters in the literary profession like so many nowadays.

Scenting danger, the Mädchen took care not to shield herself before the first stone was thrown. In what she thought a tidy manoeuvre, she pointed out that the good professor had edited neatly bound objects herself, and was even responsible for her own concoction of pure fiction. Missus Thiessen chortled, glad but also sad to be reminded of her harmonious novel that had reached an expiration date on its aforementioned harmony. Yet her edifying quest did not embolden her to divide wheat from chaff, prying her semi-comical depiction of a happy home from the adhesive embrace of those lascivious tomes full of insectile copulation. Only such a character would swan out of the religious bookstore with a drastically discounted copy of *The Metamorphosis and Other Stories*. No, the printed word was on the side of the angels. The professor unfolded an article from something called *The Province* and apprised the Mädchen of the key points.[86] What little glory the man had

---

86. Mercifully, she was not carrying one word about "Wascanagate."

garnered for himself was merely a smokescreen for an elegant avant-garde cabal in the shape of either a pyramid or a quincunx, of which he was the de facto numero uno, if not in fact aesthetic chancellor. A Giacometti figure, with inestimable influence and reach, if that helped. No, it did not, for the Mädchen did not understand a word of it. In answer to the man's strangeness, she herself was a local, but a first generation hard-fought-and-hard-won local. Was she to be shamed and shunned and strung up by her nethers as well?

But the name, countered Missus Ainsley Thiessen. Centuries back, the name that whet the passive blade of faith was her unsmiling passport. By all means, be tolerant whenever it is time to be tolerant. To study the ways of these Peoples in the name of reconciliation was one thing; to make free of oneself in their company was quite another. To her credit, the Mädchen was quick to provide a political correction of this line of thinking, or perhaps to keep it from reaching where it was headed.[87] The professor allowed herself an ounce of condescension and patted the younger woman's excellent hand. It would also be a grave error to be led down the Peguis Trail and sort this stranger with the highly honourable Cree and Métis, a man who had sprung from flamboyant island folk or, more accurately, from the original 2,264 "Indians" found by the first Prime Minister to be the most depraved and uncivilized in the province, even from sea to shining sea, on account of the ruinous potlatch

---

87. Even more mercifully, she was not carrying clippings from *Der Bote*, a local Mennonite newspaper that often promoted anti-Semitism and concepts of racial purity during the 1930s. An article from 1936 blaming the Jews for general promiscuity and accusing a particular individual of scarcely believable potency would be enough to render Farinata a double threat in cultural terms, once we factor in his intense appreciation of the fair sex.

held by them, a "savage" ceremony they were never to relinquish although the law had demanded it.

The Mädchen reddened, conceding that things were pretty weird in those days. Missus Ainsley Thiessen savoured a lick of triumph and poured the Gunpowder Green, which had steeped nicely. Things were still pretty weird. Though her issue was not with the indictment so much as with the man's reaction to it, expressed not as gushing wound or bristling indignation—not that he should be absolutely compelled to state his case like a "good Indian"—but on the verge of insufferability, abruptly jutting out with the kind of masculine pride one must greet with prostration if not overzealous genuflection on account of its coarse, alien splendour, falling deeply and haplessly into his transient thrall, flinging up consent for donning of splintered mask and application of greedy-eyed paddle to soft, smooth flesh scarcely known to the brusque touch of male society. Had the Mädchen read her loud and clear, she might have reddened again.

Transient then, on account of the way the man roves, aiming to outpace the cloud that perpetually looms over his looks, that dark obscurity of a past marked by patches of luminosity, determination, and wealth—for a poet—he managed to drink away faster than he could hoodwink his niche demographic or outstrip his supposed mentors in sheer brazenness, in this way living two or three lives instead of one. Over a hundred barmaids have screwed their lips shut on that score, on how he crawled from dive to hole to hole and back to dive in the wall again with the *folio classique* edition of *Nuits d'Octobre* in his back pocket, soggy and stained with the remainder of countless iniquities. Even so, it was not her prerogative to chasten the sottish horndogging of a mongrel, except to underline in red ink that his Olympian enthusiasm for a young lady just shy of twenty

who found herself waiting attendance upon his person—
well, the scenario was older than the hills. The Mädchen
frowned, still at an age when she felt a slight chagrin at
being taken for younger than she actually was. As for the
young-old man, he was older than he appeared, and this
fact had the obverse effect of casting their relations in a
boyish light behind the breach in the fence where she sometimes rested her bicycle. Eleven to seventeen minutes later,
she would emerge from behind that thick cluster of trees,
feeling much refreshed and ready for the late shift. There
were surely worse ways to pedal through one's life, and
worse things than a man of convenience who—generally—
operated like clockwork—his expression—once given a
quick peek at her youthful charms.

Missus Ainsley Thiessen brought down her cup with a
crash. Dare you, she countered. Dare you hope to reach
around his oh-so-precious ipsissimosity[88]—if such a beautiful word may be said to exist—when such charitable ambivalence has brought low many a lady and many a town, leaving behind nothing but a palpable atmosphere of absence
and ruination? She paused then, nearly kicking herself for
forgetting hectoring never did get a horse to drink, let alone
get a horse to quit drinking. The Mädchen—on the verge of
serving up an ounce of petulance—reined in her views in an
undeniable display of good breeding, as now and then, even
two contentious ladies may grace the air with a generous
civility, and nourish between them a contrapuntal silence
of unspeakable sublimity. Feathers from fading milkweed
that used to fill pillows in lieu of chicken plumes did not

---

88. Coined by Friedrich Nietzsche to disparage so much self-
referentiality, although Thiessen assuredly happened upon it in a
novel by Samuel Beckett; it is significant she recalls "precarious" as
"oh-so-precious."

blow this far in, although this would have been the perfect occasion for them to provide another talking point. Actually, the milkweed was next to dead at this stage but for our purposes, it was not. Therefore, the feathers filled the air around them, and there was no means available to woman-kind for rubbing away the indelible impression of that man supine and slyly tucked under the leaves with the haunted look of anyone hunting for monarch eggs. No, there was not sufficient reserve to rain on his amateur lepidopterist project that would allegedly benefit this former township. All the same, whether he meant Charleswood or Tuxedo or Unicity or Edgeland in those moist, muffled tones remained a profound mystery that nestled snugly between the life experience of the Mädchen and the chronic dreaming of Missus Ainsley Thiessen.

Fortunately for us, the Mädchen was not one to wax telepathic all afternoon. With a practiced air of over-the-counter aloofness, she wondered aloud if the stranger had ever held fast to any one place or person. The aquiline nose of Missus Ainsley Thiessen twitched and there were drops of blood on the milkweed pillow feathers right before she mushroomed up to three times her usual size.[89] You will forgive me for my dedication to my office, where the lion's share of my hours are squandered on corrections of foul corruptions and flawed interpretations of *The Turn of the Screw*. An ineluctable quaver passed through the Mädchen at the last word, although she was still pretty much getting little to none of it. The disclaimer Missus Ainsley Thiessen was coming to—even with the periphrastic approach that was her stock and trade—was that time and place were of

---

89. Subjective impression of minimal importance, and certainly not the share of grotesque realism one finds in the works of Rabelais. More simply, the professor was warming to her topic.

little consequence; it did not matter whether the event had transpired in Bienfait or Mozart or Oakville or Dogville or Enochvilleport or along a haunted stretch of Etobicoke replete with ghostly flower girls, but that the event had transpired at all. Faulkner, Manitoba was, to this day, the chief suspect.

The stranger had arrived from the true West, tossing over his shoulder like a pinch of salt those gloomily humid islands of unspeakable infamy, a man the worse for wear who would no longer touch a drop, not even on social outings, either from constant dread of imminent self-destruction or of being permanently blown like a ravaged ship into a 100-proof bottle, if not from fear of his sheer inability to return the courtesy in polite company, should wicked circumstance wend his way, for those were days of hardtack when he could scarcely boast a nickel to his name. Tongues were bound to wag. What he wanted with a woman as insolvent as himself defied speculation. Right before setting off, he was fêted by romantic fools who blogged the colour commentary of his fiery pursuit of love, while more centrally, unspoken accusations of carpetbagging began to blossom in the entrails of the envious, for if he would lay claim to nothing else but paltry chattel—meaning a few sticks of furniture and decades of worthless clutter—he would still find opportunity to swell up with pride over this newfound air of tainted respectability that would hang off his swagger for the rest of his days like some unneutered part of him. Your garden-variety millennial—the Mädchen winced—might say he aimed to do right by her, and in the process did her a kneecap-crushing wrong in the metaphorical sense, mainly on account of the passionate fever between them that for a spell spiked the water of the whole place, refreshing enthusiasms and enmities that everyone thought had died from frostbite long ago. Not one but several gentlemen were sorely aggrieved that she could link her caboose to a stranger and not to love handles hanging from one of their more homogenous and reliable stock while a few of the womenfolk began to discreetly pitch their woo in the direction of this already suspect enterprise, nourished by the hope they could topple the whole affair and sample the overhyped prize of a suitor in one avaricious gulp, if only to ultimately decide he was nothing to write home about. Sliding an echelon up or down in their social standing was a risk they were prepared to take.

Missus Ainsley Thiessen stared at the Mädchen meaningfully and repeated the part about social echelons. Another ineluctable quaver passed through the Mädchen, this time mingling with tremulousness of an entirely different character.

This strategy of setting aside prelapsarian from postlapsarian was the hallmark of a critical theorist worth her salt at a moderately religious institution, although that came about more as a convenience in the telling of that honeymoon period so beset by obscurity and obfuscation. Only the old-young woman lording it over the upper crust of that duplex could say for certain whether those cries in the middle of the night were baleful or amorous when projected through the amplifier of choice from her favourite aunt's glassware set. The newlyweds downstairs were given points from the get-go for being reasonably attractive, in a pinch. They were young enough to still get into scrapes and old enough to know better. When spotted naked—yes, their exhibitionism extended to any windows that faced the street—there were no visible scars or signs of abuse to chime along with the tongues that had been set wagging at the first glimpse of this uncanny apparition who seemed to

give the woman an extra-special glow she had not displayed
in ages. Historical evidence can only confirm hearsay about
a cosmetic procedure she would have liked to have done on
her legs and her deep shame suffered over two permanent
welts below her rib cage, not the result of belt buckle or
novelty jumper cables, but by most accounts, a violence
done to herself for some years before she was shown how
to correctly wear a bra, a violence the marks of which
were witnessed by an infinite series of gentleman callers
in the collective imagination of the town, and perhaps
the neighbour upstairs. Chirpy and not without a charm
that grew onerous, she was always the one to do all the
talking, eager to win the debate, but never grasping from
ogre-childhood onward that often with every word, she
kept beating the walls of the vestibule just outside of the
mantrap[90] she sought to escape. What was clear through
the vibrating glass on the floor—oh, expanding ear of
any haphazard Samaritan who might liberate her from a
growing sense of degradation suffered at the hands of
the town!— was that not unlike her groom, she was also
a bit touched. Since her nervous breakdown over a paper
on Jean Genet—some say Crowley—there were few witnesses to her numerous symptoms, save a Syrian engineer
who had found his fortune as a corner shop owner on
her block, only to face her manic fury every time he made
use of a bacteria-ridden sponge to pry free a sheet of bus
tickets he might as well have licked into a state of liberty.
Leave it to the addled poet in a weak moment to have his
fancy stricken by that demented Joan-of-Arc look[91] she

---

90. We cannot account for this imagery, other than to attribute it
to Missus Ainsley Thiessen's knowledge of prisons used during the
Middle Ages.

91. This veiled reference to the painting by Jules Bastien-Lepage can

got directly before they were swept away by the sticky collision of their waning bloodlines that were like two polluted rivulets whose eventual meeting only increases their pestilence.[92]

Then Missus Ainsley Thiessen rewound. She felt about to pull a Moravia. Was the Mädchen familiar with Alberto Moravia? No, she hadn't the foggiest. Not that Moravia would be taught in those hallowed halls. Missus Ainsley Thiessen explained that a faint yet fatal mistake was at the core of almost every one of Moravia's novels. In other words, the pimple of nature rudely popped. In spite of her upbeat declarations of affection, the child-in-mind-but-no-where-near-child-bride-to-be continued to nurse less than savoury connections so as to maintain the prospect of occasional set work in Brolleywood—though her pre-eminent dream to dance in the background of a Studio 58 production had long since hung up its faded tights—but to be fair, such nursing of connections did not include any kind of impromptu massage, towel-dropping, or sexy nursing. Still, her intended noticed how she hid news of her engagement with a scarcely conscious slyness in front of a fellow who hounded her with a nasty brand of lush-courage—a miserable creep who would later go on record as having beaten and strangled his own common-law companion within an inch of her life. Through a dim haze, the stranger could nose something rotten on the rise and decided to cut her loose, then and there, on Hornby—or some say Hamilton—where

---

only have originated with the groom himself, and critics in the Salon of 1800 might have seconded his aesthetic observation that the bride's amped-up delusions of grandeur were most often at odds with her naturalistic beauty.

92. On the other hand, the Salon of 1800 would have been shocked by their intense enjoyment in one another, right to the bitter end.

she begged him to change his mind and abscond with her. With the temptation of a plane ticket on her mother's credit card—they lacked credit in their kismet, this pair—and several sessions of loud yet consensual sensuality flapping in his face, he tried to mentally wainscot over that dull, rusty nail now sticking out. His chief mistake was to confuse their warped faculties and absurd frailties with those of the hopeful lead characters in Walker Percy's *The Moviegoer*, although for once, he was more like the naïve victim in an Internet tale of erotic mind control.

The Mädchen, regurgitating a key question from one of her exams, admitted that the secular and non-secular worlds were continually competing for our desires. Missus Ainsley Thiessen pointed out that the woman was of a different faith, one without colourful history or centuries of sacrifice. In accordance with its customs, the stranger whipped up a letter that would charm birds off the trees, and received the paternal blessing in ink, if not blood, and by then, you could see the meagre chattel in his eyes, and though she had told him to ask, she resented the idea of needing permission but not more than she despised the wedding gift, which was half the amount her sister and cousins had received, emphasizing with the clink of nickel after nickel the illegitimacy of not only her own modest person but that of the stranger, who was hardly the last turkey in the shop to pledge his solemn troth. All this clambering after chattel and coin formed the seeds of a distinct ugliness that would blot out the horizon before harvest time. Yet the resolve of the stranger, in a prolonged fit of madness, was to see the whole sorry business through and try and make a go of it, helped along by her variegated threats through each attack of doubt, being far from what he then called home with no more to his name than the exact cost of the civil ceremony.

Missus Ainsley Thiessen explained that the institution of marriage was the kind of machinery you could not fight any more than City Hall, once it had been set in motion and once it had you in its toothsome gears. She was not drawing on personal experience when she said that it crushed anything in its path, including any glimmer of what once was thought to be clean energy fueling the blasted contraption. Merton Densher had found his Kate Croy, and the rest of the world had better watch out! As such, he hung out the one suit that he owned while she entered into strange confabulations that were to be inscribed on the rings that never were to be, after they were wed with unburnished heirlooms that carried their own stern maledictions on either side.

On the morning in question, she applied her anxious guile to getting a free makeover while the enigmatic gentleman and the male half of their two witnesses—they were of one flesh—breakfasted at leisure on an excellent piece of pie that was portentous, given the telltale stain absolutely "Havishamed" onto his suit that no drycleaner has seen to in years. Portentous, in that the stain is more crust than fruit from not one but three berries that could be rubbed or scraped out for all its stubbornness. She came to her appointment with handsome destiny as an image of comeliness in the company of the other witness—the womanly side of the one flesh—who was already rather clapped out on account of her myalgic encephalomyelitis,[93] if not from the jittery bride-to-be's ability to drain even a stone of its colour.[94] The entire scene was reminiscent of Natalie Dessay's wedding and subsequent mad scene in *Lucia di Lammermoor*, set to the maddening glass armonica instead

---

93. Chronic fatigue syndrome on a doozy of a day.

94. Another option was "even a turnip of its turnipness."

of the flute.[95] However, there was not a soul they knew well enough to contradict this assertion or dare call them crazy. The people in line waiting for permits and pet licenses were mildly surprised and even a shade moved until the blushing bride-to-be began screaming her head off at a hapless security guard about the solemnizer being a minute or two late. One by one, each of the supportive smiles turned upside down. Somehow, the main event got underway, but with nary a happy ending in sight. Whether the bride had in her pre-marital days nabbed the true love of their ride remained a subject for speculation, although the story had been corroborated by another poetess who had suffered a similar fate at her hands, or so she told anyone who would listen.

In other words, their chariot—an environmentally affable car on loan—did not await. Though it must be said, there were ample opportunities for hotwiring and carjacking and the bride resorted to neither. No, she went from quaking with rage to beaming for about a hundred photos by herself while the groom reflected on these rumours of her past, when she had been at liberty to pluck dopey fruit from branches belonging to those slightly less aesthetically pleasing. Yet that first germination of mistrust on Hornby—or some say Hamilton—was contaminated by another outbreak directly after solemnization, setting free the broad-winged bird of apathy he had done his utmost to keep in a gilded cage, revealing why it sang with that raspy voice. So by the time the bride was yelling at the driver for waddling and not racing towards them, the bemused groom no longer gave a fig about any of it. Once the car had started, it is beyond the scope of our understanding to know for certain whether the ill-fated stranger hid his face from shame or

---

95. Mention of a blue Maïwenn in *The Fifth Element* might have struck a chord with the Mädchen.

fatigue in the lap of that backseat driver, if not to hide his eyes from the accusatory glare of that bird of apathy that trailed behind the green car. Only one day would a thousand pictures of her arrive in the post as evidence of an entirely unbalanced happiness. In spite of the harshest grudges residing in the hearts of the best frenemies and the driver's imputation of emotional carjacking, they reached the station in time to meet their train, and at the first possible opportunity, spilled piping hot coffee on themselves.

The Mädchen looked over at the coffee machine and at the new hire (who could not pour a flat white to save her life). So that was their wedding in Morse, she said. Missus Ainsley Thiessen laughed and shook her head. Mozart maybe, or some other place like that. The point was not where but how it all panned out. Admittedly, the fallout of their union was not easy to describe, no matter how many versifiers you pumped for the goods. Unfortunately, this sorry tale was no historiographic novel reimagining a cross-cultural encounter in terms of metaphor or metonym, even as in poetry where any example of metonymy can be treated as slightly metaphoric and where any metaphor can be seen through a metonymic tint, or more specifically in certain works where conceptual allegory serves as an epistemological tool for conceiving otherness. The Mädchen opened her mouth and then closed it. Suffice it to say that VIA Rail could not rush them away from themselves, and even if it could, such expedient service would be out of their price range. The rest was open to speculation. Perhaps they had died of ecstasy in a hot tub in front of a ground floor window along Grand Allée, or perhaps they had met a similar demise on the Plains of Abraham that was explosive enough to wake Champlain with a shudder, or perhaps they had simply wasted away from weeping all over the grey stones of Vieux-Québec. The Mädchen saw her chance to point out that to the best of her understanding, they still walked the earth in near-perfect physical health, although (with a slight cough) she could attest more specifically to the vigour of the male specimen. Missus Ainsley Thiessen let that one slide, assuring her that no amount of stamina in any corner of the globe could have saved them from the cloud of despondency laced with awareness of their own bloated ignominy that followed them back to Morse or Mozart or wherever, filling their minds with static that was the equivalent of an unending migraine forecast until they were too confused and afraid to dare lick even one of their private wounds or manglings. If they were alive, they were imbecilic, and constantly on the verge of uncomfortable laughter.

Missus Ainsley Thiessen sighed. The last straw eludes us too. Within less than a month, the witnesses were called over, still believing that the worst was behind them, including the pie stain and the free makeover and all the caterwauling but no, there was sufficient testimony that the honeymoon had never really begun before the stranger had packed his bags, claiming she had screamed him out of sleep and her short fuse had blown one time too many and he would not sleep under that roof any longer, lest she give him heart failure or draw a blade across his traitorous throat in the night. He was no Rochester but in that instant, he had the look about him of someone who could lock up one spouse in the attic—more than likely with the old-young woman on the top floor of that duplex—and board it over and send up scraps of day-old remainders in a basket on a rope while striking up a feckless dalliance with the first curvy mail carrier to happen by. Fatigued as ever, the female witness was charged with the awkward task of marching the recent groom—much as the Comte d'Artagnan had done, famously, with Superintendent of Finances Fouquet—to an automatic teller where he was instructed to draw out every last nickel to his name. Fortunately, a professor, a friend, and an old flame (in that order) had each provided a plane ticket in his name, and he was free to choose the best flight home. The weary witness was also compelled to oversee the deletion of a number of risqué photographs from a party with an Aleister Crowley theme, ensuring he would never be able to use them against her at any point in the future. Then he fled, going against the grain of the frigid weather. But for her, he still remained—lurked, more like—in what she called sardonic and watchful triumph.

The Mädchen exuded nonchalance, only vaguely aware that conniptions might come later. It sounded to her like a fling that had gotten out of hand. She had heard of such things. Missus Ainsley Thiessen snorted then checked herself. Granted, she no longer knew what marriage meant. But for the stranger and his wild bride to see the spectre of midlife happenstances just around the bend, only to have their respective hopes dashed upon the rocks of reality— how could there not be invisible scars wherever they had been gored on that arid safari known as fleeting love?[96] As in countless other townships, he had laid the community to waste, leaving its denizens to parrot this wretched tale of their own ruination, for he had wooed them all with love's sweet song and slipped through their fingers just as he had slipped through her decidedly erotic clutch. The bride, as if suddenly widowed, had not only lost her implicit status of imaginary May Queen, but she had also lost her inexpressible delight in scraping nickels together to nourish the hoard

---

96. Unless the issue was not being "gored" enough on that arid safari. One never really knows with people.

that had patiently amassed around bubbling pots of bulk
pasta—there are too many varieties to enumerate here—for
she was a hoarder to the point that the horrified groom
could scarcely move for all her clutter, presumably encouraging the life cycle of those large translucent arthropods—
if not mutant crickets or silverfish—he had been obliged to
gruesomely splat out of this world and into the next, each
time inciting another erotic spark within his new bride.[97]
It would despoil the ears of any decent folk to let them
hear of the cajolery and raillery and extortion that ensued,
immortalized in a separation agreement that drove one legal
representative into utter befuddlement and another into a
doleful crematorium.[98] At first, it superficially wounded the
stranger, to find that his meagre affection had been crudely
converted into baser material, until he felt himself beck-
oned towards the middle of a bridge on many a dark night,
his heart wrung out with despair.[99] Worn down by painful
taunts, he soon agreed to hand over the second lump sum
she wanted, transforming the whole Babylonian deal into a
four-hundred-a-night arrangement, to put it despicably. Yet
it is said that even with their tax status inexorably altered,
they can feel vestiges of their wanton cruelty turning them
into amorous gargoyles still oozing a feverish passion,
a ghostly heat that only the stone of civic dedications to
cantankerous despots or half-crazed martyrs can absorb,
and that a controversial statue in St. Boniface swallows the
bulk of the poet's loneliness on his way to fields of milkweed, where he withers among prairie dwellers, eating up

---

97. Think David Cronenberg on William S. Burroughs.

98. Think J.J. Abrams' restoration of the 1979 cult horror classic,
Phantasm.

99. This turned out to be a common phenomenon—the result of
seasonal affect on the West Coast.

dust from the Red River Valley while awaiting her return, either to squeeze out a few drops of redemption from her still-girlish flesh, or merely to expand his flatland campaign of pitiless revenge, the undeniable remains of his ancestral praxis, which is another way of saying obstinate shame culture amid obdurate petroglyphs wailing just above the intertidal zone.

Orange light filtered through bare limbs. All I am saying, offered Missus Ainsley Thiessen in conclusion, is that he may invite you to look for butterflies or deer in relative seclusion. It was not her place to proffer a strenuous warning, but in a manner of speaking, there it was. *Caveat amator.*

Missus Ainsley Thiessen stretched her arms and stood up. Her final word on the matter was not retained by the Mädchen, who watched her depart until she was devoured by the Great Hall. Then she took the regifted heap of thorny sabra fruit outside and dumped each prickly ovoid into a recess for wild creatures to try their luck with, entirely unaware that the professor would have appreciated this startling resonance with the end of an Elizabeth Bowen short story about daffodils. Pretentious meddler! After all, what did she know about prickly amours? The Mädchen had already been to see the butterflies and the deer and they were sensational! Besides, if the stranger was such bad news, why had "Greasy Thiessen" sent her through the forest with him on that fateful summer day, hmm? The Mädchen did not even live over there!

Realty and Reality

To say they had never been close would be an understatement. Yet a mutual indifference without any studied enmity, glimpsed quickly in the rear-view mirror, was perhaps something to cherish. Joey Cavalcanti had certainly made his way. Even in adolescence, his good looks, his athleticism, and his attention to his wardrobe had presaged a soft landing in life. After a couple of decades, Farinata could give the man his due, and admit that his easy-going manner and his sportive powers of concentration had helped to clear a comfortable path. The rear-view mirror would show that our friend had only ever managed to beat Joey once at the short distance run around their high school, presumably on an off day. Similarly, he had always lagged behind on one of the long-distance runs that began at the doors of the gymnasium and ended after a lap around the lagoon through which Pauline Johnson's paddle had once sung. A number of the boys would hide in the bushes and cheat, although after a satisfying smoke, they were always inclined to let Joey Cavalcanti keep his first place record. What Farainta had taken for stubbornness—or even stupidity—he now remembered as stamina with a touch of integrity.

Come to think of it, Joey Cavalcanti had never taunted or tormented him. There had even been one or two words of encouragement for his maniacal defensive hustle or a rare swish. Joey Cavalcanti was the team player so many job applications asked for, nay, demanded. They had only ever been briefly aligned by their mutual interest in a drama club that never really got going, the production budget having been reallocated by democratic decision to upgrade the basketball backboards. Though he doubted Joey Cavalcanti had any time for the Bard these days. A future advocate for Schopenhauer's brand of pessimism tempered by kindness to animals, Farinata had found that his grim outlook and invariable black ensemble threw him in with a small circle of Goths and/or Morrissey fans. Well, there were not so many choices, and everyone had to make do. If he had ever distinguished himself, it had only been through an amusing composition he had read aloud, and a rather bleak invective in one of the yearbooks he had left behind after one of his breakups—good riddance all around!—and his first collection of poetry, which had unnerved his English teacher—in spite of her enthusiasm for UFOs, shadow people, and sunbathing in graveyards—earning him a one-to-one with the visiting school psychologist.

Given the amount of non-history between the tortured poet and Joey Cavalcanti, the invite had come as a surprise. A mutual Friend had wanted to let them know about a family store that was about to disappear from the old neighbourhood. Suddenly, all of those apparitions came back, still tenuously linked to one another, shimmering in the gelatin mould that had preserved them for two decades. Though in some ways, it was marvelous to get one's school reunion over with in milliseconds. In summary, most of the men of his year had lost hair and gained weight, and had at least one kid in tow. Just about everyone had stayed in the same city. Not Joey Cavalcanti though; his exciting work took him across the country. His short message said as much. He was visiting the Peg on business, and he wondered if Farinata wanted to meet for a drink and quick catch-up. Yes, "quick" had been right there in sans serif, something of an escape clause if things took an awkward or unpleasant turn. Farinata took a peek at his profile, and discovered that the man had assembled a beautiful family to go with his personal style. He existed with his golden-haired wife and his three children in a perpetual Christmas card.

The absence of Joey Cavalcanti's high school sweetheart had come as the greatest surprise. Amid other waxen statues of the past, that couple had persisted like marble lovers caught in mid-embrace by Bernini. In those days, Farinata had let his mythic imagination string him across the incalculable hypotenuse of an Arthurian triangle, which had somehow left him maybe fourth or fifth in line to her ladyship's enjoyment, or at the very least a Thomas Wyatt figure worth an abstruse sonnet or two. Her chilly beauty had always terrified him, not to mention the fact that she had rarely missed an opportunity to make a monkey out of him, clearly the key component of the attraction. She was as extraordinary to behold as ever; the only thing capable of aging her was the same thing that always had—a strained, slightly peevish expression she often wore. In addition to all the beauty and the terror and the peevishness, Allegretta— because that was her name—had snagged a prize for writing in elementary school. From then on, his mercantile imagination had always placed them shoulder to shoulder, piecing together articles for *Elle Canada*. Instead, she had joined the ranks of so many others in his home city who were "making do" selling false hope to the anxious, the depressed, and the sleepless. Along with expensive oils, vitamins, and SAD lamps, part of her trade involved the dissemination of positive memes—glowing, throbbing declarations of peace and love.

Too bad there's not time to set the stage for the old flame who had provided shelter on her family farm just outside of Saskatoon. We need only say that she had helped the walking wounded to limp his way out of a corn maze. Once the precautionary mouth-to-mouth was out of the way, she had reminded him—or planted the repressed memory, maybe?[100]—of the affectionate notes he used to stuff into the pockets of her coat in the elementary school cloakroom.[101] No, there's not time to do more than present this ethereal rescuer as a victim of the diabolical Allegretta. After the innocent farm girl and Farinata had been separated for over four years, she had entrusted Allegretta with a letter that encapsulated the totality of her feelings for him, a letter than never reached the recipient. Whether an act of wanton cruelty or mere negligence, it (belatedly) gave him an existence he had hitherto been unaware of. Once again, there's

---

100. Not to be confused with the girl who used to play Claudio Simonetti's theme for Dario Argento's *Creepers* on a piano in the corridor, and at a time when everyone was hung up on *Labyrinth*. Let's not get the wrong idea—she would sooner send a bottle rocket your way as look at you.

101. How convenient for all these notes to be irretrievably lost when her mother (allegedly) threw her coat in the washing machine!

no time to get into everything that was revealed to him upon those sacks of grain in the ice house.

Leave it to their other schoolmates to let off bottle rockets in the old neighbourhood. Joey Cavalcanti had larger haddock to hawk. Farinata did not really regret his failure to expand his own small business, or his gaining the dubious honour of having survived a giant merger that had decimated all but a handful of the temporary hires, mainly because he was a gentleman of letters. His descent into the underworld of the printed word is yet another twisted tale. Not the same for Joey Cavalcanti, who had always been set aside for greater things. He had paved his own way, securing location after location for franchise after franchise until he was ready to try his luck with his own projects. We would require half a novel by Theodore Dreiser to tell of the rise of the modest realty empire associated with the name Joe Braul, just as we would require the other half to tell of the fall of Farinata. Now squeezed between two other passengers on the Portage-Kildonan bus, the latter was impressed that Joey Cavalcanti—whatever he was calling himself—had kept a steady pace during the long-distance run of life, putting on a good show—no, more than that—winning!

Farinata passed the Artspace building and considered how much of his life was bound up with most of its floors and offices. It was typical of Winnipeg, this repurposing of a masonry warehouse erected about a hundred and twenty years ago, a six-storey building described as Richardsonian Romanesque with features such as rusticated stone sills, interconnected hood-moulding, and corbelled brickwork. Farinata especially liked the Roman-influenced arches over the second and third-storey windows, a mark of the building's upward evolution over three years. This impressive relic gave him some respite from his hermetic ways, in addition to one-third of an attic in a Wolseley house that served as his own temporary office—also typical of the Peg as far as publishers were concerned. A young barista from one of his café haunts stood half a block away in front of a faded sign that read HAM AT ALL LEADING STORES. She had just started as a part-timer at the local poetry magazine and was sizing him up for a submission (through opera glasses, and in a blue kimono). On any other day, he would have been bowled over to know he was reflected in the compelling blue eyes of a certain brunette, but not on this afternoon[102] when he was prepared to relegate everything he knew to the past, aside from his meeting with Joey Cavalcanti.

Farinata reached King, where he suffered one of his attacks of self-doubt. He could already picture Joey Cavalcanti in his suit and overcoat, handing over a cigar intended for a gentleman's club that would only yawn open for exclusive visitors and their plus ones. By way of contrast with his vision of Joey Cavalcanti, Farinata was layered in cotton and fleece and covered in dog hair, a necessary hazard of the publishing trade. Peel away the layers and what would you find? Not the ornamental quality of a heart of lettuce; not even the provocation of a particularly mean onion. The King's Head was not especially fancy, but his impecunious situation had kept him from returning there since the night of his mysterious arrival at the meeting of two rivers. In a novel, usually, something has to happen; in this town, the brunette with the compelling blue eyes might pursue him across the boardwalk—say, beneath a pair of playful magpies—at the wildlife preserve, only to lose him among the taxidermic creatures in the touch museum. Years would

---

102. His inability to face his heart's ideal suggests that she is merely a product of wish fulfillment. If she did not exist, she would have to be invented.

pass in this fashion, with the operatic apparition of Santuzza, Tosca, or Turandot hot on his trail, and still not one poem squeezed out of him. Of course, there were edicts as old as the Artspace building about soliciting poetry on a public street. All of this to point out that things were moving faster than usual for our friend.

Farinata shrugged off his usual confusion and climbed the stairs. The bar was quiet for mid-afternoon on a Thursday. Joey Cavalcanti dominated the scene in an orange Gucci tracksuit. Leaning against the counter with his feet planted far apart, he reminded Farinata less of Elton John—who had once pulled off this look—than the celebrated Hans Holbein of Henry VIII. This was not a slight; Joey Cavalcanti had filled out into a man of means and substance. Just then, a man of neither brushed past Farinata and made his way to the centre of the bar.

"The towing guy is here. Is that your car out there? The towing guy is here."

The local crier hopped about in a circle, seeking out quiet drinkers in every corner.

"Ma'am? Sir? Is that your car? The towing guy won't wait, you know!"

Joey Cavalcanti waited for the crier to finish his speech. All the world was a stage, and the former schoolmates were nothing if not critical.

"I swear, the towing guy is not kidding around. Never mind ... you'll be sorry!"

Farinata could not resist smiling, and Joey Cavalcanti went along for the ride.

"Must be 3:30."

"What are you having?"

"Water's fine. No, make that cranberry and soda."

"You won't try some of this Glenmorangie?"

"I can't ... I don't ... I used to ..."

Joey Cavalcanti directed him towards a table, but Farinata eyed it apprehensively. On a supporting post beside the table, there was a plaque that read **OFFICE BULLPEN.**

"Whoa, what's the matter?"

"Nothing. One of the publishing gods used to sit here on many an afternoon. Called it his office. He has passed on, and the plaque's a way of remembering him."

"Uh-huh. So ... you're a writer, hey?"

"Yup. And it sounds like you've done really well for yourself, Mr. Cavalcanti."

"Actually, I go by Braul in all my dealings. Joe Braul, a name more solid than the materials. Aww ... don't get me started on all these shoddy parts from China ... instead of the element, it's cheaper to replace the whole oven. As for the walls, they're ready to come down the second you put 'em up—"

"Cavalcanti's a great name. The name of a fascinating poet."

"That right?"

After they clinked glasses, Farinata began to peel off a few layers, feeling self-conscious about his fleece outer layer and smelly hoodie and woollen base layer, all of which had picked up a fair amount of fur shed by the office dogs. He was eager to explain the futility of his situation, but knew that the vim and vigour and apple cider vinegar he applied to his battles with the basement washing machines in his apartment building—hopelessly infused with fabric softener bombs about as beneficial to mankind as cyanide pills—would not make for a convincing story. Anyway, he was mortified to still be losing the war on neurotoxic terror, especially on the domestic front. He glanced at the plaque again, and realized they might have met elsewhere.[103]

"You know, Joe ... I remember you being in a play in school. Shakespeare, methinks."

"Heh ... back in the day. There's never time to read now. Later, when I retire ..."

"Bits from *Henry IV*, that's what it was."

"You know, it doesn't really ring a bell."

"OKAY, I TALKED TO THE TOWING GUY AND YOU HAVE ONE MAYBE TWO MINUTES. I CAN'T HOLD HIM OFF FOREVER."

Joey Cavalcanti sat back in his chair and studied the post-work frown lines on Farinata's face.

"Funny. We're the ones who got out in the end."

"We are?"

"I'm based in Cowtown myself. Get over there much?"

"I would, but the chinooks cause me problems. Edmonton's more my jam these days. Though you must be on the go a lot. Then we have Little Big City here, as I call it."

"Sweet. Cozy, even. When you travel for work, there's a sameness to everything. I put on a good show for my contacts, but it's all the same to me. I'd rather be in my own comfy chair."

"Comfy, yes. It is comfy here."

"There's something I've been meaning to ask you. I don't suppose you have any pull here?"

"Pull? In the King's Head?"

"Actually, I figured you might be able to do me a small favour. I could use your influence in the community."

"Influence? I don't really know any big wheels here."

---

103. Naturally, we are thinking of the Garrick Hotel, evoking the tense acquaintanceship between Jesse James and Robert Ford, as depicted in the novel and film about said subject.

"Let me say what the stumbling block is. A few acres of land fell into my lap and my hope is to put up some units— homes for people in Winnipeg. Thing is, we've got to brush aside the trees to do it. As you can imagine, the protestors are on parade and a shitdrizzle has started in the press. Well, I'd still like to get through to those people and change their minds about Sun King Condominiums. Hey, do you want another?"

Joey Whoever ferried their empty glasses to the bar counter. Farinata had heard about the development project without connecting it with his old schoolmate. If he remembered rightly, "a few acres" were closer to sixty acres of wetlands and aspen forest, and "some units" were closer to two thousand micro-homes. The protestors were interested in preserving ecological habitats, as well as an historic Métis settlement. In response, the alter ego, Joe Braul, had installed a fence with floodlights, and had brought in a private security firm to conduct surveillance on the fifty or so "trespassers." A second cranberry and soda was set down, accompanied by a canny grin.

"Say, how's this place treating you? There must be *some* work for a brain like yours."

"Okay. I get by."

"Sure, sure. I was just thinking you might like a change."

"What kind of change?"

"You'd be my mouthpiece in Winnipeg. My man! We can cook up a title—for now, let's call it Outreach Coordinator."

"Huhn."

"I need someone on the frontline, especially as I can't be here 24/7. You can talk to the beast-huggers and get them to see the big picture. If all else fails, you can smarten up our image. Keep the wolves at bay, keep them from hurting our brand—"

"Actual wolves?"

"What? No, of course not. Look—this is good money for making a few statements, maybe writing a couple of articles, or getting a few of your writer friends to stickhandle for our side."

"Our side?"

"Oh, the importance of housing and all that. What are a bunch of trees compared to the lives of men and their families? I mean, women, too. Can't forget them. With your smarts, and with your background ..."

Farinata sipped at his cranberry and soda, losing the most salient points of Joe Braul's spiel. He was thinking of the family store in their old neighbourhood—a connecting memory—that would soon be no more, if not turned into something too ghastly to contemplate. Joey Cavalcanti had heralded it the end of an era, a happenstance wholly independent of his life and ways. What about the crows whose roost had been removed to make room for a car dealership? Now they were crapping all over the car lot and dive-bombing nearby property owners in a relentless campaign of Hitchcockian horror. So much for the old neighbourhood.

"Joe, that sounds like quite the opportunity, but I'd better sleep on it. Also, I really need to head off."

"You do, eh?"

"Yeaaah."

"Okay, see you, then. Don't be a stranger."

So far as his former schoolmate was concerned, Farinata had already sorted out his woollen and cotton and fleece layers and had left to make room for the next applicant. There was probably some prof who could see both sides of the issue. Joey Cavalcanti resumed playing with his phone, which had carried on chirpily without him. Joey Junior had scored a hat trick, and Opal was fighting off her cold like a tigress. No snowflakes, his kids. Melanie was looking forward to his return. Too bad about the quarter-breed poet plodding home, but if there was one thing he could not stand, it was a man who spat in the face of a golden opportunity. Funny how he remembered that play though. The passage of time had not erased all of those lines[104] from his memory, partly because one sleepless night, he had heard them again on TV. The old king was that British dude from *Damage*. The words had come from a million light years away, before he had ever dreamed of becoming Joe Braul.

Joey Cavalcanti reached into his bag and pulled out a stack of mail he had forwarded to his base of operations in Winnipeg. He selected an envelope marked CONFIDENTIAL and opened it. He read the contents of the letter carefully before folding it up and sliding it back inside the torn envelope. He looked up. The plaque that read **OFFICE BULLPEN** stared back at him.

"JUST SO YOU KNOW, THE CAR GOT TOWED. IT'S GONE. WHERE … WE'RE NOT SURE."

---

104. *Canst thou, O partial sleep, give thy repose*
 To the wet sea-boy in an hour so rude,
 And in the calmest and most stillest night,
 With all appliances and means to boot,
 Deny it to a king? Then, happy low, lie down!
 Uneasy lies the head that wears a crown.

Escapade in Esnesnon

Cat Fingers somehow dragged it out of him. There was an old schoolfellow in a position to appreciate the latest crisis to beset a poet, being a wizard at the guitar in the age of post-music. One of the top twelve sounds in the Western Hemisphere, and still nary a venue to be found. Other than the odd bat mitzvah, Cat Fingers had left the building—or any building—having been virtually auto-tuned out of existence. As for those anarchistic Marxian drinking chums of yore, one by one, they had decided to destroy the system from within, and were clearing close to 100K per annum. To be fair, every man occasionally rode the bus back to his cul-de-sac where he futurized his anti-poverty manifesto. The remainder of Cat's kvetches reached Farinata in what Milton had called "fallen language," more recognizable to our ears as the garbled murmurs that have always chastened Charlie Brown. Something about "owning the Showboat" and the trail going cold for a certain Dick or Deryck Thurston, who by all accounts had been carried away by a mighty Inuk. Purportedly at the Funky-Winker in a land perpetually enshrouded by mist.

Farinata had nothing germane to add, except that in a Village bar on his trip to Toronto, with the utmost decorum, a gay Anishinaabe man had stopped singing along with Toto's "Africa" to single him out for gorgeousness among the gorgeous, even with representatives of at least three of the Six Nations at his table. For a moment, the proposition and the keyboarded eighties ambience had made him forget the ghost of a beautiful settler he had encountered in Etobicoke. Farinata had already spent far too many tea breaks puzzling over that one, and in the fashion of the Romantics, he wished to relate a dream that was not a dream, the like of which he had not known since a one-way flight to the Peg under the influence of a potent relaxant. Unless the relaxant had been potent enough to transport him directly to the Forks; he had no evidence to the contrary. Cat took a hit of his smoke and a puff of his friendly and a gulp of his pint to prepare himself. If you are of age and not currently driving or operating heavy machinery, you are encouraged to do the same. Farinata's eyes brimmed over to recall many a time when Cat would do likewise with a woman on each arm. Each was a stage hero by the other's lights, and no amount of former hedonism or horridness could expose the substandard insulation and imported wires beneath those lights. For example, one frantic night on the cliffs with a man only known to them as the English Major. One frantic night they had agreed never to revive in word or deed again.

Ahem. Back to the dream. The initial scenes were jarringly specific. Those in the back, tabbing or tapping or swiping away, may take the Greyhound terminal to be a

Dantean symbol, although it was anybody's guess which would arrive first: the bus or Judgment Day. He lined up to flash his passport, an object that was more hard-won than we will ever know.[105] His existence having been confirmed,

---

105. If Farinata had been magically transported from a square full of food trucks to certain festivities at the Forks, he had still required his stiff unbendable indenture to do so. Neither troll nor gnome under bridge barred his way; the only obstacle was a stolid clerk who had been brought into the passport office and nursed there and cultivated into this extraordinary specimen who had held his post, man and boy, until his thirtieth year, and we pray, ad perpetuum.

Farinata had waited, presented his particulars, faced the music, phoned the guarantors that time forgot, waited again, greeted more small print and toothy snags, waited again, and so on. The clerk had taken exception to our poet's sporadic employment history, failing to grasp the concept of a "freelance" existence, or at best aligning it with a heap of "free-lovers" at a folkloric setting. Need he add for both their benefit they were not living in Florence, and there was not one Medici to dole out monies in aid of writing a so-called "book." If such a thing were to ever happen, the government would surely collapse. The clerk had been on the verge of checking the box for "Post-CCF Freebooter" when he had smelt the opportunity for a teaching moment. Take his brother, the bricklayer who had no mind for math. He had persisted at laying bricks, and as luck would have it, he had been accepted at the Saskatchewan Polytechnic during a strike year, and had been permitted to take a compressed program. Long story short, the man had gone on to lay bricks wherever he pleased.

Farinata, by then an awfully sweaty bundle of nerves, had offered the view that putting one's mind and elbows to work building the foundation for even the shoddiest domicile seemed an occupation more noble than walling over the travel hopes of others. Yet to labour a rather obvious analogy, his own vocation of setting down words and worrying about the amount of "pale mortar" between each of them was not exactly the opposite of bricklaying. The clerk had let that one go, mainly because his demonstration was not

even in a dream, he was asked to form the letter T while he was scanned for implements of destruction. Being a fair-minded citizen, he gave a number of Native passengers the benefit of the doubt that they were actually transporting massive boxes of breakfast cereal to their remote homes and not plotting to sabotage a public transportation system already in rapid decline. After all, that was the government's job.

Once aboard, Farinata assumed the lotus position and never left it for roughly twelve hours (in dream units). In this multi-dimensional two-seater of his subconscious, he was capable of countless Kegels, resulting in improved prowess between the sheets and unbelievable bladder control on the go. Portage la Prairie was, in part, a way station leading to the surrealistic regions; it always had been. Meandering up through continual midnight, his head fell back between the hands of the last stylist to manage his mall-cut, a woman

---

finished. Take the bricklayer's only brother. He had been selected for the "service," presumably for the same kind of qualities that divided candidates for MI6 from those for MI5. As he explained in detail to everyone with the pipe dream of one day boarding a plane again, the training had been extremely intensive; it was no secret that few survived. That said, the government issue Status Card was outside of his purview. Farinata had retorted—as gently as possible for someone on his third Take-A-Number—that the notion of demanding two or three pieces of identification from anyone whose territorial ancestry went back at least 15,000 years, not to huff and puff too heartily over the land the bricks were being laid upon, was a mere line dance away from absurdist theatre. The clerk had remained unfazed; his training had prepped him for the wildest amount of circumspection. Before those aforementioned ancestors had even begun to traverse the land bridge, surely his ancestors had already been waiting on this continent, trained up and ready to receive them with open arms, provided their documents were in order.

who had understood his scalp issues to the core. She had advised clarification in bottle form and had asked him about his imaginary studies, keen to give him a student discount. Floating in space with his eyes shut, Farinata could not deny that a dollop of Borges combed through his hair would be in perfect harmony with his operatic poses. In short, the olive-eyed hairdresser had shorn away the years. He had kept it to himself that even with her clippers and snappy conversation, she was no match for Amanda one province over, who with scissors alone could deliver the mall-cut as an extensive array of scarcely perceptible crop circles for passing admirers to decipher.

Cat Fingers inhaled deeply and nodded. Pacing was an essential part of storytelling. Still, he was nearly where he needed to be. Proust has suggested that shifting into a funny position in the night can result in a whole person, someone who is born from the placement of our thigh or a bit of pressure upon our ribs. We needn't be too surprised that the folded legs of our Greyhound yogi, not to mention his self-improving thrusts, birthed something during that long journey. Cat was athirst with anticipation when Farinata made another dodge, citing a number of books since Goethe's *Faust* that had kept up the tradition of a *Walpurgisnacht*, or at least had adapted it into a literary interlude of incoherent abandon. Cat went for another beer, primarily to give himself a well-earned pause. In life, the party began and ended with himself; in the tiger trap of the short story, one had to keep a clear head and not wave one's arms between the bars. No, he was thinking of a shark tank. Speaking of which, was it in fact true that the original islanders from *Jaws* were dedicated to screening the film on the beach year after year, and if so, did their neighbour join them, none other than special guest James Taylor? Cat contributed this and many other things into the open cooler. He was still humming the guitar accompaniment to Carole King's "So Far Away" when he returned to face Farinata's clear disapproval. William S. Burroughs, for one, had never forgiven Peter Benchley for letting some upstart knock off a sequel.

Once he had recovered from his fit and subsequent tirade, our dear flapper-of-gums picked up the thread again. Cat was about to interject with an astute remark about Carver, but the ball got away from him and rolled into a corner that would remain uninvestigated for several years. The landscape at first light had a stony look to it, and would best be described as Precambrian.[106] **NOW ENTERING ESNESNON.** When the bus rolled into the border town, our man was the last passenger; the boxes of cereal had already been stowed away in other burgs along the way. Farinata followed the road that wound between the rock formations. At the edge of town, he admired a group of symbols painted upon the uneven stone surface. The graffiti defied his understanding and unnerved him a little. It would have been just his luck to raise a pickaxe to the carmine ink and receive a geyser of memories in the face, things best left behind or even fossilized. For example, that frantic night on the cliffs with the English Major. A sandwich board outside the Sprawlmart— even Esnesnon has one—displayed an arrangement of bright, green letters that elucidated nothing.

BEASTIE FOR COUNCIL

---

106. Compare Alice Munro: "Personal fate was not the point, anyway. What drew her in—enchanted her, actually—was the very indifference, the repetition, the carelessness and contempt for harmony, to be found on the scrambled surface of the Precambrian shield." On second thought, please don't.

Farinata could not miss the one eating place and stepped inside. The breakfast special was placed before him with a rapidity that was not alarming in a dream. He had begun to describe the dimensions of the waitress—not to mention a lone sausage poking through two fried eggs—when Cat pointed out that everything had been on the psychosexual side thus far. There was something fishy about the way the waitress sat herself down during her busiest shift and unfolded a country song of honking trucks and heartless betrayals, leaving a funny taste not unlike the hollandaise. Even for a dream, thought Cat out loud, it was more than just a side of coleslaw slathered in the improbable. The way she was blowing smoke into the fluorescents in slow-motion was sheer Wong Kar-wai, and the way she was stretching her legs and gaining height was positively Wisteria, a fact which was presumably lost on Farinata, Cat, and Wisteria herself who was in her bed dreaming about failing a marketing exam she had actually passed. If he would be so good as to promulgate the whole business for the world and present company, Cat would be much obliged. Farinata frowned, and took a pee break, which gave him time to append "promulgate" to his roving glossary. Proust would have frowned to encounter such an unnecessary phrase as, "He washed his hands with characteristic thoroughness and returned to his chair," although we certainly feel much better. In this instance, there was no dress code; the waitress chose to exercise her agency and encourage coolness anywhere near the non-proverbial heat of the kitchen. Add to her gratuity the wages of deer-in-headlight gratitude, and not exclusively from the male persuasion. As for our friend with his eyes full of sleep, flashes of bosom and thigh reached him no more than a Man Ray weft of overlapping androgynous flesh. Yet as with a drowsy hand dipped into warm water, there would be an undeniable result for the sleeper.

That "come-hither" entity was the forerunner. Woman was born from womanflesh, already the stuff of dreams, ready to be strained through a literary filter or the rusty sieve of a mind—take your pick. She was a composite of the highest order, and on the surface, a real character. Each of her dark eyes were gifted from Trish, and were prepared for their close-up in *Un Chien Andalou*, if need be. Unwittingly, the Mädchen had donated her freckled nose and her eyebrow game. The pouty mouth, a veritable Sephora of possibilities, was on layaway from Piper, although with various structural reinforcements, courtesy of Gemma. The stature of Wisteria we have already addressed, now holding up the television smile of Alma Smatterson. He had secretly prized the chestnut curls of his former missus—offset by the odd grey spiral that had reminded him of Sonja Smits in the role of Morag Gunn—but he had relinquished them in accordance with the separation agreement. There was only enough wiggle room to choose a chin based on a true chin, albeit with slightly less prominence for legal reasons. In warmer weather, she bared the pastrami-grinding arms of Esther Schmelz and the piano-petting hands of Laura Horowitz—ladies in our future unless you read from back to front or entirely at random—although she had inherited her efficiency at shelving books[107] and her defensive block from Lucia, who was making progress at the Regina Public Library in spite of numerous cutbacks. We are embarrassed to admit that Ashley made the greatest contribution to this subconscious project. Cat felt it apropos to revisit

---

107. Scholarship has shown that the majority of her charm and efficiency can be directly traced back to the lovely librarian in the Toto video.

his controversial interpretation of *The Cherry Orchard*, by
the strength of which he had advised Farinata in greener
years to plant the seeds early for the best odds of reaping a
mouthful in the autumn of his years.[108] Had it been a spec-
tacular yield, or just another crop of the doolally?

---

108. It is not ours to reason why editorial concerns, production
costs, or time constraints have excised from this text the lengthy,
rousing speech made by Cat Fingers—indeed, one to rival Strether's
inspirational chat with Little Bilham in *The Ambassadors*, marked by
what Henry James had called "a principle of aboriginal loyalty" in
the lower case, indicating sole upon native soil of native land, etc.
and the pleasing delusion of a binding principle therein—because
the measure extending from the first chord of *carpe diem* to this
blurred fermata of *caveat cursetor*, should you forgive this sixteenth
century Latin neologism, sounds the minstrel from his lowest note
to the top of his compass. It would suffice to hear some of Cat
Fingers's most popular licks underlying the "Sweet Little Kiss of
Life" he was likening—in a way that would startle Missus Ainsley
Thiessen right out of her own Aspern Papers—to the rattling tin
cup of the blind sojourner, sad and dreadfully plain, into which, a
helpful jelly, one's consciousness may be poured instead of newly
minted coinage, unless he was thinking of the syrup stuck upon
table into which the university student's fingernails dipped to
retrieve a few pieces of silver, the very image that would ensure
his cycle of futility in a short story in some old-timey high school
anthology with a broken spine.

Amid his ninety-five theses or disputation on the folly of
analysis-paralysis, a pay-what-you-can royalty lyric offered an eerie
echo of the Mädchen's uncouth discarding of the regifted Sabra
fruit, which in turn had echoed the young women rejecting the
daffodils in the Elizabeth Bowen story: "When life would hand
me flowers / I would push them out of my way and sneeze."
Surprisingly, Farinata had only interjected once to speak of a poem
one of Cat's daughters had written when she was still a little girl,
showing a glimmer of non-conformism so precious to the pair of
them at that time. Had they not drunkenly chanted the poem over
and over again until the moment was ripe to set a Norton anthology

The librarian's soothing accent had blown in from an African prairie outside of Johannesburg, or possibly had been lifted from an erotic French film that was vaguely about colonization, along with her name, Emmanuelle.[109] There was nothing to hold back this lovely chimaera at the Esnesnon Library. When it came to handling inter-library lending between provinces, she had no equal. To survey her domain was to behold the picture of purgation, for once with more than adequate toilet facilities. Free to dwell in possibility, Farinata was happy as a prize hog in you know what; dream had softened the edges of his multifarious appetites. Other than periodic cups of nettle tea and a cheeky wedge of lemon cake, he wished for no more than to flip through *American Insects: A Handbook of the Insects of America North of Mexico* (2nd ed.). Towards this prepossessing composite, he exhibited behaviour free of all the usual objectifications.

---

ablaze in the yard, a marvel in the darkness for anyone riding the rapid transit line overhead? They agreed that the notion of regret was best summed up by Art Bergmann ("I just wanted to be good / like the Beatles in Hollywood") and that if there were a perfect time for James Taylor to storm into the *mise-en-scène* and demand satisfaction from that fake shark at Universal Studios, it would be wonderfully convenient at this age of maturation. We have leave to set down—without full pauses, straight dashes, and breaks for micturition—his closing cri de coeur, which was to push aside all manner of pedantic dreaming and do more than recalibrate one's muscles with a Yogic lunge, do more to accept as cynosure the countless positions in the Khajuraho Temple much as ascetic eyes did in an indifferent universe beset by cruel mortality, yes, to actively fling one's fervour and one's frailty with abandon towards that "Sweet Little Kiss of Life." Then, to punctuate his exceptional brologue, he sneezed.

109. We may wonder if the flight attendant of the same name is our friend's soulmate, revealed only through his subconscious leanings? Such speculation is beyond the scope of this book.

There would be neither rhyme nor reason to her gasping in a buckled leather corset, reshelving in stilettoed thigh-highs, or ascending that articulated stepladder in a grass skirt. These hankerings set aside, he was free to mull over the ineluctable modality of the visible,[110] or the light that reaches stellar bodies long since extinguished. Going by his mystical ear, he perceived a soda-coloured sofa, and cautioned himself against obsessing over every sensuous crinkle in the leather that cried out across their illuminated limbo. No, the erotic torments of his salad days—and even his cabbage days— were merely flaccid aspirations in such a haunt. The only allantoid eruption to offer mild trouble kept to its sturdy bough outside. We dare not penetrate the rapturous opacity of Emmanuelle a micrometre deeper, although we may take her thoughts to be aligned with those of every Esnesnonian, marvelling at her swift-footed ingress.

"Emmanuelle Dythers."

"You don't happen to have a lanyard? Without a well-hooked serif, names escape me."

"Well, when in Roman orthographic …"

"Ha!"

"Try this on for size. Eee-man-uuu-ell-uh."

"That post-penultimate particle is sheer Massenet."

"Not Gounod or Bizet? Why have you come here, weary traveller?"

"Look, I have the impression this border town has no more existence than an undigested root vegetable."

"What a Dickensian move! I assure you, where I am from, yams are quite real, and nary a bite goes down the wrong hole."

---

110. At the same instant (even in dream-units) another ineluctable quaver passed through the Mädchen, almost like a warning whistle for a train going on a long journey, never to return.

"So far, I have never known such a pleasing interlude—"

"These intermezzi are the cream of a bookish life."

"You know, I am fond of the way you talk."

"The way I talk?"

"Your voice is more soothing than a whiff of *Werther* or *Thaïs*. Yes, this biscuit certainly takes the cake, and has a taste more uncanny than all of Kleist. My only regret is that it came when life is roughly half the packet short."

"Just think of that hackneyed nugget about the guy dreaming he was a butterfly dreaming he was some guy. Why not a tattered, careworn monarch dreaming us into the rocky bassinet of Esnesnon?"

"Maybe a viceroy, with only the outward show of toxicity."

"I see. That would explain the milkweed corset."

"No, the monarch eats milkweed, not the viceroy. Wait, what?"

"Your mind is like an old school card catalogue to me."

"And you're two-thirds an Alice Munro character,[111] maybe thirty years earlier ..."

Naturally, the miraculous Ms. Dythers had her rock at home, and her rock spent the better part of the day analyzing rocks. A very interesting fellow who does not come into the frame, primarily because Farinata did know much about rocks, let alone how to dream about them. Not that our poet had lain with her. Let's be up front about that for once. Nor she with him in the weakest of moments. One time she had tousled his hair; another time he massaged the ball of her left foot. However, he was easily mollified whenever she brought out a big picture book and read him some local history. For example, FF, the founder of Esnesnon, had diverted his attentions from his bacon-and-cheese

---

111. Once again, this is just some weird romantic rhetoric.

concerns, not to mention his many admirers, to journey into the depths of the planet inside a mechanical fish, a sort of Jules Verne bass.[112] Emmanuelle could scarcely get going before Farinata would nudge her—more impatient than a child—and start in with an inchoate fragment of his own. Then she would tap his hand like an overindulgent school-marm, and without an ounce of condescension, declare that he had come up with quite the romp. Thus emboldened, in the dreamy voice of an anonymous matelot, he told her about an incident that had happened the day the Maestro died.[113]

---

112. Rhymes with "ass." Just saying.

113. Yet another tempest has separated the tender Chatham from the HMS Discovery. The next appointed rendezvous is in Matavai Bay, but not before the Chatham's cutter has been dispatched to investigate a tasty bit of *terra nullius* Captain Cook called "No Body Knows What." A darker key is required for this ombra scene, although it is no fantasy in the musical sense of the term. Set in alla breve, prior to the tragic part. Let us not forget that clumsy andante keeping time for the opera buffa that passes for the world. Look, give us at least one sforzando shock, one blistering chord that jolts us right out of our elbow chairs! No, it is not hard to picture a piece of lead that is being nailed to a tree near the beach. It reads like so:

His Britannick Majesty's Brig Chatham, Lieutenant William Robert Broughton commander, the 29th November, 1791.

This may leave a strange taste on your mother tongue; if you dig around, you will unearth a bottle that contains the same intelligence in Latin. Here, we watch ourselves gavotte upon a dreary shore, keeping time to stilted rhythms that echo the insolence of our mock salute.

Voglio far il gentiluomo
e non voglio più servir …
no, no, no, no, no, no,
non voglio più servir!

The good Lieutenant has named this place after the Earl of
Chatham, although Chatless Island would have been more fitting!
What a desolate place! The canoes are not even up to snuff. Made
out of something very like bamboo, they are more accompaniments
to frivolous baskets and hand barrows. Well, the purse nets
fashioned out of hemp are not bad. There are no grand houses
to greet us, only signs of fires extinguished some time ago. Opera
buffa or not, this is really the bush. There are a few trees to be had
but none we can dignify with the appellation of a timber tree. When
the natives finally do show up, they spend an eternity rubbing noses
with one another. We try to interest them in our trinkets, as it is our
custom to give away things we hope to never clap eyes on again, but
this is a waste of our efforts. Only one fellow became enamoured
with a looking glass and ran off with it.

Lieutenant Broughton fires his gun, mainly to get their attention.
They all back off, except for an obstinate old man who holds
his ground and appears ready to do battle. He's quite all right in
our book. The natives are putting away their spears—which is in
their best interest if they want to keep them out of the British
Museum—and are waving heavy pieces of driftwood. No, they do
not take too kindly to us, or to Mr. Johnston's attempts to learn
their secret for swiftly lighting a fire. Obviously, the brackish salt
water they offer us is not our cup of tea. Our little gavotte lands
on the dominant seventh over and over again. Portentous or not,
something is in the offing. The Maestro is not long for this world,
and his destiny is to be dropped ignominiously into a pauper's grave.

The natives are agitated. They are even making faces at us! Our
boat is being made ready but in the meantime, we are obliged to
fend off some rather sharp sticks. Note that the petulant knocks
upon Mr. Johnston's musket hang from a descending chromatic
line, spread out into three two-measure lengths by a counterpoint
of tritone and resolution. A complementary chromatic ascent is
sufficient to club the musket out of Mr. Johnston's trembling hands.
Then in a heroic panic, he dives for it and fires at his assailant. That
sets off the other men, who also fire their pieces without orders.
The diminished seventh in F minor makes me fear the worst. Time
is arrested by an unexpected fermata; the tempo is cut in half. One

Here, Cat Fingers took a great toke and nodded agreeably. One day, they would Hellenize—if not Indigenize—that island and various other locales in which their headlining aesthetic dictate would be to sip from a coconut in the sun. He also swore an oath that if Farinata could not drive all the celebrated eco-poetic settlers from his unceded ancestral island, or for that matter, from all manner of "cottage country," then together they would reclaim Turks and Caicos for their own private amusement. They were rapidly approaching the rubber glue of the Universal, a cheery eventuality that would lead to a quiet piddle in the garden with no more peeking than Beethoven's fraternal brotherhood would permit. Yet there was one itch left to scratch. The dates were slightly out of whack, and besides, Mozart went into the ground with money in his pockets and a fatal case of strep throat.

Such enchanted powers of description, make us wonder if Ms. Dythers is not the non-toxic butterfly after all,

---

of the natives has fallen. A ball has broken his arm and passed through his all-too-trusting heart. Surprisingly, the strings are still marking time with triplets ticking gravely over a dominant pedal. One fellow dares to sully the innocent's final moment with a deep and plangent dissonance, a sympathetic cry that emerges as if from the depths of some foul nightmare.

Ah! già cade il sciagurato!
Affannosa e agonizzante
già dal seno palpitante
veggo l'anima partir …

Then, with a barely audible Phrygian inflection, the man shuffles off his mortal coil. A chromatic line in the oboes descends from the dominant, marking the flight of his soul from his ruined body. He was not a composer of inimitable genius responsible for the Great Mass in C minor, but he has also breathed his last breath, and in a place far more miserable.

dreaming Cat Fingers and Farinata—and dare we say, ourselves?—into existence. Indeed, she had forsworn his bedroom eyes and company outside of library hours, and made trudging up and down the famous hundred steps her penance. Then over her desk, her head would droop, inside of which her scofflaw of a dream could freely poke at its own moth-eaten ginch. A slight tickle of nostril, and she would stir within the gutter of some geological surveys, or worse yet, ship's journals that chronicle the amicable conquest of New Albion.[114]

The ill-fated captain's words roused her. Something was different. The smokestack had stopped. The smelter was gone. Brahms had put away his Serious Songs and history had turned out to be little more than a nightmare to wake up screaming from. Not since the arrival of FF, the founder of Esnesnon, had there been such a champion to usher in a new age of artistic endeavours, cuddled snugly under the subsidiary of an umbrella company with its own tagline: *Live mere steps away from aesthetic truth*. In accord with the expanding puddles of his consciousness, the library became a widening circle of such illumination, open to half-frozen refugees and unbaptized ideologues alike. Members of his fanbase camped outside through the holiday weekend so as not to miss a line-by-line breakdown of his most scurrilous long poem. It was before these hordes that Mr. Emile

---

114. "To describe the beauties of this regions, will, on some future occasion, be a very grateful talk to the pen of a skillful panegyrist. The serenity of the climate, the innumerable pleasing landscapes, and the abundant fertility that unassisted nature puts forth, require only to be enriched by the industry of man with villages, mansions, cottages, and other buildings, to render it the most lovely country that can be imagined; whilst the labour of the inhabitants would be amply rewarded, in the bounties which nature seems ready to bestow on cultivation."

Dythers, a pillar of the community next to BEASTIE, wondered aloud if Farinata would be so good as to "go in unto" that bittersweet column of quiet he had known since his (Mr. Dythers') porridge days. Emmanuelle seconded the motion, adding the proviso that Farinata had to be dressed as a glowing proton in the dark—he had once acquitted himself nicely as a neutron giving a monologue in an amateur theatre production—to preserve a modicum of decorum. Our jejune Jude the Obscure had wet eyes when he recognized a lone credit that had been an insurmountable impasse between him and his grand Honours; this millstone had been melted down and fashioned into a medal from the people of Esnesnon for indubious doings and accomplishments in a field scarcely a stone's throw from the spires of higher learning. His eyes were made into more milch than ever when he looked past the trays of oysters and saw a cake with his face on it.

Cat Fingers laughed softly. Was the sun not brightest right before it set? He knew our friend and the erratic pattern of his sagas well. The epigraph might have read: *A wet paper bag cannot hold a plenitude of groceries forever.* In the background, the jobless crowd began to sour. To pin all their hopes (and funds) on a stranger to produce an heir for their avant-garde entail did not scan as the most feasible plotline at this point in their lives. A portrait of the culturally diverse—within the confines of this dream—civic policy-makers, something akin to a Rembrandt of a quilters' guild, would be just the thing.

It was at that instant his one undeflatable adherent gave him a sign of solidarity. Was it a sparkle of spoke or twitch of handle brake or waggle of saddle hazarding provocation? Perhaps a certain bounce in the tires. Unless the commonality was that they both needed air. Cat Fingers snorted.

His good comrade was pushing the image a mite far. Nevertheless, the lustre of that scarlet frame had him all fired up. Already, he was making tacit promises to care for the chain. If Farinata was right to intuit that Esnesnon was a border town without locks, then this would be the very first bicycle theft in its history, provided that nine-tenths consent did not warrant possession. He inched towards the entrance where Isabelle was waiting, and once he had thought of her as a "her," there was no way to backpedal out of it. Meanwhile, Emmanuelle, not unlike a number of beauties in this book, had her heart set on some kind of fertility rite; we did not want to put too much stock in the gamecock baster next to the trays of oysters, although awareness of it is quite the "what-the-shuck?" moment. She could not bring herself to do injury to his person outside of the sundering bed prepared for them—the quilters had outdone themselves—but she took everything out on his reading copy until even remaindering was out of the question.[115] Oddly, this was not the first time a bibliophile had attacked him or his words, or, for that matter, drooled over his latest. No one we know or care to remember. He carried his wounded epic in his arms and laid it in the gleaming rear basket and gave Isabelle a nudge like a lover in the night. A grim chorus began to encircle him as he mounted that elegant creature, by literal definition, the town bike. Then one graceful leap, and they were off!

The general hypothesis stands that he reached either the Manitoba or Saskatchewan side within a few minutes of riding. The most reliable witnesses were not satisfied with a shock pump-powered deus ex machina amid the quacking song of wood frogs alongside the road. Instead, their binoculars had confirmed Farinata's rescue by a "swoop" or

---

115. Clearly symbolic of the deep claw mark in Marian Engel's *Bear.*

"siege" of sandhill cranes bent on making him an essential part of the aurora borealis.

Cat Fingers finished another beer, his eyelids heavy. The one thing he intended to do before hitting the hay was set the whole caboodle down in three or four paragraphs for the sage consideration of a screenwriting graduate. He mumbled his intention with the utmost care, but Farinata was already long gone on another of his buddy-buddy crying jags.

The Heart of Harkness

It was the cruellest moon, which is to say National Poetry Month, a blessing and a curse for all concerned, and especially those unconcerned. Accordingly, Farinata had ejected himself off the #66 at Harkness Station to escape some kind of irritant—be it lotion, perfume, or shampoo—and observed one other person in the transparent anteroom, lest we call it his shelter of exile. At first, he thought it was a young man in a cap, but under closer inspection, it turned out to be a young woman in a tarboosh. This did not appear to be any sort of traditional decision, and he could only think of Sainte-Beuve's appraisal of Flaubert's penchant for such headgear.

"Hark! Do you know what 'Harkness' means?"

"Was he not at the helm of some grand ship?"

"Good guess, but it's probably toponymic. '*Heargness*,' or, 'dweller at the Temple-Headland,' in the old tongue."

"God's hooks!"

"Hark! Like my hat?"

"The spit of Flaubert."

"My sentiments, exactly."

She eyed his ring nervously. Evidence of a terrible upset, whereby several shortlisted writers had fallen out of the running due to some mysterious ailment or calamity, and Farinata had risen to the forefront of those considered worthy to wear the Aleph Beth Ring,[116] although we cannot stress this enough, more as finger model than as unanimously declared recipient, for a period not exceeding one year, until the next champion of versification could be found amid the wilds of life. One limited time advantage of this alphabetical bling was its ability to bend poets to the will of its bearer. The young woman put her tarboosh at a rakish angle, steeling herself to fight off the ring's great attraction and introduced herself as Jayde Garland, hailing from Kansas or Idaho or some other agricultural haven. In addition to half-assed handshakes, partial curtseys were exchanged.

"You know my books, I trust?"

"Yes and no. There are so many brilliant books, especially at this time of year … it really gets me down."

With that prevarication, she admitted that such books were there for the consumption. Without the gestalt of those words, there could be no grand recombinant project! Farinata raised an eyebrow and coughed politely. Another proponent of erasure poetics he did not need. Not to say they could not dip a biscuit or break bannock if the impetus

---

116. Sadly, this much-coveted prize for unusual literature has no definite origin story. We are able to reassure ourselves that Winnipeg has absolutely nothing to do with it. Frequently repeated rumours put its means of distribution on either side of the most fluent vowels of the Outaouais.

arose. It did. Jayde was tossed a tasty bone—the opportunity to interview Farinata about how it felt to nearly win something for roughly half a life's travail.

Neutral territory had been agreed upon. Jayde was morally opposed to making a trip to River Heights, a stone hammer's throw away from a former Indigenous ghetto known as Rooster Town, and by now rightfully reclaimed by our pioneer, or so we would like to believe. High upon this hillock (or butte), Farinata ruled with wisdom. Had his private life been able to withstand an ounce of scrutiny, he would have succumbed to the few enthusiasts who wanted him to run for public office. As such, his executive decision was to return to Jayde's neighbourhood. He hopped off the bus when he recognized the Flaubertian tipoff at the junction of four traffic arterials. Jayde was standing there, transfixed. Farinata also fell into a stupour as he peered up and saw that the wealthy woman with her diamonds of choice had been replaced by a grinning Mädchen raising a steaming mug of how-do-ye-do. Apparently, she had a new gig at the café down the road and the owners were requisitioning her wholesome looks to move product. We rejoice in the knowledge that he would not have pimped out his heart's desire so readily. However, he was not about to spend all day drooling over a billboard, not when there was more than just himself to watch out for.

"Happens to the best of us."

"Huhn?"

"Confusion Corner has sealed the fate of far heartier souls."

They went single file along Osborne. Is it so terrible to evoke the tugging of a lead or the holding of a piece of sugar under the nose? In any case, Jayde followed the way a goat follows a donkey it knows and trusts, drawn forward by the

gleaming letters of the Aleph Beth Ring. Farinata was doing
fine until he perceived the nearby presence of the Mädchen;
he reared up, raising his hooves. Jayde waited patiently until
the erotic shock had tapered off. A lifeline emerged in the
kitty corner competitor, Grounds for Delight. The flame
that wavered within the Aleph Beth finalist shot up again
as a ginger-haired woman leaned over the counter, flashing
her amplitude.

"Jayde Garland! Unreal. What can I do you for?"

Farinata horned in with his order. Too much water in his
Earl Grey was not to his liking. Fusspots were not to hers.
Only once his beverage was besleeved and he was seated did
the cooing resume. Mozart would have had to construct a
special clarinet just for these two. Jayde fobbed the matter
off and between sips of her iced coffee, itemized a variety of
organisms she had *hooked* in the cyber-dating cesspool. Her
very own words! As for the ginger charmer with managerial
potential in Grounds for Delight, that was simply not on.
Yet she was a foil to Farinata's dark-eyed Dulcinea, the sov-
ereign beauty of Queen City who deigned to consort with
all manner of fusspots. After brandishing his own backlist
catalogue of encounters, our confessor brushed aside any
clinical definition and declared himself a neuroromantic
(within earshot of the ginger server, who whistled softly).
Jayde brushed off this concept, tending towards nullity. You
might say she experienced a power outage just as the lights
on the ferris wheel in her companion's head were beginning
to whirl. A herd of neurons was already breaking free and
running amok! How they swarmed with rapid-fire associations! Farinata likened it to a flow chart on a whiteboard that
kept filling up beyond capacity. He was about to say that
the simplest of contradictions was capable of short-circuit-
ing his entire logic diagram, but Jayde shook her head, still

grappling with the neuronal synecdoche. Then she stood up, holding hat over heart.

"At least you can think. With me, it's the exact opposite."

Farinata flashed the Aleph Beth Ring at her and Jayde sat down again. The same old piddling contest, followed by the same old debate. Madness before method or method before madness? Jayde chose to see it as the wing flap of a wounded bird in a predatory world. Farinata, already boosted into a nitrous oxide *accelerando* thanks to his condition, sided with a kind of butterfly effect in a world where the seedy solipsist could get a bit of his own back. Causation aside, he divided craft from condition with a minimum of overlap. Case in point, the afflicted soul who knew not a whit of Allen Ginsberg, or the careerist collagist—with several letters after his or her name—for whom passionate agitation did not factor in. There was no concord on treatment either.

"Get help. So they say. So they keep saying."

"You don't like the dialogue, then."

"Meds work for some. Not for everyone though. Sometimes the side effects can be—"

"You don't like the dialogue, then."

"Environmental factors! I don't mean history or family! Are we to be prisoners of trauma forever?"

"You don't like the dialogue, then."

The longer Farinata sat there amid a clatter of teaspoons, straining to hear himself over the grinding of beans, the more confused he became. In fact, he found himself turning red and his voice rising in tremulous increments, especially the more he deplored the state of media feeds. Jayde, stalwart as the statue of Gandhi in rain, sleet, or snow outside the Canadian Museum for Human Rights, stuck to her mantra about unsatisfactory dialogue. Luckily, the ginger-haired server was making her rounds and was stocked with a few theories of her own. She clutched Jayde and cradled her vacant head to and fro. We do not infer that Jayde's head was empty, merely that the contents were temporarily out of reach. Sadly, this is another oversimplification that will leave us none the wiser for the sake of a chinless dramatic pause.

Farinata cast down the non-neutral key to the men's and splashed cold water on his neck, cheeks, temples, and forehead. His analogy of preference likened his frontal lobe to a clogged engine that all too easily overheated in the desert of semi-polite society. Yet the prickly calyx of a plant first identified by Theophrastus was always waiting to pierce him through. He returned to the table with this half-assed analogy to find Jayde in excellent spirits.

"So you don't like the dialogue, eh? There are some good doctors I could recommend. They did wonders for me."

They resumed their idle exchange like a pair of Geulincxian clocks,[117] giving the outward show of a causal connection that kept in perfect synchronicity. Farinata may stand in for the unpredictable mind in this *Gedankenexperiment*, and Jayde for matter that inclines towards a state of rest. On another day, they might have switched positions. Please rewind to find that the agitated rant of our loss leader betrays an ontological objective. In his own words, he would have wailed that such a shot across the bow proves that the island of the mind is not the same as the island of common stuff. Unfortunately, Jayde had receded into a quicksand akin to

---

117. To explain away supernatural causation, Arnold Geulincx (1624-1669) coughed up the idea of two concurrent clocks that keep time not because they influence one another, but because they are what they are, more or less. Here, we've taken a running jump, connecting this analogy with Leibniz's emphasis on the relation between mind and body, all for the sake of a meagre simile. You know, some days, it's not worth getting out of bed in the morning.

catatonia, hammered and not helped by Farinata's barrage of elusive arguments, and therefore she was in no position to appreciate the plight of the fellow sufferer caught between the general practitioner with his pharmaceutical panacea and the holistic huckster with her crystals and oils. Even the effects of traditional medicine were moot, wherever the benefits of a meditative root fast are counteracted by an atmospheric disturbance that may be driving an entire tribe to extinction. There was a general outcry to call in more doctors to swap bad drugs for good drugs, and to offer a few words of cheery advice. No, without reducing the whole business to a branch of souped-up phrenology, the dialogue was not something to be liked. One's cranium is bound to be measured for suggesting that environmental affinities may hold more value than any amount of so-called "understanding," save the unconditional love of a non-judgmental pet. Better a grey comma sip his sweat than social parasites drain him dry!—present company excepted. Add to his burden the perpetual emphasis on emotional intelligence. One saving grace for Farinata had been his discovery that his thoughts more or less corresponded with whatever passed for reality when not subject to the polarity (or see-saw effect) of two chemicals in particular, brought into a state of imbalance because of the neurological logjam we have already witnessed, which gave him the reputation of being an up-and-down guy. In summary, Dr. Gabor Maté was his trigger warning.

Jayde emerged from this conversational morass, wheezing. The doctor highest in her estimation, finding herself unable to unearth sufficient historical or familial trauma, had pinned the entire thing on budding love in the wake of a woolly adolescence. A contrarian to the core, Farinata amended this diagnosis to treat calf love as symptom instead of source, although that theory cast a swath of his own poems to the four directions. Was there a point to objectification in a world full of objects, should even the otherworldly reveal itself? The tender udders of love aside, we must admit that Farinata had spent the greener years of his life whining about a small yet shocking injustice committed against his person that mingled the earliest stirrings of infatuation with a sense of chastisement, teaching him that one must alternate between whip hand and raw, raddled booty. Could such a sorry iota of human experience have switched him off like an electric kettle? We cannot raise action against the public school system for his loss of good cheer, or for turning him into the aloof and moody soul we recognize with ease. What a relief then, to realize that the pathetic fallacy panned out, except in reverse! Given that he was a melting pot of Northern bloodlines from Indigenous marauders to melancholic Celts, the cumulative effects of those first gloomy years had taken their toll. With Proustian delicacy, he could recall the sound of a train passing through the rain on many a morning when the barometric pressure was holding him down in bed. Feigning sick, he read, doing himself more harm than good. Before long, our autodidact was bound to find women in a continual fog. Years and years of self-medication drifted by. Around the time he was storming out of literary salons, he was thought to have the artistic temperament of your garden-variety genius. He had oiled his hinges to combat this atmospheric heaviness, with pint after pint and shot after shot, but a plethora of stimuli had still tormented him, and by the nychthemeron. The result was countless pages of post-Joycean miasma, and the undying yet irreconcilable adoration of a fair sourpuss with a Swinburne fetish.[118] On a related

---

118. The letter from her proves she can be fairly jolly when she's had a few.

note, during this neoclassical era, there was an upsurge in the number of esoteric odes left (in lieu of a gratuity) for barmaids in their late twenties. Fortunately, he remembers little more than falling off a stool in an establishment that is now an incredible opportunity of a luxury condo in the Land of the Lotophagi.

Then Farinata emerged out of the dark dank to find himself exposed with all the floodlights turned on. Madness was dispatched to our friend from the living sky, much as it was to Herakles. Yes, a period of adjustment on the bright prairie was inevitable. When tearing his hair out in the square town that felt to him like a sanatorium, he saw visions of another city of sinuous rivers that circumnavigated around oneself, happily discharging all the positive energy that was so debilitating to the human nervous system. He had heard tell of such a place directly to the east, where even the most disenfranchised denizen could recline by one of the rivers like a Whitmanesque "rough" and cast his imitation nymph into the muddy water. We will not keep you in suspense— there he went and there he remained, even as pen is pressed to foolscap. His valiant attempt to be grounded (or to find an outlet) had led our poet to seek sustenance in wall sockets. The purpose of the stinky mat was to connect him with the earth, even from a fourth floor apartment. Eventually, he switched to the overpriced sheets (and matching throw) that helped him unload all that positivity while he slumbered. Another beneficial option that also stank was the leather sandal customized for the foot of our Lord (or Roman reprobates, take your pick). After a proper soaking, provided that the toe-hold held and the wearer held out, he or she would cease walking and start *earthing* in no time flat. Perfect for the hipster part-timer on the go! Nine out of ten aging hippies approved. The only drawback was during the frequent summer lightning storms when a rubber sole suddenly regained its appeal. The odds of being struck and becoming a prophet had gone up exponentially. Farinata raised the ring to drive his point home, if there was one. Jayde scrunched up her eyes to take in the four letters[119] and nodded. Remember that for one "creative," the icebox was filling up with verbose fridge magnets and for the other, they were rapidly quarking out of existence. All the same, Jayde managed to rattle off a list of renowned writers with mental disturbances. Then she froze.

"It's time. Show you, time to show you. Time."

"Sorry, what did you say?"

"Not far. Hark … Harkness."

Jayde led them this time. Were it less difficult to scoop up the temporary bearer of the Aleph Beth Ring in her slim arms, she would have done so. Were it convenient for them to form each end of a polka dot donkey, that would have been most apropos. In hardly any narrative time at all, Jayde was ushering him up some rickety stairs. The two-storey exterior sported the bright technicolours of a Douglas Sirk film from the 1950s. Once they had creaked upward to the top, Farinata was disappointed to enter not a garret or a mansard, but an attic she introduced as her studio. Their whistles still wet, there was no thought of tea. Jayde merely gestured towards the longest wall and turned a ghastly white.

The wall was white too. Not the iridescent white of the raised wings of a checkered white upon a shoot of alfalfa, nor the white of manuscripts contemplating the vast icy backdrop of an idealized and/or horrific North, where

---

119. The Aleph Beth Ring contains four adjustable rings of letters, which, to the bearer's delight, can spell the profane or, on occasion, the sublime. The recipient of its four-lettered command is obliged to answer in kind on a weekend.

the last dregs of a post-colonial romance could occur. Still a thing, apparently. Jayde understood. The first time, an onlooker needed reassurance. She asserted with verve that a poem was there to behold. Certainly the finest poem she had ever been involved with. Possibly the finest poem to ever come about. In spite of her annual membership in the dubious club of half-mad geniuses, Jayde would never dream of taking credit for a single word, let alone a lick of white. For quite a spell, Farinta saw nothing. Notwithstanding, to let drop a remark too early would destroy his reputation as an aficionado of all things scrivenish. Finally, a cloying notion rose up out of that naked expanse, one that jounced wildly between his polarities. Those of us familiar with his experimental fiction (stoically full of promise upon a few pallets in a small warehouse that also functioned as a garage) would, in close reading, detect a semi-autobiographical note in his use of the *Orgelbüchlein* to indicate that one of his characters was having an episode. Yes, Bach's *Little Organ Book* was a testament to the spectrum within many surfaces. We cannot resist a cinematic cliché firmly established by Andrei Tarkovsky and others, allowing the most famous of those chorale preludes to go round and round in Farinata's poor head while he stared at the wall. Though he hated to admit it, Rilke had been right. The visible *could* bring to light the invisible. Unless that was just a scrap of Merleau-Ponty, a delicious earworm that had somehow gained entrance to his hearing. Out of nowhere, he remembered walking out of a student film and bumping into a man in a seersucker suit who had reminded him of a Rococo Pierrot. The entire incident was almost making sense. Farinata rubbed his eyes as torturous lines began to appear, covered with countless layers of marginalia, scratches, strikethroughs, and white-outs that displayed the meticulous care of a true collagist.

No one would dare raise his voice over the cantus firmus to ask what the poet meant or where her ideas had come from. A poem of preternatural silence could get by without gradient or depth. As for Jayde's ideas, they came from nowhere and took up not one inch of unnecessary space. In fact, the white wall had out-erased all the erasure exercises in the known world.

Then Jayde caught another glimpse of the Aleph Beth Ring on the anathematizing finger of our protagonist and the profundity drained right out of her. The ring did not read **L**-**O**-**V**-**E** or even **L**-**I**-**K**-**E**. Alas, she could feel her convictions slipping away. The clutter Farinata had brought up with him was no better than aesthetic baggage. As for our deviser of standardized letters, he could not bear to hang around in the presence of that sickly green—prominently featured in Sirk's *Written on the Wind*, where Lauren Bacall's dress matches the shutters—now dripping from a broad paintbrush down the ineffably white wall. DIY sabotage was simply not his jam. Jayde painted away in silence, fully resigned to becoming the temporary owner of one green wall. Rest assured, the four traffic arterials of Confusion Corner were not to blame for this one. There were at least half a dozen similar casualties every year in the heart of Harkness.

Horror at Chez Horowitz

By the start of May, Farinata was losing patience with the straggler ladybugs who could not decide whether they wanted in or out. He was terrified of the karmic consequences, lest one of them set out across the Sahara of the hardwood floor and die of dehydration. Over the past week or so, he had shuttled numerous parties of three or four down to the lawn at the base of the apartment, weather permitting. In the interim, they had not been without their amenities. He had learned that the lid of a jam jar or vitamin bottle—turned upside down and upgraded with less than a millimetre of water—was their heart's delight. Once they had slaked their thirst, they were content to scurry around the rim of the lid over and over again. He prided himself on his efforts, suspecting that these workouts and a subsequent show of fitness after a long spell of wintering would fast-track the mating process like nobody's business. Of course, the excessive care and generosity he showed them was a measure of everything he had squandered only a few weeks earlier.

First, his mind reeled back to last Yom Kippur, which he had enjoyed rather obliviously at Schmelz's Deli. To be fair, the Mennonite University had thrown a curveball at his atonement by engaging him to give a reading from his various tomes. As a man given to appetite, he had forgotten all about fasting to cast out the bad, choosing to replenish his spirits after the event with a Reuben and a kosher beef dog. He had been at the apex of his digestive process when the accusatory text from Laura Horowitz chimed right into his back fillings.

> i knw wht u did on yom kippr

No, she was no fanatic. It was her father, Councillor Morry Horowitz, who would have wondered what kind of man—without the bloom of youth on his side like Jacob Bloom—thought he was above "cleaning the pipes" in the spiritual sense. Only a poet who lacked any sense of propri-ety—the way he said "poet" implied a lack of initiative in worldly affairs—would feast his eyes on the busy hands of Esther Schmelz as they assembled and heated his contro-versial sandwich. The kasha knish on the house was a hurt-ful fiction, and practically impossible for anyone who had a business to run. Farinata could rend his heart in sackcloth until the cows came home, but only when his famous stom-ach was appeased. Even so, Laura knew what her father was getting at. While you're fooling around with that schle-miel—Morry actually would have called him "nebbish"—a catch like Bloom will slip the net. He'll sidle up to another student of proctology and you'll find yourself ordering onion bisque from your former paramour, mark my words.

In spite of this inauspicious start, events had unfolded splendidly from late October through April, partly because Farinata was adept at concealing his personal views. Picture the incredible Enrico Caruso singing *La Juive* at the Met to try and win over his father-in-law, even post-elopement. For Farinata to confess to there being a non-practising Jew in his little pinky or a Socratic Atheist in most of his bones would have been preferable to the admission that he believed less in theological constructs than he did in Dante Alighieri's roadmap through romance or hell or both, if one was not the other. A dash of melancholic eroticism— the early churning of Kierkegaard—surely could not hurt. Of course, it could. Laura Horowitz had an inkling that he would prove a tough date to digest. Flight from pogroms in turn-of-the-century Poland had not bolstered the faith of his particular strain in Orwell's Britain—if anything, suspicion had increased. Was it not his great-grandmother who had railed against the divorced woman who got pride of place at the synagogue simply because she was a gener-ous contributor? She might have agreed with Molière that the only thing you cannot criticize in society is hypocrisy. During her declining years, her decision to eat nothing but pork hocks and jellied eels had been interpreted as a form of dementia rather than defiance, although no one could have said for sure. As for the British soldiers in the family who had smuggled arms into a flowering Israel—only to be treated shabbily in an American POW camp—was that more about the tidy profit than the cause itself? Worst of all would be to let on that Laura Horowitz was in possession of all the allure of a Petrarchan conceit, which for Farinata was fair praise indeed, but not necessarily the kind of thing one likes to hear.

The one dragonfly in the borscht—scooping up some of the Ukrainian blood-memory that had originally flowed into Poland—was the no-longer-debutante often manning the Schmelz counter. Though all the kosher butchers with Richard Tucker singing a Schubertian *Silbertönen* from the depths of their hearts had shut up shop in the city, here Esther Schmelz survived with her refined physical exposition and overt athleticism. To paraphrase the shin-kicking Three Stooges, Farinata knew it would not do to "hock a chynick"[120] by haunting about the door of Laura Horowitz during those precious hours of idleness before dark—how wrong he was!—so he elected to frequent the deli instead. Let's face facts: Esther would not have paid him any mind during a warmer, busier season. But a man who would brave a few blocks in blizzard conditions to pull up a stool in her presence was worth pause for thought. She appreciated his rugged, outdoorsy demeanour during the winter months; a rabbi would not be caught dead in leather hunting boots with little gun dogs upon the eyelets on Yom Kippur or any other day. She would tend to the chicken soup or run his pastrami through the slicer, and he would hear something akin to Mahler's *Klavierquartettsatz*, although it would be David Bowie or The Weakerthans or Neil Young he was actually hearing.[121] She would raise her tongs and transfer a wet pickle to his sandwich basket, allowing him to relive his grandmother's delight over a plastic container with three

---

120. Larry, Curly, and Moe, would it have been any clearer to say "knock a teakettle?"

121. Unbeknownst to our friend, what he was actually hearing was Young's "Safeway Cart," priming his subconscious for the less wobbly return of a woman from his recent past.

baby gherkins inside. Then he would assume his usual stool and stare dreamily up at a framed vintage CPR print advertising Indian Days in the Canadian Rockies of another era.

Haimish tendrils filled the air between them and steamed up the front windows even more than the delectable anodyne in her soup pot. Though Farinata had only ducked into the deli to sidestep his own baser nature, he encountered his carnal appetite there as well. You, or any impartial observer, would be hard pressed to understand what it was this shrewd, robust woman—with a partial share in the profits generated from an influx of brawny construction workers who downed more than a pound of prosciutto in one sitting—might see in this skin-and-bones poet, no matter how soulfully he wolfed down his fare. Here, we would be remiss not to hammer the point home that Esther Schmelz and Laura Horowitz were each on the frightful side of thirty, and would not have given Farinata a second look seven or eight years ago. To call these lovelies relatively accomplished is not to call them down. We are as surprised as you to learn that Papagena is not quite content without her Papageno, or that respective bird-person in the middle of the road of his life. It was all too easy to picture the long winter walks ahead, with Esther dutifully jogging circles around him. She was a true huntress of the urban wilds, given half a chance.

On the other hand, if he wanted someone more upmarket who seemed to have stepped right out of the nineteenth century—or so the shadchan had promised—Laura Horowitz was closer to the mark. A fatal mistake during a music competition had handed her the programme for the rest of her life, even if that flaw made her quite a catch in his eyes. There would be no lonesome nights spent wondering where in the province or country or world she had swanned off to, or even worse, what she was getting up to. Nor would she be testing his patience with the likes of Elliot Carter or György Ligeti. Come evening, she would tie back her dark hair and sit in the parlour and knock out a few études. In addition to her sonnetish appeal, her performance of Chopin's Nocturne in C minor (op. 48) had shaded in her personality with a sense of mystery. Once she applied herself, that ounce of effusiveness would colour selections from *Harmonies poétiques et religieuses* splendidly, and if she revealed a gift for interpreting Liszt, perhaps she would try out a piano fake of the "Dante Symphony." A tuneful future was all mapped out, provided he could keep from doing anything so distasteful as be himself.

Farinata's prospects had improved since his atonement fail in October. For one thing, he had been nominated for a national award for a volume of his poetry, resulting in a slim column and picture in the *Winnipeg Metro*, copies of which Mrs. Norah Horowitz distributed wherever she could. All of a sudden, Councillor Morry Horowitz was a great patron of the arts, nursing a talented daughter and encouraging a prospective son-in-law who was, by all accounts, an *agent provocateur*. If he could secure those famous evenings of music and poetry in their parlour for the movers-and-shakers over fifty, he would have no more worries about securing his civic seat. The fact that Farinata had taken a graceful powder pleased both the literary award oddsmakers and Laura Horowitz, who was touched by his noble defeat. There would be no lonesome nights spent wondering where in the province or country or world he had buggered off to, or even worse, what he was buggering. When he was not in one of his moods, he would put aside his incomprehensible lines and read her some Keats or Shelley in the parlour. To say he had wormed his way into the heart of Chez Horowitz would be unjust. We cannot rule out the reciprocity here, which is to say the associative chicanery of family life, pushing him along with its own momentum and pulling every string on his behalf.

Farinata's improved status led to a number of evenings on which no Horowitz would probe any shadows in the parlour too closely. The most controversial privilege was that he and Laura could listen to selections from Wagner's "Ring Cycle" at a low volume. It was a matter of some discretion just how many knees had quivered in his grip during the first act of *Die Walküre*. That being the case, he could never completely detach his amorous pursuits from the baleful enchantment of the incestuous Wälsungs. The otherworldly modesty of these evenings resulted in an invitation to the first night of their Passover Seder, and not only that. The measure of this mensch would find his inside leg while he served as ancillary supervisor for the evening preparations. He came highly recommended as one who enjoyed a sense of order and was inordinately fussy about his food. While each Horowitz was at temple being softened up by the Song of Songs, Farinata would be playing Childe Roland and keeping an eye on the Seder table. He would clear away any stray bit of *chametz* that spontaneously appeared to challenge all of creation and the gluten-free, and most importantly, he could be trusted to comfort the gun dog, who was confined to the backyard until after the meals on the first nights of Pesach.

Bartók (Béla to his friends) defies our powers of description. On the surface a large, amiable yellow lab, he had a certain ingenuity that went unobserved—the skills of a safecracker when it came to hidden kibble or rawhide treats. The first time Bartók had offered his paw to Farinata, the shake had told him everything he needed to know. Yes, he had sized up this guest quite nicely. Beggary would lead nowhere; the world would end with a whimper. His strategy was sound. He stood on his hind legs and tapped at the parlour window with one paw, letting out an emphatic yawn—an authoritative bark would have toppled the whole enterprise. For anyone up to speed on their *terza rima*, the adverbial *caninamente* was unavoidable. A hint of a conspiratorial grin sealed the deal. Rest assured, Bartók would fulfill his end of the social contract. A pat down around the flanks was all he was after, or so he swore with his paw upon the window pane.

There would be no protagonist to speak of without *hamartia*, or a divine comedy of errors. His first error was letting Bartók in as a secret between them. His second error was to abandon his station in front of the Seder table and retire to the parlour where he could anticipate the prospect of a future guided by the sage hands of Laura Horowitz. His third error was to recline comfortably with a copy of Spinoza's *Ethics*, especially without taking into account that Schopenhauer complained about that philosopher's lack of understanding where dogs were concerned. We cannot quite stomach the idea that a compassionate angel—who knew the Hebrew for every item on that plate—roused our hero with his own snores. The fact that Zeus had sent him a prophetic dream is already a lot to take in.

Ten years or more down the line, Farinata was walking in the company of his two children, Francesca and Belacqua, along the traditional route for many a mensch that extends past the boundary, connecting civilization with a blind diverticulum[122] on the other side of Edgeland. A dream is no place to meditate on the *Yekke*, or the slightly stuffy German uptown Jews who arrived in the late 1800s and settled in the South End, or the more expressive Eastern European

---

122. Fancy term for "cul-de-sac." Here, we ask our protagonist, and not for the first time: "Are you really up to being a mensch?"

Jews who followed their trail and settled in the North End, especially when Esther and Laura were both on the *right* side of the tracks. Our social climber wore a yarmulke, and his sidelocks were longer, clearly dividing his overactive frontal lobe from the more sensual rear part of his brain. Three deli sandwiches sandbagged a container of bisque, balanced perfectly in plastic looping through his left hand. The children walked (safely) on his right. His wife was away, on a lecture tour for her book on tactile music therapy, which he had, in part, ghostwritten. It turned out that people would shell out quite a bundle to come in contact with The Sage Hands of Laura Horowitz. Life was unfolding so smoothly he did not see the red-tailed hawk at first. Bless him, his first thought was the little ones and not the mice of the field. The shelter he gave his kids left him uncharacteristically vulnerable in other ways. He would only be negligent about a fresh meal in a dream. Also, in reality, the hawk would not have plummeted as fast as a peregrine falcon, just as it would have left the cumbersome bisque behind. The plastic bag crinkled in the wind, hanging from its hallux-claw overhead as a snort—or snore—emerged from its beak.

Farinata awoke with a fright. Rubbing his eyes, he rose from his future chair and went to perform another status check on the Seder table. Though a plodder when it came to cultural homework, he was still able to review the centrepiece. The parsley was the *karpas*, expressing the flourishing condition of the Israelites to be dipped into salt water that represented their tears during enslavement. *Charoset*, the mixture of wine, honey, and nuts, stood in for the mortar the Israelites used to construct buildings for Pharaoh. It pleased Farinata greatly to find significance in the optional addition of apples, a nod to midrashic tradition and a time when the women would sneak away into the fields to lie with their husbands under the apple trees. This was a subtle allusion to the obstacles thwarting love, although a smattering of dates and figs would have been pushing his luck. Endives were the *maror*, passable as the bitter roots and leaves that had made up the slave diet. An aunt on a flying visit had left an inexplicably phallic horseradish to soak in a bowl of water, but everyone at Chez Horowitz was too intimidated to touch it. *Chazeret* was really just a placeholder for more bitterness, and lettuce was fine for that. The *beitzah*, or roasted hard-boiled egg was a tad abstract and seemed open to interpretation. Not for the first time, we blush over Farinata's caddishness, and the birdy quote from the Bard[123] that flitted across his consciousness.

The sight of leaves only brought to mind a bit of hoary alyssum, an invasive species that seizes its opportunities along roadways and railway lines. In the *charoset*, he could make out a pair of feet planted firmly under a table, and so on. Yet he was not a seasoned Seder-goer, or he would have known that the absence of the roasted lamb shank bone was no great cause for alarm. Nor did he know this was not the first occasion when the Z'roah had disappeared. In fact, Bartók had become quite ritualistic about his hiding place for the ceremonial shank bone. Farinata called the golden picture of innocence by his more informal name and directed him outside, scolding him over his misappropriation of the mimetic sacrifice.

There was still time. Farinata just needed a second

---

123. *And being fed by us, you used us so*
   As that ungentle gull, the cuckoo's bird,
   Useth the sparrow—did oppress our nest,
   Grew by our feeding to so great a bulk
   That even our love durst not come near your sight
   For fear of swallowing …

opinion. He used the key under the mat to lock up and sped over to Schmelz's Deli. Esther saw him coming and straightened her sanitary pigtails. The tune he loved to hum between bites—Wolfram's "Song to the Evening Star," also perhaps familiar to anyone who has watched Charlie Chaplin cook his shoe for dinner—thrummed faintly underneath her Winnipeg Jets cap. He was babbling away—something about a section of beef or a chicken wing doing the trick. It was not yet her prerogative to slap him. He was and was not a baby and not her baby, but she took hold of his shoulders anyway and joggled the histrionics right out of him. Pastrami or smoked meat on the Seder plate? She shook her head and led him behind the counter and into the back. The mood was noticeably different from the time when he had leaned in close and notified her of his allergies. She savoured the air of intimacy between them as she opened a Styrofoam container to reveal two lamb kebabs resting peacefully upon a bed of rice. Her own *chagigah* sacrifice would be weightier than a mere egg. Farinata accepted half of her lunch with the note of solemnity it warranted, although once again the omen dispatched by Zeus was lost on him, even when their hands touched over the bamboo skewer. When was life not just like an Eric Rohmer film?

Back at Chez Horowitz, Farinata sliced off strips of the lamb cubes as cleanly as he could, scraping off stray grains of rice, and gulped down the remainder. Still warm. If he had been better acquainted with the Book of Numbers, he would have realized he was being commanded to eat the lamb with unleavened bread and bitter herbs. Once he had whittled down the kebab, he placed the skewer on the empty space on the plate. Then he crumpled up the pink wax paper from Schmelz's Deli and pressed it down into the garbage bin under the kitchen sink. When the Horowitz tribe returned, they divined at once what had happened and derived great merriment from Farinata's Seder innovation. One of two bubbehs gave him a beetroot to deal with. Apparently, the Jerusalem sacrifice could be represented by a beet because it was blood-red and the Talmud gave this practice a thumbs-up. After he had pared the beet, more laughter ensued over Farinata's futile handwashing technique. He had been caught red-handed, etc. Laura Horowitz looked down a long narrow road towards her intended. If not the best of mensches, at least he was not a complete schlemiel. After all, he could stare down a comical horseradish without flinching.

When it was time for each guest to offer a show-and-tell celebration of liberation, Farinata surprised everyone by putting on the third act of *Nabucco*. Naturally, they already knew the story of Nebuchadnezzar, king of Babylon; they did not know that in 1842, the Italians were so moved by Verdi's "Chorus of the Hebrew Slaves," they used the composer's name and music to help mobilize resistance forces to overthrow their own oppressor, the Austro-Hungarian Empire. Even Morry Horowitz felt a mild stirring in his chest, for he was quickly taken in by the drama between the reformed blasphemer and his wayward daughter. After the finale, Farinata could not resist giving out the rallying cry of the Risorgimento movement—"Viva VERDI"—a codified call foreshadowing the 1861 ascension of the King of Sardinia, Vittorio Emanuele, Re D'Italia. Jacob Bloom could not keep from wilting into the smudged ink of his optimistic newspaper article about Israeli-Palestinian relations. Bitter roots and leaves, indeed.

Dusk ushered them into the parlour. We do not know if Elijah the Prophet tagged along. Presumably so, because Laura Horowitz had broken protocol and prepared a treat for their living, breathing guest of honour, and more of the apples, dates, and figs variety. If anything, it was a liberation of the murky underpinnings of her budding love—all of these turbulent emotions that she was otherwise incapable of expressing. As Laura reanimated the majestic figure and noble brow of Liszt, each Horowitz was happy that neither Art nor Poesy had passed over their house this year. When she turned towards the interruption about twelve minutes into her slow interpretation, the proud smile vanished right along with Elijah. She carried on bravely, peering down at the mysterious trail of garbage. Then she saw the ingenuous grin of Bartók. Then she saw the torn square of pink wax paper and the *Funérailles* died under her fleshy fingers.

Laura experienced a rare but life-changing flash of insight. On the way back home, she had stopped to pick up an extra box of matzahs at Schmelz's Deli. She knew she would have to pay an arm and a leg, but that would be better than hazarding the supermarket on the first nights of Pesach. The woman in the Jets cap had given her a stranger look than usual. Laura had pointed at the box she wanted, after waiting for her to finish assembling and wrapping some sandwiches for a standing order. Imagine, handling pastrami on Passover! Then everything clicked. It was just like that Eric Rohmer film, the one about the girl at the bakery. Only it was her soulmate in the clutches of a deli siren with a dainty nose, taking contraband from her slender fingers. Laura thought she could smell even more than Bartók could in those crinkled creases of that pink wax paper on the carpet.

Farinata was still hooting and clapping himself into oblivion. For the sake of appearances, she turned back to her piano and began to attack the arpeggi from the Intermezzo to *Cavalleria Rusticana*.

The coyote was no longer visible from the window of the train. A sudden jolt had startled him, but it was nothing to write home about. *Home.* To this day, the concept eluded Farinata, or he it. Directly across from him, Piper was flipping at random through a copy of *Dreamboats.* Large yellow lettering on the cover read **HOW TO MAKE A WATERPROOF MANTRAP.**[124] Stealing a quick peck crossed his mind, but he decided against messing up her makeup. Piper was dolled up as Sofia Heartstop, and once they reached the cosplay expo in Saskatoon, she would help others do likewise. Yes, her costume and cosmetic kits sure went like hotcakes. He had long ago learned to suppress his critical faculties on this score, and a score it was indeed. Comparatively—when compare he did—his prosody held no such place in the free

---

124. Sadly, the genuine article about eating a Bronut off your man was censored here.

market. Still, it had not been such a bad match. Just then, somewhere down the aisle, a cloud of sound announced its presence with the distinct swells of Gustave Mahler's unfinished symphony.

Farinata knew better than to get underfoot at the expo; he set out on a walk by himself and found his way across the university bridge. Along a gravel path, he conversed with a few magpies. Though he had been living in Friendly Manitoba for what felt like donkey's years, he still retained the prejudices any Reginan worth their flax fire would actively demonstrate in that "Paris of the Prairies" with its fancy river. The same rule applied to any S'tooner compelled to spend one night in Regina, undoubtedly on business. It was fitting for Farinata—who embodied the civic pride of his Florentine namesake, when not doing a runner—to identify with the defiant attitudes of the founders who had insisted on cultivating a capital city of the then North-West Territories that would rise out of the muck with the stateliness of a freshly kissed leopard frog. The magpies bore the brunt of his less-than-impartial views on the matter, and they were intelligent enough to understand him and also to know that his words[125] had little to no bearing on their seed caches.

---

125. There is a place everyone just drives through and everyone says that because there is no gigantic moose maw on the highway to guide you inside. In the second half of the nineteenth century, a cylindrical heap of buffalo bones appeared and the mound began to grow and grow. For the longest time, it was thought to have been the "happy hunting ground" of Indigenous hunters, although it's hardly a stretch for the bones to have been a ghostly admonition about the small pox epidemic. In other words, by no means should you hunt there. Though the name stuck, and the area was known as Pile o' Bones, Manybones, Bone Creek, and more exotically, as Tas d'Os. "Oskana," the Cree word for bones, was mistakenly taken down by Captain Palliser as "Wascana," and that name stuck

too. Can we argue that our poet is not stuck in the Palliser Triangle right now? A lot of things stick there, and perhaps that is because the city was built on soil that has been described as "gumbo clay" that adheres to whatever it touches with the tenacity of molasses. Indeed, to this day, there is no record in the census of how many boots fell victim to this unpaved muck before roads and pavement were poured in.

Leave out your Stegnerian idyll. In 1882, when Edgar Dewdney, the Lt. Governor of the then North-West Territories, posted his announcement that this land was marked out for government use, it had already been surveyed for the CPR, and it would not have been lost on the Right Honourable Mr. Dewdney that it was cheaper to build on flat land than in a more fetching valley. In 1886, the honest, plain-speaking folks of Queen City resorted to some sleight-of-hand on the occasion of Prime Minister John A. MacDonald's visit, rounding up all the green trees they could find to line the muddy procession route with indigenous flora. The decision to drop precious civil servants into a place with a poor water supply, inadequate sanitation, and acres of mud—covered with showers when not plagued by drought—was lampooned in innumerable cartoons—including one depicting the Lt. Governor watering a pile of buffalo bones in the hope of somehow growing a city out of them.

Lucky for everybody, in 1883, Nicholas Flood Davin, editor of the newly founded *Regina Leader*, took up the cause and became the city's champion. In those days, there was a little more spirit in what was said, and a little less fear over saying what was said. Davin was a tall, charismatic Irishman with a fount of eloquence, never merriest save when launching scurrilous jibes and barbs at critics of the new capital of the then North-West Territories, thus grooming himself for a life in politics. Of course, in those days, there was honest-to-goodness poetry in the paper, and you settled your differences in published verse. In answer to opponents scratching their particulars in wonder at such questionable *creatio ex nihilo*, Davin was only too happy to prettify the city in becalming lines, calling her "a pleasant city on a boundless plain." It is common knowledge that a contemporary admirer of Davin who launched a newsletter in the same spirit was soon crushed by scandal, but that was over a hundred pages ago. Who remembers?

In any case, the year before the Prime Minister's visit, a man with a bushy black beard was dressed as one of the mounted police among six hundred and fifty guards—for his own protection—and escorted into the Mesopotamian temple on Scarth Street that served as a courthouse. The jury took sixty-five minutes to reach a guilty verdict, with a request for mercy. That man, who is considered a madman, a statesman, and even a hero—depending on who is doing the telling—was hanged at the barracks on November 16th. Historical hauntings aside, it is not surprising that the city enjoys a good ghost story and most everything is thought to be haunted. Seems the more we try to change the names, the more the ambiguous legacy of the pile of bones comes back to us; the drought that followed the typhoid fever epidemic; the drought that followed the path of disaster a tornado left in 1912; the drought that followed the market crash; and the drought that accompanied the grasshopper plagues to chew away at the vestiges of world-wide Depression.

What is it, then? Some define it as *defiance*. Defiance to build a wooden dam and make a beautiful lake where there was none, under conditions that need not be repeated. Defiance to have four hundred acres of marshland, to populate it with crowfoot, cattails, plantains, red-winged and yellow-headed blackbirds, coots, terns, grebes, muskrats, frogs, water striders, and something called a fairy shrimp. For the Stegnerian touch, some eye-catching wolf willow, and for the surreal taste, floating space for quite a few pelicans. The streets are lined with elms with attractive black "bug belts" that show how much they are cared for. There are countless geese, and at migration time, you are likely to see them forming an arrow in the sky pointing south, and flying, dare we say, with defiance. The wry remarks of the outer world need not touch the securely melon-headed, when, in the last few seconds, the quarterback suddenly barrels through and takes off like a jackrabbit through the hapless opposition and, decked out in green, the crowd roars and beats kettledrums not because it is the only game in town, but because they share in that fleeting instant of defiance and feel it in their very bones.

The magpies launched into rattled cries and Farinata cut short his civic pacan. Not surprisingly, the Saskatchewan River had flooded the conference floor of the majestic hotel, which resembled a misplaced castle. As such, the cosplay expo had been moved upstairs, and arrangements had been made to utilize business suites and even some of the lower rooms. Farinata made his way through the milling crowd, scarcely able to identify any of the popular female characters with everything popping out. He was jostled by a familiar figure and came out with a quip about being more antique Roman than Romulan, but this gesture was in vain. The man's equally alien daughter dropped her quinoa treat and burst into tears. In spite of his misgivings, every Sofia Heartstop who prodded him with the spear of Cockglen became a matter of personal pride (and pocketbook).

Farinata watched from afar as Piper pitched her sales woo—or wooed her sales pitch?—at groggy passersby. In just under five minutes, they too could become Sofia Heartstop! He knew from experience that once she was whirling about in that bubble of commerce, there was no way to reach her. Another soliloquy was in order. In spite of rather inauspicious beginnings, he had come to accept the undulating rhythms of their relations, and they now fit into one

---

If you are a newcomer, cheerily deboning your food truck chicken dinner or smoked roast in the grey public square, then you may only be coming to the realization that a few degrees minus zero is truly "balmy" and that the night belongs to you and you alone in the short-lived vanity of darkness, when for once, the snow is not falling and the wind is not biting, and along the storm drain, amid bounding rabbits, there is just you with your extremely long shadow under the moon and the stars in relative quietude, save for the sound from the highway of people just passing through the place where the bones are.

another like mangled android hand into frayed steampunk glove. Nor was it lost on him who was on top. Never— never!—had he taken what they had for granted, knowing that he was better off with a little looking after. For one thing, there were no more copious tears when he was in his cups. Just a sip from a snifter and straight home! He had to agree that as a minor bard with a bit of stability, he had shot up a notch in the estimation of others, and before long, he would be composing alexandrines for special occasions and blessing official inaugurals with pinches of sage. He watched Piper's chin wagging and wondered aloud why most of the books made and tales told had been of nascent love, tragic love, deceived, faithless, or unlawful love, but so seldom of lukewarm compromise that, notwithstanding, warmed the cockles on wintry nights. In the words of his own cosplay maven, they would die together, so they had best get used to the idea.

The concierge showed his respect for Farinata's soliloquy and waited for him to finish. He passed the time by humming along to the short Purgatorio movement from Mahler's unfinished symphony, which was originating from somewhere in the hotel. *Tod! Verk!*[126] Once Farinata appeared to be on excellent terms with the limitations of his mortality, the concierge cleared his throat and held out a Delta envelope. The glowing lanyard around our poet's neck was as good as a flashing billboard. Apparently, some months ago, hotel staff had extracted a letter from the mail chute with his funny name on it. The fact that he had returned was serendipitous, or so the concierge said, waving aside a tip in hope of satisfying his nosiness. The romantic fool! Farinata tore open the envelope and unfolded a piece of stationery.

---

126. Presumably an abbreviation for *Verklärung*, that long awaited transfiguration.

F,

So you're at this cosplay thing. Awesome sauce.

Maybe at the end of the day, you're the real deal.

I'm in Room 603 if you want me.

T

Trish must have been at the event a year ago—before
Sofia Heartstop had taken off—when Bambi Bamboozle
was all the rage. The concierge coughed once after a reasonable pause. Farinata asked if a Trish Portsmouth happened
to be staying in Room 603. The concierge raced over to the
front desk and went into a lengthy song-and-dance about
privacy in the information age before looking up the room.
Then he smiled and straightened up.

"I think you'll find everything to your satisfaction, sir."

Ach! Ach! Ach! Leb wohl mein Saitenspiel![127] Farinata
knocked and feared at once that his knock had been too
comedic for the occasion. When the door opened, he drank
in the deathly image of Leonora Bloodlust. Trish put down
her bloody carving knife and quiver of poisoned arrows. He
stepped inside and she turned away to face the river.

"Ah, so it's you. Right on time."

"I only just got your note."

"You are here with *her*."

"Yes. She is my—"

"Shhh. Help me bloody my cleavage. Then we'll talk."

---

127. *Farewell, my strings!*

A mere kiss and the corset was off.[128] The dizzying heights of the subsequent *scene d'amour* defy our powers of description, but it is safe to say the whole ordeal was less cringe-worthy than usual, more milt upon mermaid than alien tentacle action. Trish vowed on her hallowed soul-snatcher that they would improve. Farinata was admiring her grim determination when he nodded off, and that seemed to be the deal-sealer, for never in his wayward life had he slept so peacefully beside woman or man. When he rose from his power nap to find an encore taking place, he was wearing a rare decisive look. Maybe it was just the pheromones talking, but it was abundantly clear he would have to leave Piper and the Peg. Yes, he would have to cast off amiable "Peggy" for the infinitely more difficult Regina, which would give him the occasional icy or mucky shock his aesthetic process required. Or was his inner monologue soaked through—rather like the sheets—with intoxicating fibs?

When Farinata returned to the conference floor, the concierge winked at him and made a repetitive gesture with his free elbow. Gratitude and gratuity were well deserved but Farinata was distracted by the appearance of a stately septuagenarian in a grey suit. The man smiled and raised his fedora politely. He struck Farinata as someone he knew, or at least knew of. The concierge took his cue out of the air and gave up the goods. The man had been a poet and novelist of some small repute who had settled on the prairie in his later years. These days, he just wandered around the hotel, waiting for a conference or festival that never arrived. The

---

128. If only it had been that easy. They got the wretched thing off in three-quarters of an hour. Consummation of their mutual interest was but a blink of an eye, comparatively. One of those times that is neither terrific nor terrible. They do happen.

older fellow started walking away, and then turned around again, perhaps attracted by the telltale glow on the kisser of another poet.

"Oh brother, another Manitoban! So you're here as well. How is long poem country, then? Is the Times Change(d) High & Lonesome Club still hopping or have they been knocked down, too? If I remember rightly, I once wrote a poem about the old Eaton's—"

"The hockey centre now brings joy to so many!"

"So they got the team back, hey? Will wonders never—"

"Sorry, but I'm in a bit of a rush."

"Well, mind how you go. I got off the train here and could never bring myself to get back on. Though now I've seen you, I feel like I'm on the right—"

"Okay, see you!"

> *Leb wohl*
> *Leb wohl*
> *Leb wohl*[129]

When Farinata caught up with Piper, he found her going over the day's takings in the guise of Agent Buxom. With a breathy grin, she informed him that they were about to dine in style, or at least for one night, money was no object. After he had helped her pack up, she gave him a deep kiss and he felt his resolve weakening. He watched her critically throughout dinner but could find no target for his critique. Instead, he resorted to one of his finical bugaboos about the heavily peppered steak—his second attempt at steak in S'toon that day—and she supported his world view with no stinginess of heart. Not one but three hotel guests paid

---

129. Though these "farewells" cannot bring Mahler's unfinished symphony to life, we are doing the best we can.

her a compliment on her costume and, despite her genuine delight, she was still shrewd enough to give them her particulars. Life with a walking advertisement was not such a chore. He felt a profound sense of weariness as he began to picture himself working shoulder to shoulder with Trish's father, trying to cultivate exotic mushrooms for Regina restaurants and the farmer's market. On some level, he knew that he was still in denial about his inability to return to that life of chicken and waffles. Since his reunion with Piper, who had been working at a health store at the time, he had switched to pulses, lentils, beets, with jicama sticks for a treat. Bread was also out, but he was allowed to have as much cheese as he liked on rye crackers. In fact, he had lost count of the number of times she had saved him from turning bright red and breaking out into hives. Even as he choked on peppered shovelings in the hotel restaurant, it dawned on him that he was bound to her by hundreds, possibly thousands of little habits that no illicit roll in the proverbial could scatter to the four directions.

Then she was gone. Whither? Had she paid? Farinata could hear the muffled beats of a formidable bass drum. He walked up and down the restaurant, asking diners if they had seen Agent Buxom's departure. Stifled laughter ensued. He hurried back to their room and found no trace of her. Not a lipstick or sunflower (loaded with antioxidants and an excellent source of calcium, iron, manganese, magnesium, selenium, and zinc) or more surprisingly, not a single red or purple hair. He rushed outside and ran across the university bridge. Unfortunately, this experience brought back a traumatic incident from childhood when he had gotten lost—or had been forgotten—in the toy section of a large department store. Suddenly, in the middle of his panic attack, Farinata remembered that he had arranged to meet Trish in time to catch the evening train to Queen City.[130] Variegated mushrooms it would have to be! The onset of a manic attack got him to the train station at extraordinary speed, even on foot. There, the train was pulling out! He ran, careless of where his belongings had gone, and managed to climb aboard at the last second. The conductor glared at him and announced that he was in charge of the sleeping car, which appeared to be empty. Farinata was quick to describe the costume of his beloved, bloody cleavage and all, while a sinuous flute solo[131] echoed his lornest sentiments. In short, she looked like death warmed over, only kind of hot. The conductor waved his baton angrily, and suggested that if the good gentleman wanted off the uranium express, he'd best be sharpish about it before the train picked up speed. In poetic fashion, Farinata selected a hillock (or butte, actually) and flung himself directly at it in the fetal position.[132]

Manics and panics over. He lay there on the thick, cool grass, enjoying his ignorance of visible stars above. A coyote ceased chasing a jackrabbit to stop and size up this indistinct lump. No, too much trouble. Even the familiar nocturnal chill was welcome. Life alone in this wide open expanse would wipe out his memories of much sorrow and much joy. Finally, he would be at peace. If he was not yet

---

130. Why not? Mercenary resilience had gotten him this far.

131. Certain critics of Mahler's unfinished symphony have found this nod to flautists incomplete and perhaps even insipid in spite of its impact on a century of cinematic moments we have come to cherish.

132. Whenever facing uncouth adversity, a tried-and-true colonial trick was to curl up like this and picture oneself in the cradle of civilization.

that venerable poet in the grey suit and the fedora, he would do his best to become something like him.

The woodwinds were heaving genteel sighs when the train went off the rails. There were several casualties, including our poet, but—praise the living skies!—the cargo turned out to have been some safety sand that was sorely needed in Manitoba. Farinata had been heading home to his wife[133] when the accident occurred. The last of an unhappy race, as they say in Italian operas.[134] With whom he crossed paths, once transfigured in that wide open expanse, we haven't the foggiest.

---

133. Not Piper or Trish, but someone we should have seen coming around the bend. Stay tuned.

134. For once, this reference to the tenorial wrap-up in *Lucia di Lammermoor* is spot on:

> *Tombs of my fathers,*
> *receive the last son*
> *of an unhappy race,*
> *I beg you.*

Ashes in Assiniboine Forest

FECK, FARINATA, ON A CARGO TRAIN.

This news came as a shock to the second Mrs. Feck, although she had been the one to choose the words with economy. A crying shame, considering he had seemed a shoo-in to one day do the obits himself. His contemporaries were still too young to enter into profound reflection for more than a few zeptoseconds, if that. His snort of a mortal sentence had come to a full stop, and that was that. A few breezy conjectures about his slender corpus and wealth of humanity, and that would indeed be that. As for the lovely ladies he had loved and/or pestered, they had given their fainting couches to the junk people some time ago. The first Mrs. Feck laid claim to the role of surviving widow, and much to the surprise of anyone who would listen, now had nothing but good things to say about his eccentricities and dependencies. Who would now keep items on the kitchen table in tentative symmetries? Sure, there had been the odd time when she had despised him for shaking himself like a wet Bernese over the porcelain seat; now she would know that clammy sensation beneath her shivering thighs in darkness no longer, all because of a few lines of print.[135]

One shock may follow another, once we realize that the second Mrs. Feck was in fact the yam activist, Yella. After her breakdown, she had packed in theatre life for good. Then she had crossed paths with a mystic who had divined in her more than a few shamanic tendencies. It is not our concern how she obtained the funds necessary to take the essential workshops, only that she visited the temple steps of Khajuraho[136] with paradoxical reverence. Suffice it to say, she was soon rubbing stones and minerals into frail flesh for cold hard cash; magic never seemed quite as effectual when one could not monetize it. Her first show of personal power was to scatter the owners of Tie-Dye Curios, taking possession of their premises and sad-eyed feline. After a hasty prescription had triggered an especially nasty episode, Farinata came to her seeking alternative treatment, which involved a great deal of tapping on his cortices.[137]

---

135. Romantics should note, belatedly, he had come round to her opinion on a number of subjects, including bog roll direction, the proper way to turn the tines of one's fork, and the best way to avoid impeding one's circulation during sleep. The absence of a comma between city and province on the envelopes containing subsequent billets-doux crafted by hand remained the most irrefutable echo of her influence. Let us agree that even the shortest union in history is still a vast universe unto itself.

136. The erotic stone carvings at this site already showed their stewardship in Farinata's dream about Esnesnon, and it is touching they did not cut him loose when it counted.

137. One tapping soon led to another, or so she would quip in later years.

Yella regretted the whole foofaraw about the so-called yams, but that did not matter because Farinata was unable to place her until well after they had begun to writhe in a Khajuraho of their own. The way she fondled her healing stones was more than enough to beguile him. For once, we can agree that the anxious hand of fate pushed him back on a stone bed; there, the corners were bedecked with red carnelian to avoid carnal routine; there, the ornate stonework of aragonite and jasper could do no less than magnify his animal magnetism, even as it cranked up his libido. For reasons unknown, the hand of fate had gone to a lot of trouble selecting a dark camisole laced with rough tourmaline that was increasing her own sensual tactility beneath her healer's robe. Such were the circumstances leading up to the first and last happy ending[138] her business could boast. By the time he felt the cat nuzzling up against his left foot, his fate was sealed. The rest, as they say, is mystery.

The legal ritual was scarcely worth a mention. No Wagnerian bier awaited our erratic hero, but his final wishes would be honoured. The worms would not get at what was left of him any more than blubbery words or reptile tears. The capable giant saw to it; he returned with the ashes, and that was that. Yella sensed that it would have been too much to size him up at this juncture in spite of how wonderful in black she looked. Off he went without even a cup of Dilmah. Yet the universe was obstinate in its design. One door closed and another opened.

Atmoo made an incredible entrance and whistled at the fresh widow. Then he recalled the nature of the occasion and clammed up. He squeezed her right shoulder in sympathy, enduring the bittersweet farewell of Siegfried and subsequent funeral dirge that was playing in a loop. Atmoo

---

138. Euphemistic or not, depending on how your mind works.

attempted a Nietzschean stance, but choked up instead, knowing full well there would be no rebuttal forthcoming.

He sat down on the sofa and began to unburden himself. For some reason or other,[139] he had taken Farinata out for birthday roti and had launched into a fervent attack on his personal value system—admittedly sketchy, and ultimately a subset of a systemic conspiracy against the squishier sex, to use a ghastly phrase—while the poet's stigmata from a recent romantic crisis were still dripping all over his flatbread.[140] That was years ago, and they had not spoken since. Filthy ashes, where be thy enlightened tribalism now? Yella deferred to Atmoo's peculiar world view, not wanting to be left alone with the palpable absence that had taken the place of her spouse. Even so, decorum prompted her to make a face about his having nowhere to stay before relegating him to the lumpy sofa upon which he sat.

Rousing Atmoo in the morning was no easy matter. By way of contrast—not that she was comparing tart apple slices to prominent bananas—the bonds of wedlock had increased Farinata's need for more solipsism than usual, for which reason he had shot out the door before daybreak and wandered around the trails in Assiniboine Forest, guided only by the stretch of light that precedes the definitive emergence of the sun. Yella had respected his show of independence, resenting it all the same. Why should he have hurried to that dark wood at first thing when the bed was still warm and she infinitely languorous? A clandestine assignation was pretty much out the question at that hour, but it was entirely possible that he went to the forest to review some faultier

---

139. There's probably a good one.

140. Before Yella had made an honest fellow of him, flatbread had been one of his favourites.

prototype[141] who lacked everything she had brought to the table as the supreme Mrs. Feck. He would return, brimming over with arcane chatter and the prospect of a few decent lines—or words, or particles, or vowels—before another fruitful nap could catch him within its warm depths. Now cloven, she felt a sense of relief that was in danger of running slack and expanding into unfathomable space, if left unchecked. Gone was his isolationism and his asceticism, not to mention his aesthetic *bêtes noires* that threw a wrench into the smallest casual gathering. This was not something she would have breathed aloud, this feeling that her mortal flesh was off the hook, so to speak.

Atmoo on the other hand, was making the most of a sad occasion. He found that the cool air in the forest was easing his migraine and that his mind felt sharp. Once again, he was surprised to find himself caving in to another of Farinata's crackpot theories, namely the one about the mammalian brain evolving solely to maintain the function of temperature homeostasis. Whether the deceased would have called it sublimated cannibalism or Social Darwinism was beside the point because Atmoo felt it was his duty to wrap himself round that inchoate mass of curves before she did herself a mischief. He clasped her hand and faintly paddled her palm, still on the side of the angels. They made their way into the narrow meadow, which as we should know, was possessed of the most unpredictable erotic properties. Though the ground was still frozen and the plants were still devoid of leaves, the warmth of Schubert's *Winterreise*

---

141. We rely on a hint of omniscience to tell us that at the instant the fatal train derailed and Farinata went the way of the safety sand, the Mädchen ceased her sign language in the lower left corner of public television screens; her hands fell eerily silent.

enveloped them, courtesy of the Mennonite chamber choir
and a guest bass-baritone.

Es zieht ein Mondenschatten
Als mein Gefährte mit,
Und auf den weißen Matten
Such' ich des Wildes Tritt.[142]

Atmoo spoke a few words, touching upon timeworn customs concerning kinship and chattel. The mournful Mrs.
Feck did not fully grasp what he meant. She stared at the
box in her left hand and saw a ship on the horizon with a
flapping flag that convinced her habitation on this island
of grief need not be more than a flying visit.[143] She opened
the box and brought out the plastic bag. She bit her lip and
unfolded the bag, shaking out the contents into a sudden
gust of wind. Then without warning, she dropped bag and
box and sought comfort in an embrace that was absolutely
gravid with meaning. Her imitation fur opened in mid-ca-
noodle. In spite of his excitement, Atmoo felt obliged to
express that such a continuation was exactly what Farinata
might have wanted. Kisses spurred on bold caresses beneath
the faux fur.

Fortunately, we are saved from the duel of their drool
by a young white-tailed deer who was still uncertain what
feet were for. After hammering them with its hooves, the

---

142. *A shadow in the moonlight*
  is my companion
  and over snowy meadows
  I follow the feet of animals.

143. We forgive our fresh widow for mixing up her imagery here.
There was no longer anyone to suggest otherwise.

deer returned to its affable gambol among the poplars with a prideful air that instantly trampled any suspicion of metempsychosis.

Rest assured, the mourning cloak butterfly that had been attracted by their exchange of precious moisture was a far more likely candidate for the speedy transmigration of our troublesome poet. The prospective lovers watched it fly off, and that was that.

Acknowledgments

Many thanks to the folks at Turnstone Press for their zeal about publishing this sprawling text. A special word of thanks to Melissa McIvor for her astute and insightful edits that made this a better book.

Gratitude to Warren Cariou and Katherena Vermette for publishing a section of this novel in *Prairie Fire*, and to Allison Crawford for including a section in *Ars Medica*.

A loud shout-out to Coby Stephenson whose quirky novella *Violet Quesnel*, along with her unwavering enthusiasm, inspired me to write this book.

And a wave of the antennae to Dan Johnson whose insectile expertise made this a better book.